BRIAN FLYNN

THE FORTESCUE CANDLE

With an introduction by
Steve Barge

DEAN STREET PRESS

BRIAN FLYNN
THE FORTESCUE CANDLE

BRIAN FLYNN was born in 1885 in Leyton, Essex. He won a scholarship to the City Of London School, and from there went into the civil service. In World War I he served as Special Constable on the Home Front, also teaching "Accountancy, Languages, Maths and Elocution to men, women, boys and girls" in the evenings, and acting in his spare time.

It was a seaside family holiday that inspired Brian Flynn to turn his hand to writing in the mid-twenties. Finding most mystery novels of the time "mediocre in the extreme", he decided to compose his own. Edith, the author's wife, encouraged its completion, and after a protracted period finding a publisher, it was eventually released in 1927 by John Hamilton in the UK and Macrae Smith in the U.S. as *The Billiard-Room Mystery*.

The author died in 1958. In all, he wrote and published 57 mysteries, the vast majority featuring the super-sleuth Antony Bathurst.

INTRODUCTION

"I believe that the primary function of the mystery story is to entertain; to stimulate the imagination and even, at times, to supply humour. But it pleases the connoisseur most when it presents – and reveals – genuine mystery. To reach its full height, it has to offer an intellectual problem for the reader to consider, measure and solve."

BRIAN Flynn began his writing career with *The Billiard Room Mystery* in 1927, primarily at the prompting of his wife Edith who had grown tired of hearing him say he could write a better mystery novel than the ones he had been reading. Four more books followed under his original publisher, John Hamilton, before he moved to John Long, who would go on to publish the remaining forty-eight of his Anthony Bathurst mysteries, along with his three Sebastian Stole titles, released under the pseudonym Charles Wogan. Some of the early books were released in the US, and there were also a small number of translations of his mysteries into Swedish and German. In the article from which the above quote is taken, Brian also claims that there were French and Danish translations but to date, I have not found a single piece of evidence for their existence. Tracking down all of his books written in the original English has been challenging enough!

Reprints of Brian's books were rare. Four titles were released as paperbacks as part of John Long's Four Square Thriller range in the late 1930s, four more re-appeared during the war from Cherry Tree Books and Mellifont Press, albeit abridged by at least a third, and two others that I am aware of, *Such Bright Disguises* (1941) and *Reverse The Charges* (1943), received a paperback release as part of John Long's Pocket Edition range in the early 1950s – these were also possibly abridged, but only by about 10%. These were the exceptions, rather than the rule, however, and it was not until 2019, when Dean Street Press released his first ten titles, that his work was generally available again.

The question still persists as to why his work disappeared from the awareness of all but the most ardent collectors. As you may expect, when a title was only released once, back in the early 1930s, finding copies of the original text is not a straightforward matter – not even Brian's estate has a copy of every title. We are particularly grateful to one particular collector for providing *The Edge Of Terror*, Brian's first serial killer tale, in order for this next set of ten books to be republished without an obvious gap!

By the time Brian Flynn's eleventh novel, *The Padded Door* (1932), was published, he was producing a steady output of Anthony Bathurst mysteries, averaging about two books a year. While this may seem to be a rapid output, it is actually fairly average for a crime writer of the time. Some writers vastly exceeded this – in the same period of time that it took Brian to have ten books published, John Street, under his pseudonyms John Rhode and Miles Burton published twenty-eight!

In this period, in 1934 to be precise, an additional book was published, *Tragedy At Trinket*. It is a schoolboy mystery, set at Trinket, "one of the two finest schools in England – in the world!" combining the tale of Trinket's attempts to redeem itself in the field of schoolboy cricket alongside the apparently accidental death by drowning of one of the masters. It was published by Thomas Nelson and Sons, rather than John Long, and was the only title published under his own name not to feature Bathurst. It is unlikely, however, that this was an attempt to break away from his sleuth, given that the hero of this tale is Maurice Otho Folliott, a schoolboy who just happens to be Bathurst's nephew and is desperate to emulate his uncle! It is an odd book, with a significant proportion of the tale dedicated to the tribulations of the cricket team, but Brian does an admirable job of weaving an actual death into a genre that was generally concerned with misunderstandings and schoolboy pranks.

Not being in the top tier of writers, at least in terms of public awareness, reviews of Brian's work seem to have been rare, but when they did occur, there were mostly positive. A reviewer in the Sunday Times enthused over *The Edge Of Terror* (1932), describing it as "an enjoyable thriller in Mr. Flynn's best manner" and Torquemada in the *Observer* says that *Fear and Trembling* (1936) "gripped my interest on a sleepless night and held it to the end". Even Dorothy L. Sayers, a fairly unforgiving reviewer at times, had positive things to say in the *Sunday Times* about *The Case For The Purple Calf* (1934) ("contains some ingenuities") and *The Horn* (1934) ("good old-fashioned melodrama . . . not without movement") although she did take exception to Brian's writing style. Milward Kennedy was similarly disdainful, although Kennedy, a crime writer himself, criticising a style of writing might well be considered the pot calling the kettle black. He was impressed, however, with the originality of *Tread Softly* (1937).

It is quite possible that Brian's harshest critic, though, was himself. In *The Crime Book Magazine* he wrote about the current output of detective fiction: "I delight in the dazzling erudition that has come to grace and decorate the craft of the *'roman policier'.* He then goes on to say: "At the same time, however, I feel my own comparative unworthiness for the fire and burden of the competition." Such a feeling may well be the reason why he never made significant inroads into the social side of crime-writing, such as the Detection Club or the Crime Writers' Association. Thankfully, he uses this sense of unworthiness as inspiration, concluding: "The stars, though, have always been the most desired of all goals, so I allow exultation and determination to take the place of that but temporary dismay."

Reviews, both external and internal, thankfully had no noticeable effect on Brian's writing. What is noticeable about his work is how he shifts from style to style from each book. While all the books from this period remain classic whodunits, the style shifts from courtroom drama to gothic darkness, from plotting serial killers to events that spiral out of control, with Anthony Bathurst the constant thread tying everything together.

We find some books narrated by a Watson-esque character, although a different character each time. Occasionally Bathurst himself will provide a chapter or two to explain things either that the narrator wasn't present for or just didn't understand. Bathurst doesn't always have a Watson character to tell his stories, however, so other books are in the third person – as some of Bathurst's adventures are not tied to a single location, this is often the case in these tales.

One element that does become more common throughout books eleven to twenty is the presence of Chief Detective Inspector Andrew MacMorran. While MacMorran gets a name check from as early as *The Mystery Of The Peacock's Eye* (1928), his actual appearances in the early books are few and far between, with others such as Inspector Baddeley (*The Billiard Room Mystery* (1927), *The Creeping Jenny Mystery* (1929)) providing the necessary police presence. As the series progresses, the author settled more and more on a regular showing from the police. It still isn't always the case – in some books, Bathurst is investigating undercover and hence by himself, and in a few others, various police Inspectors appear, notably the return of the aforementioned Baddeley in *The Fortescue Candle* (1936). As the series progresses from *The Padded Door* (1932), Inspector MacMorran becomes more and more of a fixture at Scotland Yard for Bathurst.

One particular trait of the Bathurst series is the continuity therein. While the series can be read out of order, there is a sense of what has gone before. While not to the extent of, say, E.R. Punshon's Bobby Owen books, or Christopher Bush's Ludovic Travers mysteries, there is a clear sense of what has gone before. Side characters from books reappear, either by name or in physical appearances – Bathurst is often engaged on a case by people he has helped previously. Bathurst's friendship with MacMorran develops over the books from a respectful partnership to the point where MacMorran can express his exasperation with Bathurst's annoying habits rather vocally. Other characters appear and develop too, for example Helen Repton, but she is, alas, a story for another day.

The other sign of continuity is Bathurst's habit of name-dropping previous cases, names that were given to them by Bathurst's "chronicler". *Fear and Trembling* mentions no less than five separate cases, with one, *The Sussex Cuckoo* (1935), getting two mentions. These may seem like little more than adverts for those titles, old-time product placement if you will – "you've handled this affair about as brainily as I handled 'The Fortescue Candle'", for example – but they do actually make sense in regard to what has gone before, given how long it took Bathurst to see the light in each particular case. Contrast this to the reference to Christie's *Murder On The Orient Express* in *Cards On The Table*, which not only gives away the ending but contradicts Poirot's actions at the dénouement.

> "For my own detective, Anthony Lotherington Bathurst, I have endeavoured to place him in the true Holmes tradition. It is not for me to say whether my efforts have failed or whether I have been successful."

Brian Flynn seemed determined to keep Bathurst's background devoid of detail – I set out in the last set of introductions the minimal facts that we are provided with: primarily that he went to public school and Oxford University, can play virtually every sport under the sun and had a bad first relationship and has seemingly sworn off women since. Of course, the detective's history is something not often bothered with by crime fiction writers, but this usually occurs with older sleuths who have lived life, so to speak. *Cold Evil* (1938), the twenty-first Bathurst mystery, finally pins down Bathurst's age, and we find that in *The Billiard Room Mystery*, his first outing, he was a fresh-faced Bright Young Thing of twenty-two. So how he can survive with his own rooms, at least two servants, and no noticeable source of income remains a mystery. One can also ask at what point in his life he travelled the world, as he has, at least, been to Bangkok at some point. It is, perhaps, best not to analyse Bathurst's past too carefully . . .

> "Judging from the correspondence my books have excited it seems I have managed to achieve some measure of success for my faithful readers comprise a circle in which high dignitaries of the Church rub shoulders with their brothers and sisters of the common touch."

For someone who wrote to entertain, such correspondence would have delighted Brian, and I wish he were around to see how many people enjoyed the first set of reprints of his work. His family are delighted with the reactions that people have passed on, and I hope that this set of books will delight just as much.

The Fortescue Candle (1936)

> "He did not pass in purple pomp, nor ride a moon-white
> steed;
> Three yards of cord and a sliding-board are all the
> gallows' need."
>
> *The Ballad of Reading Gaol*, Oscar Wilde

AFTER dealing with the sale and theft of antiquities in *The Sussex Cuckoo* (1935), Brian Flynn, not one to write the same kind of mystery twice, turns his hand to politics and the death penalty in *The Fortescue Candle* (1936). Albert Griggs M.P., the Secretary of State for Home Affairs, aka the Home Secretary, is considering whether to rescind the death penalty for a pair of brothers, and chooses not to, thus providing a possible motive for his inevitable murder.

The actual Home Secretary of the time of publication was The Right Honourable Sir John Simon, a member of the Liberal National Party. He was one of only three people to hold, eventually, the positions of Home Secretary, Foreign Secretary and Chancellor of the Exchequer. He also went on to hold the position of Lord Chancellor. Whilst he was not particularly liked as a politician, according to politician and political historian Roy Jenkins, he was still a far cry from Albert Griggs.

Griggs, it seems, is a philanderer – another motive for his murder is presented when a neighbour accuses Griggs of "molesting" his daughter. It should be noted that, while by no means a positive word, the meaning in the 1930s was not the same as today's. He also has an obsession with an actress in a stage play, Phillida Fortescue, and it's not altogether clear how he became Home Secretary, given that he apparently isn't a competent public speaker! It is also odd is that he doesn't seem to have any security or bodyguards with him at any point . . .

Needless to say, there is more to this story than the murder of the Home Secretary. Most notably there is the death of an actress, somehow poisoned in the middle of a performance, one that Griggs was attending. With the barest of links between them and a plethora of suspects, Bathurst is, for once, apparently clueless throughout this one until he sees the light at the end of the tale – it's rare to see him baffled, although the reader can sympathise as, on the face of it, the two crimes do seem to have little in common.

Brian Flynn's love of Sherlock Holmes is again on display. Whereas *The Horn* (1934) may be considered a full-on tribute to the great detective, here there is a smaller nod to one of his cases – without spoiling it for the reader, the format of the message sent by the organisation in question was a signal feature of that particular Sherlock Holmes story. More evidence, following *The Triple Bite* (1931), that Anthony Bathurst and Sherlock Holmes occupy the same fictional universe.

One other thing worth mentioning – the reader may recall that, in *The Billiard Room Mystery* (1927), Bathurst is quite rude about Father Brown's methods of detection. It may well be that Brian was angling for an introduction to the Detection Club by 1936, as in *The Fortescue Candle*, Bathurst praises "the marvellously clever creation of the mighty brain of Gilbert Keith Chesterton". If that was the intention, the invite never came.

Never reprinted since its initial publication in 1936, it is a real pleasure to be able to help bring *The Fortescue Candle* back into print, not least in order for other people to sample what is, perhaps, one of my favourite motives from Golden Age detective fiction. I do hope you agree . . .

Steve Barge

Chapter I
THE FIRST PORTRAIT

THE Rt. Honourable Albert S. Griggs, M.P., Secretary of State for Home Affairs, sat at ease and personal comfort in the library of his house at Great Astill in the county of Kent. For one thing, he had just dined—and dined well—and for another, he had, in the earlier part of the day, put through an astute piece of business in a little matter of oil that must ultimately, should there be any reliance on precedents, prove extremely lucrative to him. As he turned the cigar in his mouth he felt that his horizon was beautifully clear—save for that one rather troublesome problem that must be settled within the next twenty-four hours at the most generous estimate.

The Home Secretary frowned at the mental reminder. It was the affair of those two brothers condemned to death a month or so ago at Marthwaite in Yorkshire. A girl had been murdered. A servant in the house which these two men, intent upon burglary, had entered late in the evening. The defence—and it had been in extremely capable hands—was that the two men had left the house with the stolen articles at least an hour before the murder had taken place. The medical evidence had been a little conflicting and on this account the counsel for the defence had built strong hope. But the verdict had been for the Crown and the appeal that inevitably followed had been dismissed.

The Home Secretary had reached the stage of his final decision. He was now the sole arbiter of life and death for two fellow-creatures. He had the various documents of the case in front of him. He had also a glass of old brandy which he enjoyed from time to time with the cool and appreciative savour of the connoisseur. He prided himself on what he described as his positive reaction to humanity. It may be observed that he was inordinately fond of the word "reaction". He read with care and deliberation the judicial comments on the Marthwaite case of the Hon. Sir Maurice Ogden Bromley—the Mr. Justice Bromley who had passed sentence of death on the two men concerned. The two men who now lay in condemned cells at Armley Gaol—the lives of whom were now balanced on the palm of his hand.

The Home Secretary, as he read, shook his head slowly. Truly, this was a terrible, almost affrighting responsibility. Greater than should ever be allotted to the individual. He went through the papers methodically.

Let us take stock of him as he does so. Age—the late fifties. Medium height. Brown, bird-like eyes that were always restless. He wore a new light suit. As it happened, his wife and two daughters were away. He had dined alone and had therefore decided not to change. He knew his own mind. He had the courage of his opinions. "A politician," he said, "was gone to-day but 'ere to-morrow. Keep your eye, then, on the to-morrow." He looked spruce sartorially and alert mentally. Although on this occasion his face was slightly flushed, it was not altogether unpleasant. Fleshy and congested perhaps—but good-natured. His shoulders were bulky and thick-set, and even his waistcoat seemed to crease in folds of flesh. A doctor, looking at him carefully and noting the pounding of his temporal arteries and the darkish suffusion of his forehead, would have quickly diagnosed high blood-pressure. "But," as the Home Secretary himself would have said, had he been informed of the fact, "can you wonder at it? Look at the strenuous life I lead! My motto—as you know—'as always been service for others . . . ahem! . . ."

He turned again to the notes and comments of Mr. Justice Bromley. Then, for a second time, he referred to that dignitary's summing up. The Lord Chief Justice, at the Court of Appeal, in reply to the counsel for the appellants, had emphatically stated that in his opinion there had been no misdirection to the jury whatever, and that his learned brother's summing-up had been admirably fair and just to the two accused men. His two colleagues, it may be said, had entirely agreed with him.

The Home Secretary sipped his old brandy again. These condemned brothers had been unemployed. Men with idle hands and wasted faculties, men whose economic circumstances must be, to some extent, on the conscience of the country. Not that they were on his conscience . . . far from it . . . he'd always been sympathetic

. . . to the *genuine* unemployed. To men whose failure had been no fault of their own. Of course—there were men who . . . his fingers flicked somewhat impatiently at the papers in front of him.

"Walter Fowles . . . aged twenty-nine . . . and Harper Fowles . . . aged twenty-six . . . the elder married . . . with two children. . . . Harper Fowles . . . single."

Albert S. Griggs tossed the stub of his cigar into the fire-place and brushed at his nose with his fingers. The habits of the years are difficult to break, and it must be admitted that this particular action was an improvement upon the predecessor for which it had been substituted.

He betook himself to the settee and arranged himself thereon with a maximum of comfort. Before coming to a decision he would read again the notes on the evidence of Dr. Newbiggin, the doctor who had been first called to the body of the dead girl, discovered huddled up on the hearthrug in front of the burnt-out fire in the kitchen. Death had resulted, Dr. Newbiggin stated, from a fracture of the skull caused by three heavy blows from a blunt instrument—such as a poker, for instance. The kitchen poker, however, that lay in the fender, bore no traces of having been used by the murderers. No other weapon of a similar nature had been found in their possession or proved by evidence to have been in their possession.

On the other hand, however, there were on the kitchen linoleum footmarks that fitted the boots of the two condemned brothers . . . who did not deny having been in the kitchen, *after* they had ransacked the upper rooms of the house. The purpose for which they had entered the kitchen was to obtain food and drink. They had left the house, they swore, at twenty-two minutes past eleven with the spoils of the burglary and without having even as much as "set eyes" on the girl who had been killed. There were spots of blood, however, on the waistcoat of the younger brother, Harper Fowles, and this damning fact had weighed heavily in the scale against the two men. The man's explanation of this blood-stain . . . a previous attack of nose-bleeding that he had been unable to staunch . . . the Rt. Hon. A.S. Griggs shook his head dubiously as he read . . . that particular gag had been pulled so many times before. He determined to concentrate, for the time being at least, on Dr. Newbiggin's evidence as to the probable time that the dead girl had been murdered.

Called to the body about five forty-five on the following morning, the doctor had given it as his opinion that death had taken place "somewhere about six hours previously," that is to say, about a quarter to twelve. The Home Secretary brought himself to the condition of mental calculation. A quarter to twelve. Eleven forty-five. The Fowles brothers swore that they had left the house at eleven twenty-two and stood up in the witness-box extremely well to a merciless examination from the Crown counsel.

Griggs knitted his brows. The margin to spare was very small. A bare twenty-three minutes! And two men's lives at stake. Again he shook his head. After all, this doctor chap's statement, at the best, was but an opinion and an approximation at that. The jury, however, had regarded it as antagonistic to the defence's theory. It lent strong colour, indeed, to the accusation put forward by the Crown—that the murdered girl had surprised the two housebreakers, in all probability, on the point of exit, and that they had almost instantaneously struck the girl down and made their escape. The weapon that had been used had probably been thrown into the Marthwaite canal, postulated the Crown, although all attempts made on the part of the Police to find it had proved unsuccessful.

Griggs again went through the salient points of the case. The condemned men had each a relatively bad record. Each brother had served a term of imprisonment. For robbery. But—let it be stated—*without violence*. Griggs stressed the fact mentally. He turned up the papers with which the Police had supplied him that dealt with Harper Fowles's previous conviction.

Strange! Undeniably strange! A maidservant had figured prominently in this affair. After having been tied to a chair, this girl had shown signs of faintness and physical collapse and Harper Fowles, realizing her distress, had actually filled a glass with water and handed it to her. With regard to this action the Home Secretary evolved a grim jest. "Not robbery with violence. On the contrary, rather, robbery with extreme consideration." *But*—the facts of this previous case against Harper Fowles were definitely disturbing. Criminals, in the Home Secretary's experience, usually ran true to form. They rarely varied as to general principles of method. Here were distinct differences.

The Home Secretary, as has been stated, was a firm believer in, and keen student of, psychology. *Was* there a reasonable doubt? *Had* the Crown proved its case beyond the vestige of reasonable question? They were the points which he had to consider. Four of His Majesty's Justices had already given their expert opinions.

He searched amongst his papers for the photographs of the two men that he had specially requisitioned. The faces at which he looked were of ordinary, commonplace type. In fact, the elder Fowles was surprisingly like the young member for East Hammersley, young Victor Bowman. Funny . . . he hadn't noticed the resemblance before, although Fowles's face had been in the Press constantly for some time now. Strange how Fate plays with men for pieces. It was but an infinitesimal difference that so often lay between the two impostors, Triumph and Disaster.

The Home Secretary pulled moodily at his upper lip. He must avoid the quicksands of sentiment. He glanced at the clock. H'm—getting late, as he feared. He rose, put the various papers on the table again, and walked across the room to the fire-place. He must decide—the die of Justice must be cast one way or the other. He looked up at the ceiling and came to his decision. A scrawled phrase on the top document told the whole story. He could find no reason why he should interfere with the course of Justice. The Home Secretary had decided that Walter Fowles and Harper Fowles must die . . . be taken to a place whence they came and be hanged by the neck . . .

CHAPTER II
NO CHAPEL

THE morning of Wednesday, March 3rd, broke wet and wild. The sky was sullen. Its red streaks which the wind had seemingly whipped into the cheeks of the clouds boded ill for the hours that were to come, and for the shepherds that were to live through them.

A knot of people had gathered outside Armley Gaol because there were two men within the precincts of the prison who were doomed to die that morning. They would walk from their cells to the execution-shed . . . at different times . . . and . . . The hangman, with his little bag, had shuffled through the gloom on the previous evening, and all was ready within the prison for the last grim scenes to be enacted.

Neither Walter Fowles, nor Harper Fowles, his younger brother, was calm—or, by any means, resigned to the inevitable. Each, indeed, burned with the blaze of resentment. The Chaplain, kindly and low-toned, had pleaded with each of the condemned men for the conditions of confession and repentance. The brothers had sturdily and steadily resisted him and his ministrations. Their souls flamed with the sense of the injustice that was being meted out to them.

The stilled hush that hung over the gaol was eloquent evidence of the state of affairs that prevailed within. Outside, a tall, lean, heavy-jowled man who rode a bicycle joined the group of people who were standing waiting, and after a fragment of conversation upon dismounting, he turned away from them and stood with his cycle on the fringe of the expectant crowd. His face was heavy and brooding. With a high-beaked nose and strongly jutting chin. The line of his jaw was clearly defined in its rigidity and his black eyes smouldered.

Several people in the knot of watchers noticed him and nudged others to a closer attention. Whispers passed from mouth to mouth concerning the man's identity. But he paid no heed. He stood in silence, watching the high brick walls of the prison that separated the living from those about to die. He constantly looked at his watch. He accepted a handbill demanding the abolition of capital punishment, and he read the handbill before screwing it up and tossing it away. Beyond that, he made no movement.

At twenty minutes to nine, a detachment of the Salvation Army arrived, and a grey-bearded man, rallying his forces, led in prayer. The tall man flung a contemptuous glance in his direction.

His long, upper lip curled disdainfully. But the man of blood and fire came to the end of the prayer and announced, with a strange enthusiasm, the first line of a hymn. The tall man who watched, wheeled his bicycle a few yards further away and his face contracted in a spasm of pain. He brushed his eyes with his hand.

The quavering voices of the singers rose in the hymn and, as though in protest, there came a burst of wind and flecks of stinging rain. The whole crowd, however, braved the weather. Coat-collars were turned up and caps pulled farther down . . . that was all that happened.

The Army sang on steadfastly and yet pathetically. The man by the bicycle gripped the handlebars and set his teeth. He had just glanced at his watch. The clock of Armley Gaol began to strike the hour. The crowd silently counted the nine strokes that quivered on the morning air.

One by one, each with a kind of shy, halting awkwardness, the men outside the prison removed their hats and caps, and stood bare-headed in the wind and rain, waiting for something which not one of them, if suddenly called upon, would have been able to describe adequately. A girl of the Army suddenly went on her knees.

Fifteen minutes of oppressive silence passed. The people who watched from outside seemed to have been placed under a spell, with the evil of the enchantment predominating. Except the tall man who stood by the bicycle. He was apart—in every sense of the word. Cut off from all of them. Separated and distinct. The part that he played was different from the parts that were being played by all the others.

He stood there in a state of splendid isolation. The forms of fear that during the night had filled the empty corridors of Armley Gaol now danced their grisly masque around him. He saw them clearly as they tripped on pointed tread and they mocked—alas— not the moon—but him.

Suddenly a door, that appeared from the distance to have been let into the prison wall, opened and a man came out. He held a paper in his hand. He turned his back on the silent crowd and affixed the paper to the door as a public notice. This accomplished, he returned to the prison by the way that he had come.

The more curious of the watching crowd surged forward.

"Sentence of death . . . passed upon Walter and Harper Fowles . . . was carried out . . ." Cold and stark and cruel were the words.

The Salvation Army leader raised his voice to lead in yet another prayer. Many of his comrades knelt with the girl who had knelt before.

The man who had stood apart raised his hand passionately to high heaven. His face was contorted with an emotion upon which it was not good for humanity to look. He mouthed words. But there was none near who could hear the words. Agony, hatred, and soul-crucifixion writhed and twisted on the man's face, like the serpents that lashed themselves as the coils of Medusa's hair. He stood there, an isolated figure, in the wind and rain under that angry, sullen sky.

After a time he put his cap back on his head and buttoned his coat more closely to him. His face now had changed. It had become the face of a man who had, after travail, dedicated his soul to a mighty purpose. The crowd watched him—wide-eyed and staring—as he hunched his shoulders and rode away.

At the inquest that was held upon the two brothers some hours later medical evidence stated with pontifical exactitude that "Death, in each instance, had been instantaneous." When the Governor was asked by an indiscreet juror as to whether either, or both, of the condemned men had left a confession, he had replied that he was not required by duty to answer that question. He glared at the juryman as he made the statement.

Twenty-two miles away, the tall man wheeled his cycle into a shed and knocked at the door of a squalid house. A dark, slow-footed, heavy-browed woman came to the door. Her face looked as though every feeling had been mercilessly hammered out of it. Dull despair brooded in her eyes, and her cheeks were stained by tears.

She followed the man who had entered silently, into the kitchen.

"No miracle occurring—your boys have gone," he said harshly.

She nodded, as an idiot nods. Then sat and wept silently with shuddering sobs.

"But the case, please God, hasn't finished yet."

"What do you mean?" she gasped wonderingly.

"Never mind what I mean! To-morrow is also a day."

But the woman stared blankly and shook her head. She didn't understand. What she *did* understand, though, terrified her . . . she was frozen in her grief for the sons of her womb.

CHAPTER III
THE SECOND PORTRAIT

THE Rt. Honourable Albert S. Griggs, M.P., Secretary of State for Home Affairs, sat at ease and personal comfort in the library of his house at Great Astill in the county of Kent. If such a thing were possible, he exuded even more self-satisfaction than usual. At the particular moment of description, he found himself in the direct and lineal descent from the illustrious John Horner, the producer of plums.

He caught sight of his reflection in the mirror that hung opposite to him, and it says much for his condition that he actually extracted pleasure from the sight that he saw there. He had always been easily pleased in some directions, and in one or two respects—unique.

The paragraph in the evening paper that informed him that the brothers Fowles had walked calmly to the scaffold he did not linger over. He read it, on the contrary, extremely quickly and then turned equally quickly to other parts of the paper. After all, he might have missed reading it altogether. But the thoughts that the paragraph had occasioned were not so easily subdued. That had always been his trouble. From the days of his early youth. He could push almost everything that troubled him *away* from him, *except* his thoughts.

As a boy he had been inordinately afraid of shipwreck. The idea of being drowned at sea in the dead of a dark night had haunted his dreams for years. At this present age he shivered at the thought. He remembered how an illustrated magazine that had belonged to his father and mother had a vividly arresting picture of the sinking of the *Princess Alice* in the North Woolwich reaches of the Thames on that dreadful evening in September, when hundreds had lost their lives. The colour-scheme of the picture was black! Dark and dreadful. Bodies in the water, with despairing looks on faces appallingly white, contrasted most horribly with the ebony blackness of the sky, of the water, and of the boat itself. Albert Stanley would be given this book to look at as a special Sunday evening treat after the singing of the hymns. He knew almost to a page where this haunting picture came, and for minutes before he actually turned to it, his soul cowered before the thought of what soon his eyes would see. Note that he need not look at it—but always did!

So now, in the full flower of what he called his career, he was always clumsily fugitive from the unhurrying pursuit of his thoughts. Which fact annoyed him. He would much rather survey himself in the succession of mirrors that Life brought to him than be concerned with a moment's unpleasantness. Even though that unpleasantness might be in no way attributable to himself.

A second paragraph in the paper, however, caught Albert Stanley's eye and changed his horizon. His face almost beamed as he read:

We are pleased to announce that the Rt. Hon. Albert S. Griggs, M.P., and Secretary of State for Home Affairs, has arranged with the B.B.C. to give a series of broadcast talks under the description of "Some of the Problems of a Home Secretary". These talks, we may observe, will in all probability be five in number, and are likely to commence during the first week in June and to extend, we understand, until about the third week in July. It may also be stated in this connection that the British Broadcasting Corporation is hopeful of engaging the services of yet another Cabinet Minister—the Chancellor of the Exchequer—so it is whispered—who will follow Mr. Griggs in the early weeks of the autumn. Other equally distinguished gentlemen are likely to broadcast before the close of the year. We heartily congratulate the B.B.C., not only upon the success that has so far attended its enterprise, but also upon the idea that parented it.

Albert Stanley Griggs repeated the phrase aloud after he had read it: "Some Problems of a Home Secretary." He found that it held a rich flavour for him. He rolled it round his tongue and let it caress his palate. The world would listen to him!

What a marvellous thing modern science was, reflected A.S. Griggs. He chuckled to himself. What a triumph for him to have all his old colleagues of the Transport Waters Federation and Boilermakers' Union listening to him! They'd be green with envy. Although he owed them a great many things, they had failed to keep their place during these last few years. Didn't realize . . . wouldn't realize all that he had done for them. After all—there were limits! And times changed considerably. Just consider the conditions of the two Unions at the present day with those of, say, ten years previously. Why—there was no comparison at all! Their hours of work, their rates of pay, their service conditions, security of tenure—he loved that phrase—were all immeasurably superior for the men of the rank and file since he had been first returned to Parliament . . . to the . . . er . . . Mother of Parliaments . . . and he prided himself that he had played no small part in bringing about these ameliorative changes. He had made the statement many a time in his Election addresses. Lots of men whom he knew, were they in his position, wouldn't have troubled themselves half as much as he had done.

There were one or two things that he might reasonably introduce into his broadcast on June 8th. He had been considering them ever since he had come to terms with Broadcasting House. They certainly came within the category of "problems" and it would do the general electorate good to hear of them. A tap sounded on the door of the library and checked his meditations. He knew who had tapped, though—it was his butler, Jayne.

"Come in, Jayne," called the meditating Home Secretary.

There was a second's interval and Jayne entered.

"You will pardon me, sir, but there is a person here who states that he wishes to see you. I have remonstrated with him, sir, and amongst other things have pointed out the lateness of the hour and that he has no appointment with you. But the person insists, sir."

Jayne coughed. The cough was an apology in itself.

The Home Secretary frowned. "It's a man—you say? Who is he? What's 'e like?"

"A person of some coarseness, sir. I used the word 'insist'. In connection with his general attitude his demands might even have been described as 'overbearing'."

The Home Secretary's frown became more pronounced. "H'm. Did 'e indicate what 'e wanted?"

"Not altogether, sir. He stated that he would rather give his name to you privately. All that I was able to extract from him on the general subject was that the interview with you would be of a particularly personal nature."

The Home Secretary glanced at the clock on the mantelpiece. "It *is* damned late, as you say, Jayne. I suppose that I'd better see 'im. But I don't know whether . . ."

Jayne came in again. "The person—it seems to me from my short acquaintanceship with him—*might* be disposed towards violence, sir."

The Rt. Hon. A.S. Griggs bristled. He lacked many qualities, but courage was not one of them. "Oh, might he? Well—I ain't afraid of 'im. No earthly use being afraid when you've a job like mine to do. If I refuse to see 'im, it might make 'im worse. You never know with these fellers. Infuriates 'em. Show 'im in, Jayne."

The butler's eyebrows expressed polite disapproval. "Is it a wise decision . . . sir . . . pardoning me for the expression of the opinion?"

"That—only time will tell, Jayne. Show 'im in."

"Let me open the window, sir, for a moment. A slight hint of dinner—if I may say so. Shall I stand by, sir . . . afterwards?"

"Oh, if you like. But I'd like to see the man that I can't deal with single-'anded. He ain't born yet, Jayne—believe me."

"Very good, sir."

Jayne departed, and the Home Secretary took his seat in an arm-chair by the fire. He carefully placed another arm-chair opposite to him.

The door opened. Jayne ushered in the caller.

"This way, if you please. Thank you."

The Home Secretary glanced up curiously as he heard Jayne's voice. The man who had entered the library at the butler's invitation was a stranger to him.

"Sit down," he said, genially indicating the armchair that he had placed in readiness for the coming of his visitor.

"Thank you, I'd rather not."

The Home Secretary eyed the speaker shrewdly. He saw a short, stout man, clad in a light overcoat, who carried a much-worn bowler hat. Undoubtedly a man of the people. None was a better judge of that than A.S. Griggs himself. The Home Secretary wondered. The man at whom he looked was clean-shaven, fair, and had light-blue eyes that showed an inclination towards watering.

"My dear man," said A. S. Griggs, "you can't stand all the time. It will be thoroughly uncomfortable. Sit down and get it off your chest—whatever's worryin' you I mean. Now, tell me, don't beat about the bush, what's your trouble?"

The man stood in front of him and over him. "I told your servant-chap, who talks like the Pictures, that I'd give you my name when I got in here. I will. My name's Wells. Fancy you've heard it before, haven't you?"

The Home Secretary's intelligence came to attention. The tone of the man's voice was unmistakable. Griggs began to understand better where he was. Ridiculous nonsense! Why couldn't the fellow understand things and adjust himself to modern conditions? He spoke quietly to the man who had questioned him.

"Wells? Oh—yes—that's right—I know the name quite well. Run across it more than once in my time. Well, Mr. Wells, what can I do for you?"

Wells made an impatient, almost menacing, gesture with the hat.

"You're clever. They told me that. Got the gift of the gab. Perhaps my initials may help matters on a bit. Give your memory a bit of a kick. I happen to be C.D. Wells. I live at Ransford. It's a village you know . . . quite close to Brook. I rather fancy that you know it almost as well as I do. Now—how do we stand?"

The man's face held an ugliness as he spoke. Griggs realized it and played for time.

"Oh yes . . . Ransford . . . I know it. I've been there. Pretty little place. Well . . . what about it? What can I do for you with regard to Ransford? Want me to open a bazaar or something?"

"Don't you come that stuff with me, you lying swine. Suppose I mention the name of Constance Wells? Connie to us at home and Connie to you. . . .You bloody old Mormon!"

The Home Secretary raised his hand in protest. "Sh! . . . My dear Mr. Wells . . . please don't raise your voice like that. People might hear things that weren't intended for them. Well, supposing I 'ave met this young lady. What about it? What's your game?"

"Game? No game at all. I'm not one of that kind. I'm not here to put on the black. I've come to give you the straight tip . . . that's all. I can't wipe out the damage that you have done already, but I'm takin' good care that you don't do any more. Get that, you old rat. Connie Wells happens to be my daughter. The only girl I've got. See? Well . . . lay off! That's what I've come to say . . . and I've said it."

The Home Secretary expostulated. "But, my dear Mr. Wells . . . as far as I'm concerned . . . your daughter—"

"Has given you a lot of pleasure already, eh? Yes—I know that. I found it out the day before yesterday. I'm an old-fashioned man, you see. What you might call a bit Victorian. I don't hold with these modern goings on. And I get no thrill from my daughter going to hell because it's a celebrity who's takin' her there. Now you know—Mr. Albert Griggs. *Celebrity!*"

The Home Secretary again raised his hand. "The theatrical stuff cuts no ice with me, Mr. Wells. You may as well know that from the start. Your girl's old enough to know her own mind and to live as it suits her. As for going to hell—as you call it . . ." The Rt. Hon. A.S. Griggs shrugged his shoulders to express his complete unconcern.

Wells opened his mouth to reply, but Griggs was too quick for him.

"And now if you'll excuse me," he said, "I must request you to leave. My time is valuable. Jayne!" He raised his voice on the last word.

The butler came immediately.

"Show this man out, Jayne."

The butler advanced with a certain amount of diffidence. Wells, however, pushed him aside contemptuously and went a pace nearer Griggs.

"You needn't worry yourself. I'm going all right. You ain't much to look at, you know, and many's the morning paper that your ugly dial has spoiled for me. I'm stayin' just long enough to say one thing more. Listen. Because it's worth hearing. If you keep on molesting my girl—I'll let daylight into your ugly carcase as sure as my name's what it is. And don't say I didn't warn you! Out of my way—Kensitas."

Jayne fell back in astonishment. Wells swept him to one side and made his exit by the way that he had come.

Jayne found words: "As I said, sir, at the outset of the matter—an extremely coarse and disgusting person. I wish that you had taken my advice, sir, and refused him admission."

The Home Secretary laughed unpleasantly. "That's all right, Jayne. We needn't worry about him."

CHAPTER IV
THE THIRD AND LAST PORTRAIT

THE body of the Rt. Honourable Albert S. Griggs, M.P., Secretary of State for Home Affairs, was discovered by Ada Cracknell, rosy-cheeked chambermaid employed at the Lansdowne Hotel, Lokingham, in Berkshire, at approximately a quarter to eight on the morning of June 22nd. A morning when death and the thought of death, were outrages on seemliness.

Knocking on the door of his bedroom and entering immediately with the morning cup of tea, as was her invariable habit, her eyes had caught sight of a ghastly figure lying half in and half out of bed. And there was blood in some considerable quantity. Instantaneously, Miss Cracknell deposited her tray and the contents thereof on the carpet, uttered a piercing scream, and fled incontinently from the dread sight of the dead to the more comfortable communion of the living.

The first man she met in her precipitate flight was the hotel porter. She encountered him, it may be said, on the bend of the first staircase.

"Oh, Roberts!" she cried. "I've had a terrible shock—you wouldn't believe. The gentleman in Number Fifty-four—Mr. Griggs—'e's been murdered! There ain't a doubt of it. I just give him one glance when I took his cup o' tea in and then dropped the tray and everything on the floor. It's all smashed to atoms. It's the blood on the bed what give me the turn. It's all over the sheets and on his pyjamas! Go and look, Roberts, do—and then call the Police. It's made me feel terrible." She shivered as she dwelt on the reminiscence.

The porter, inclined at the outset to be distinctly incredulous—he was a married man and dubious of all femininity—gave her a second look of searching inquiry and was able to see therefrom that she at least believed herself to be telling the truth.

"You'd better hurry along and tell the guv'nor—if you're so certain of yourself," he volunteered nervously, "and I'll come along to him with you now. That's the best thing we can do. If what you say is true, it'll be a job for the Police all right."

Ada Cracknell nodded and followed him down the stairs.

Mr. Staniforth listened to the story that the chamber-maid gasped into his ear and almost shook himself with a strong sense of irritation. He always liked to start the morning well.

"Are you quite sure of yourself, Cracknell?" he demanded, a trifle testily. "What you say seems incredible to me, and I've no desire to waste my time this morning on—"

"Come and see for yourself, sir," urged the still shaking Cracknell. "There's nothing like seeing for believing. But it'll put you off your breakfast."

Mr. Staniforth, realizing the woman's earnestness, ran up the big staircase that led to the room of the chambermaid's discovery with Roberts and Cracknell hot on his heels. The door of Number 54 was still open as Cracknell had left it. Staniforth went straight in, and at once all his doubts of the maid's story vanished. There was the body of Albert Stanley Griggs exactly as she had described to him.

"Good God!" he cried in tones wherein horror and petulance were strangely intermingled. "Do you realize who it is? It's the Home Secretary himself. Griggs! And killed in bed in my hotel. Goodness gracious! Terrible! Terrible! We shall never live the scandal down."

It will be observed that he knew his business thoroughly.

Carefully avoiding the pieces of the broken crockery of the Cracknell *débâcle*, he approached the bed more closely and looked carefully at the corpse.

"Shot!" he exclaimed, and his agitation increased. "Roberts! Run down to the 'phone at once. Don't lose an instant on any account. Get on to Inspector Sutton at the police-station, give him my compliments, and ask him to come up here as soon as he can. If he hasn't arrived yet—find out where he is. Make them understand that it's urgent. And tell them to send a doctor with him. Tell them just what I've said and nothing more. Not a syllable! Understand?"

Roberts nodded and turned quickly on his heel. They heard the sound of his feet as he ran down the staircase.

At a peremptory gesture from Mr. Staniforth, Cracknell, the maid, followed him, and Mr. Staniforth himself, seeing her safely away, locked the bedroom door behind him, placed the key in his pocket, and quietly descended the flights of stairs. His thoughts molested him. What a frightful stroke of misfortune! To harbour the Home Secretary for one night in the hotel and then to have a thing like this happen! Terrible! Heart-breaking! Still—perhaps Sutton would be able . . . Staniforth found in the thought a crumb of comfort. His name would appear in the papers almost everywhere. Possibly also his photograph.

Staniforth twirled the ends of his little moustache. After all . . . it was an opportunity!

Chapter V
INVESTIGATION

INSPECTOR Sutton was nothing if not business-like. His brain was brisk and his manner was even brisker. The fact that the dead man in front of him had been the Home Secretary stimulated him excessively. Like Staniforth, the hotel manager, he could see opportunity ahead of him, beckoning—inviting.

He turned to Dr. Wickham after the latter's first examination of the body with a gesture that bordered closely upon impatience.

"What do you think, Doctor? Suicide a possible theory?"

Wickham grunted evasively and shook his head. "Where's the weapon, then? The man's been shot, Sutton, not poisoned with weed-killer. Be reasonable."

Sutton shook his head as the doctor had done. "Leaving the question of the weapon alone for a minute and judging merely from the position and nature of the wound—how about it, then?"

"In my opinion the man's been dead not far short of twelve hours and the shot that killed him was fired at very close quarters. Look at the mark on the pyjamas. I won't say any more than that. Bullet gone through the throat. I shall have to probe for it. But there's no weapon on the bed or on the floor. Which is eloquent! Men don't turn into magicians when they're *in extremis*."

Wickham turned away and wiped his hands on a towel from the wash-hand stand. Inspector Sutton, impervious to the sarcasm that his question had produced, looked at Staniforth and jerked his head towards the floor.

"This mess down here, you say, came from the tray that your maid dropped when she found him?"

"Yes, Inspector. That is so. You can't wonder at it. The girl came in, spotted the corpse and the blood, screamed several shades of blue murder, dropped everything that she was carrying, and bolted out of the room. After all, you can hardly blame her, can you? Wasn't a pretty sight for a girl to start the day's work with."

Sutton went on his knees and sorted out the debris. "H'm, suppose it's all right," he muttered. Then he straightened himself again and went back to the body that lay on the bed. He fired another question at the manager. "Have these bedclothes been touched at all?"

Staniforth explained. "Nothing whatever has been touched. I was particularly careful that nothing should be. I flatter myself that nobody could have been more careful. I locked the door when I sent my porter to 'phone for you. When you and the doctor arrived just now, everything was exactly as it had been when Cracknell first came in and made the discovery. In every particular."

Sutton frowned at the manager's remark. "From the way the top clothes have been thrown off and their general disarrangement, it looks to me as though Mr. Griggs was trying to get out of bed when the murderer shot him. Look there—and here! See my meaning, Doctor?"

Dr. Wickham looked at the bedclothes to which Sutton was pointing.

"H'm! Not unlikely. Took fright when he saw what was coming to him. That's about what happened."

The Inspector began to prowl round the room. Beyond the dead man's clothing, most of which was lumping in the wardrobe, and a few ordinary toilet requisites that lay on the wash-stand, there appeared to be nothing there that could be said to be of the slightest importance. Sutton continued his seemingly purposeless meandering, whistling softly to himself the while. After a time he again came back to the bed. Standing at the foot, with his hands on the end of the bed itself, he leant forward so that he could look more closely at the body. As he did so, he uttered a sharp exclamation. Turning back the clothes that had been flung towards the foot of the bed, he disclosed an open book and a folded newspaper. The book lay face downward in the bed and the paper was at its side.

"Hallo!" he cried. "What are these doing here?"

Wickham and Staniforth looked at him curiously.

His surprise—for surprise was apparent in his tone—infected them.

"I should say he was reading in bed just before he was shot," contributed the former. "Nothing unusual about that, Inspector, surely? Dozens of people do it. You'll probably find that the book's a detective story. It's the custom nowadays for all great men to amuse themselves with 'thrillers'. You know what they say, 'It isn't the blood that attracts them—it's the problem.'" There was a touch of sarcasm in the doctor's voice.

"Great men!" echoed Staniforth with immeasurable scorn and emphasis on the adjective. "You don't call this fellow a great man, do you?"

"Well, he's Home Secretary, chance it." Wickham was curt. Who was this fellow Staniforth, anyway, to give himself airs?

The manager refused to be put off. "Home Secretary! Good Lord! In these days anybody's anything. Meritocracy's run riot. The Mayor of Lokingham at the present time keeps an eel-pie shop in the High Street. What was Griggs? Where did he come from? I can tell you, if you want to know. I knew him when his reputation was distinctly unsavoury. He was a 'jumper' on the National buses in his early days, and after he'd got a girl into trouble, his Union started him off on his political career. Then he was taken up by the Boilermakers and they solidified his position. Great man! It makes me tired when I hear people talk like that."

Sutton listened and smiled. Here was political bias, if you like. Then he had his say.

"Well, we'll leave that for the time being. Dr. Wickham happens to be wrong in his conjecture. About reading a crime story in bed, I mean. Look."

He held the book out to them for inspection. It was a new one. Both its condition and appearance made that plain. The title was an unexpected one. *The Basic Principles of Elocution as Applied to the Art of Public Speaking*. Sutton, elated by his find, advanced an explanation.

"When we look also at the newspaper that we have here and then again at the chapter at which this book was lying open, things begin to piece up more satisfactorily. The book and the paper explain each other, as it were. Look for yourselves."

Dr. Wickham, impressed by Sutton's statement, took the book and the newspaper. The latter held but a brief announcement where Sutton had indicated him to read.

The Rt. Hon. Albert S. Griggs, M.P., Secretary of State for Home Affairs, will broadcast to-morrow evening at 7.45 on the National programme, on "The Problems of a Home Secretary". This talk, we may observe, is the third of a series of five which the Right Honourable gentleman will have given before the end of the summer. As we announced previously, the British Broadcasting Corporation hopes to engage the services of another cabinet Minister—in all probability the Chancellor of the Exchequer—to follow Mr. Griggs in the early part of the autumn.

Wickham passed the paper across to Staniforth and turned his attention to the open book. The author's name was Harold Oakley, Professor of Elocution, Principal of Maxwell House Academy, Erlegh. Prior to the opening pages was a photograph of the author and his wife. The chapter to which Inspector Sutton had referred was entitled "Consonantal Attack and the Application Thereto of the Principle of the Onomatopoeia".

"Obvious to a blind man what he was doing," observed Sutton. "Preparing for his job in front of the 'mike'. That's yesterday's paper. Look at the date. The broadcast was to take place this evening. I hoped at first that finding these things might help us and give us a clue to the murder. But it's all normal and just what you'd expect. There's no name on the book. He'd probably bought it recently." The Inspector turned to Staniforth. "The crime seems motiveless as far as I can see at the moment. All his belongings seem to be intact. There's one thing, though. Tell me the names of the people that you have staying in the hotel. I'll leave the staff out of it for the time being."

"We have but four at the present time, Inspector. Four who stayed the night, that is. We don't get a lot these days. You can interview any of them as soon as you like. You want the names. First of all there is Basil Palliser, the actor. He's playing juvenile lead in the Howard Baluster Number One touring company at the 'Orphic'. Let's see—what's the show? *Strained Relations*. He always stays here when he's this way—has done for years. Besides him there are a couple of fellows on the road—also old acquaintances at the Lansdowne—by name Ellis and Searle. The fourth chap's a stranger to me. Never seen him before. Let me see now—what's his name? It was on the tip of my tongue just now."

Staniforth caressed his chin in the effort to remember. His face cleared. "I've got it. Wells, I think. Yes—I fancy that was what he told me. Wells. Comes from somewhere in Kent."

The Inspector noted the names that Staniforth had given him.

"When did Mr. Griggs come?"

"Yesterday mid-day. Came in his car. Drove it himself. I was rather surprised at that. Had lunch and dinner here and said he would stay till mid-day to-day. Went out during the afternoon in the car. Came back for dinner and spent some time in the billiard-room during the evening."

"Was he expected? Had he previously arranged to come—I mean?"

"Not till yesterday morning. He 'phoned through from Binfield about half past ten—on his way down—and booked up then."

Sutton leaned against the wardrobe. He was beginning to realize that cases may break reputations as easily as make them—more easily, perhaps.

"These four people you mentioned—where do they sleep? Palliser, Searle, Ellis—and Wells. Near at hand to this room? Or are they on the . . . ?"

Staniforth reflected. To tell the truth he had expected the question and in preparation against it had turned up the admission register before the Inspector's arrival.

"Let me think for a minute. This is fifty-four. Ellis and Searle, the two 'commercials', are in next door—that's fifty-five. That's a double room, of course. Mr. Palliser is opposite, on the other side of the landing—he's in Number Forty-Nine. He always makes a special point of having that room whenever he stays here. The other fellow I told you about is on the floor below—Room Thirty-Eight, I think. I'm not sure of the exact number, but I can find it out for you if you want me to."

Sutton jotted down the information in his note-book. "H'm! What sort of a chap is this Wells that you mentioned? How does he strike you? Anything fishy about him?"

Staniforth, non-committal, shrugged his shoulders. "No. He's a short, stout, rough-looking customer. Well-dressed, though—in a way—and very quiet. Reserved. Looks as though he'd put his best suit on. For an occasion. Although he said he came from Kent—might be a North countryman, by birth, I should think. I'm judging by his speech. I rather pride myself on being able to place people in that way."

Sutton nodded. "When did he come? Can you tell me that? Before Briggs or after?"

"After. But not long after." Staniforth thought for a moment. "About half an hour after—not more."

"Well, I shall have to have a word with him, and with the others too, I expect. May pick up something important. Though why the devil anybody should want to murder a Home Secretary, I don't know! Tell me, Mr. Staniforth, how did Griggs seem during the time he was here? Normal? In pretty good spirits?"

The Inspector paused—pencil poised over note-book.

Staniforth showed no hesitation. "I noticed nothing to the contrary. But he wasn't here twenty-four hours, you know, and was out for a good deal of the time, at that."

Sutton nodded understanding.

"Yes, so I gathered. That's another of the things that I must do. I shall have to see how he spent his time while he was here. Where he went and what contacts he made. You'd better communicate with the dead man's people and make arrangements for somebody to come down here at once. The photographer will be along very shortly. I don't think that we can do much more for the present."

"I'll be getting along, then, Sutton," remarked Wickham. "If you want me again for anything, let me know."

"Thank you, Doctor, I will. I hope that I shan't have to trouble you. Mr. Staniforth, without disturbing your guests unduly, as soon as it's convenient I'll have that word with each of them that I spoke about. Also, I'll see your maid—what's her name? Ada—er—Cracknell, and after her, Roberts, the porter. What time's breakfast?"

"Nine o'clock—usually, although it varies, of course, according to the individual. The early people have it when they want it."

"In the smoke-lounge, then. That will be as handy a place as anywhere. Don't give anything away to any of them and I'd like to see our friend Mr. Wells last of all. Don't forget that. I don't quite see where he fits in. Suit you, Mr. Staniforth?"

"Very good. I'm in your hands, Inspector." Staniforth was unusually curt.

Sutton shook his head with heavy humour. "Don't put it like that, Mr. Staniforth. It sounds bad."

Staniforth stared before he understood. A remark like that, he considered, was in damned bad taste. If the Inspector had a grain of sense he'd call in Scotland Yard at once and have done with it. These local people—not good enough for the job. Too big for 'em by a long chalk. Staniforth felt certain of it.

He went to the telephone and issued certain orders. Staniforth was always *thorough*. He prided himself on the fact.

Meanwhile, Inspector Sutton, blissfully unconscious of the unspoken censure that he had raised for himself in the mind of the hotel manager, was proceeding with his various interviews in the smoke-lounge. He started with Ada Cracknell, the maid, and completed the circle with a short talk with Charles Dutton Wells, of Ransford, close to Brook, in the county of Kent. And when he had finished, Inspector Sutton was beginning to realize more and more that he was still very much in the position that had been his when he had started. For his various interviews were singularly unproductive. The Lokingham powers-that-be, who controlled him, saw no reason to disabuse him of the idea.

Chapter VI
ENTER MR. BATHURST

When the news of the Home Secretary's murder left Lokingham and became common, it ceased to be—as news! It became mere topical gossip. It was, of course, broadcast throughout the land, and in view of the fact that the man himself was to have contributed part of an evening's alleged entertainment, the announcer on the National programme whose sad duty it was to convey to the multitude of listeners the news of his death, did so in a voice that was appropriately attuned and fittingly edged with black.

Then the Prime Minister, who, by a strange chance happened to be *in* the country and not cementing peace abroad, bestirred himself. The affair was a national outrage! An international disaster! Griggs, too, of all people, who had been described in the *Morning Post* only one day that same week, as an "unsinkable" politician. The Prime Minister, ignorant, naturally enough, of the details and etiquette of Police procedure, was soon in touch with the Chief Constable of the county and then, after that, with Scotland Yard—with the Commissioner of Police, Sir Austin Kemble himself.

"Very well, sir," said the latter after a patient sitting, "I'll run down to Lokingham myself. Leave it to me. As a matter of fact, the local people have requested our co-operation. I've already heard from the Chief Constable."

The primary result of the Premier's intervention in the matter was that Sir Austin and Mr. Anthony Lotherington Bathurst entered the lounge of the Lansdowne Hotel at Lokingham about half past two on that same afternoon.

Inspector Sutton had been warned to meet them. He did so with conflicting feelings. You never knew—with Scotland Yard—and an amateur! When Sir Austin spread himself (as was inevitable), the Inspector prepared himself for the worst. But when, on the other hand, the tall, grey-eyed man with the quietly incisive voice, who was with Sir Austin, asked a question and followed it up with another, he prepared to modify his outlook somewhat. Sutton stated all he knew—from his first entry into the case to the details of his last interview with the man Wells, of Hansford, Kent.

"This man, Wells," growled the Commissioner. "I don't know that I like the sound of him at all. Ten to one he's our man, but how the devil are we going to put it over on him?"

Inspector Sutton expressed his approval of the last statement. "That's my difficulty, sir. But he can't get far—that's one thing. Neither he nor any of 'em—come to that. I've made all the arrangements with regard to keeping an eye on them."

"You've done excellently, Inspector," said Mr. Bathurst. "Nobody could have done more in the time—or better. You won't mind me having a word with these people as well, though, if I should want to? There are one or two questions that I confess I'd like to put to them."

Sutton eyed him critically. "Do you think that's really necessary, Mr. Bathurst? I shall be pleased to let you have . . ."

Anthony smiled. "Not perhaps necessary, but eminently desirable, Inspector."

Sutton stared at his nonchalant calmness.

"Only way really, you know, Inspector," went on Anthony. "Psychologies and all that. Individual possibilities and personal reactions. Always eloquent. The investigator must make contact with 'em."

Sutton shrugged his shoulders. "Yes, I know. But after all, facts must be facts and common sense, common sense. You can't alter them."

"What's the use of common sense in murder, Inspector? Murder flouts the rational, you see. Distorts normal conditions. Knocks the board over and all the pieces that were on it."

"If you prefer it, then," conceded Sutton with reluctance.

"It's not a question of preference, Inspector. I'm not here to pick and choose. I'm here against my will—believe me. I had hoped to be at Chelmsford for the Cricket Week. But the good God, in His infinite wisdom or otherwise, has disposed of the idea."

"Very well then, Mr. Bathurst. What would you like to do first?"

"Not 'like', Sutton. I imagined that I had made that clear." Anthony paced the room and then turned to the Inspector. "But I'll tell you what I will do. First of all, take Sir Austin and me upstairs to the bedroom, Sutton. Let us see the body and the surroundings. Then we shall start in the right way."

"Very good, Mr. Bathurst. Come this way, will you, please?"

Sutton piloted them along the corridor and up the staircase. They came to the bedroom where the body lay. Anthony took a quick glance at the position of the room in general relation to the other bedrooms. Sir Austin Kemble issued a peremptory order. "Take us in, Inspector . . . will you?"

Anthony Bathurst looked at the body, at the bed, and at the appointments of the room generally. Sutton supplied details. Sir

Austin listened gravely. The murdered man had been one of His Majesty's Ministers!

Sutton supplied more details. "Nobody admits having heard the shot and I discovered the newspaper and the book on the bed by the dead man, sir. But they explain themselves, I think. If you will look at them, Mr. Bathurst, you will see what I mean."

Bathurst glanced first at the paper and observed the significant column and paragraph. He then took the book and carelessly noted the title and the chapter at which it had been opened.

"A little bit of self-education there, I suggest, sir," remarked Sutton rather ostentatiously. "Getting ready for his broadcasting job. Taking the one point, that is, with the other."

Sir Austin Kemble nodded corroboration. Bathurst frowned and read a few sentences devoted to "Consonants as Continuants and General Consonantal Attack". He put a question to the Commissioner.

"What sort of a speaker was this man Griggs, Sir Austin? Any idea?"

"Pretty hopeless," returned Sir Austin with emphasis. "Made an unholy muck of the job. Every time I've heard him, that is."

Bathurst looked up intently. "In what way—hopeless? Tell me more. I'm curious."

"Well, strewed the floor with aspirates for one thing. You had to walk warily to avoid falling over them. A terrible accent too. Common as dirt. Bow Bells sounded plainly in his ears when he was born. Some of his—"

Anthony Bathurst rubbed his hands. There came the gleam in the grey eyes that Sir Austin knew so well.

"A most interesting case, Sir Austin. I wouldn't have missed it for worlds. Already I am reconciled to the loss of L.G. Crawley hitting sixes into the Chelmer. Observe, Inspector, that the Home Secretary's name doesn't appear inside the book anywhere. But let me have another look at that body."

"I had already observed your point about the absence of the name," replied Sutton stiffly.

Anthony walked over to the bed again and looked at the bloodstains on the pyjama jacket . . . at the wound in the throat. He put

his hand to it . . . the back of his hand, as though testing something
. . . a theory perhaps that he had been able to form. As the back
of his hand came to touch the breast pocket of the pyjama jacket,
a strange look entered his eyes and took possession of them. For
the hand had encountered something.

"There's something in this pocket, Sir Austin," he said quietly.
"Let us see what it is."

A frowning Sutton went to the bedside. What was this that he
had missed? Not missed—exactly, but . . .

Anthony Bathurst inserted his hand into the pocket and his
fingers closed on a small, hard substance. When he withdrew it,
he and his companions saw that his hand held a small, white cube
of chalk. The top of the cube had been hollowed out, which fact
alone made it the more easily recognizable.

"Billiard-chalk," observed Sutton, with undisguised relief,
"used for chalking the tips of the cues. The manager told me that
Griggs had been in the billiard-room during the evening. You'll
find it all in my notes. He played a game or two."

"You've got it, Sutton," remarked Bathurst. "It's billiard-chalk.
And it's found in the dead man's pyjamas, mind you. Unusual place
to put a cube of billiard-chalk! Don't you think so, Inspector?"

Sutton seemed unimpressed. "Probably brought it from the
billiard-table when he came away from the game. First forgot about
it—and afterwards remembered it. Had to put it somewhere—so
dropped it into a convenient place."

"After he had undressed, Inspector? Don't get that somehow."

Sutton was silent.

Anthony persisted. "Well?"

"Now you say so, does seem a bit strange, I suppose. Still,
you never know with a little thing like that. All of us do unusual
things at times." Sutton was far from pleased.

Anthony smiled. "You're losing confidence, Inspector. Mustn't
let that happen."

Sutton challenged. "Well, what do you make of it yourself?
We haven't heard that yet."

"All my possible explanations are quite unconvincing,
Inspector. But that cube of chalk *may* be decisive."

"You mean that the murderer may have dropped it there?"

"It's possible, Sutton—surely? And the possibility splits itself into two. It may have been dropped in there by accident. It may, on the other hand, have been dropped in there by design. Things like that have happened before, you know, Inspector. History simply adores repeating itself. Anyhow, we'll see. Had a look round, sir?"

The question was addressed to Sir Austin Kemble.

"Yes. Doesn't seem much for us here, Bathurst."

"What did the doctor say, Sutton? Tell me again, will you? Had been dead for about twelve hours, wasn't it?"

"Yes, Mr. Bathurst. That was what Dr. Wickham said."

"H'm! Any time, say, between eight and midnight for the murder. As we know that Griggs was in the billiard-room after dinner, and can easily ascertain when he came away from there, we ought to be able, from that, to place the time pretty accurately."

Sutton referred to his note-book. "The dead man left the billiard-room soon after eleven o'clock. I've checked that up from more than one person."

"Good! That certainly clarifies the situation."

Sir Austin Kemble busied himself with the clothes that were hanging in the wardrobe.

"I've been through those clothes, sir," said the Inspector. "The contents are over there on the dressing-table. If I may say so—nothing out of the way at all."

Anthony walked over and looked at the arrangement on the dressing-table. Loose coins, a wallet containing Treasury notes, stamps, and a few visiting-cards. Nothing else. Anthony looked at the cards. There were five of them in all. Two were cards of the dead man himself. The remaining three were: Sebastian Lothar, 19, Berkeley Mansions, S.W.; Harold L. Oakley, Principal, Maxwell House Academy of Elocution and Dramatic Art, Malplaquet Street, Erlegh, Berkshire; and Phillida Fortescue, c/o "Howard Baluster Productions", Henrietta Street, Covent Garden, W.C.2. Bathurst held out the second of these three cards for Sir Austin's and the Inspector's scrutiny.

"Your remarks, Inspector Sutton, concerning the late Home Secretary's attempts at self-education were only part of the story.

Judging by this evidence, he's in touch, as well, with a teacher of Elocution. At any rate, it conclusively explains the presence of the book."

"Looks like it, I admit," remarked Sutton.

"Wonder if he came straight to bed after his billiards," said Mr. Bathurst. "Where are his shoes, Inspector?"

"Shoes?"

"Yes. Those that he took off when he came to bed. They might perhaps give us indications."

"He hadn't dressed for dinner," said Sir Austin. "Look here." He pointed to the clothes in the wardrobe. "No dress stuff here."

Anthony picked up the two shoes that were on the floor by the foot of the bed. "It was damp last night. There was a drizzle where I was. Those conditions were fairly general, I should think. No sign of wet on either of these shoes. I should say that, whatever Griggs did, he didn't go outside the hotel."

"He had a car here," interjected the Commissioner; "don't overlook that fact."

"The staff can tell us if he used it last night." Anthony turned the shoes over and glanced at the soles. Then he looked straight at Sir Austin Kemble. "Come here, Inspector, will you?" he said quietly.

Sutton joined the other two.

"Chalk and chalk-marks, Inspector. Chalk has more uses than one, you see. Now—where are we?"

The Inspector and Sir Austin stared at the broad soles of the two shoes. On each of them was a drawing. In each instance the lines were crude and rough, but, at the same time, plain to understand. On the sole of the left shoe had been drawn in chalk a skull and on the right a pair of cross-bones.

"Piracy," remarked Mr. Bathurst. "The Jolly Roger on the Home Secretary's shoes. Captain Kidd, Flint, Farragut, and all the Martyr Throng. We progress, Sutton—definitely. We have no ordinary murder here, that's very evident. Look at it from the point of view of motive, if from no other. No robbery, as far as we know—certainly not for monetary gain—so that we are immediately brought back to the fiercer passions. Jealousy, hatred, revenge. Pick where you like. Any one of the three will answer the equation."

Sutton nodded. He was annoyed to a degree. To have missed all that he had missed. But who could have possibly anticipated that . . .

Bathurst was speaking to him. "Is there a billiard-marker attached to the billiard-room? I suppose there is."

"Yes. I asked the manager, Staniforth, the same question. As a matter of fact, I've got the man down on my list to be interviewed. He may even be here now. He's not always on the premises, you see." Sutton looked at his watch.

"If he's here, tell him we'd like a few words with him at once. Do you mind?"

"Up here?" The Inspector looked significantly at the bed. "The body is being removed to the mortuary. . . ."

Bathurst considered for a moment. "No. I think we'll go downstairs again. Tell the billiard-marker to come into the lounge. Ask the manager to arrange that we aren't disturbed in there. Get the marker, Sutton, and Sir Austin and I will come along."

The marker's name was Britton. He was small and spare, but looked intelligent. He had dark and restless eyes.

"Last evening, Britton," said Bathurst, "were you on duty marking in the billiard-room all the time?"

Britton nodded. "Yes, sir. All the evening. That's my one job and I don't go anywhere else."

"You can help me, then. Who was playing? Think of everybody, if you can."

Britton reflected before he answered. "Them two young gentlemen what are stopping here who are always together. Fair inseparables they are, as you might say. Mr. Searle and Mr. Ellis—their names are. Then there was that Mr. Wells, another gentleman stopping in the hotel. The 'Ome Secretary, Mr. Griggs—'im that's dead—'e 'ad a game late in the evening. Then later on, after the theatre was over, Mr. Palliser, the actor-chap, had a game. And another fellow—a stranger. Big chap. Played three 'undreds up. Came in specially. I think that would be the full packet. Can't remember anybody else."

"Who played with Mr. Griggs, the Home Secretary?"

Britton cocked his head to one side. "Let me see now. Mr. Griggs had three separate games. One with young Searle, one with Mr. Palliser, and, last of all, one with the stranger."

"Sure of these facts?"

"Quite sure, sir."

"Thank you, Britton. Now tell me this. As far as you know, were relations friendly in the billiard-room throughout the evening?"

"How do you mean, sir—exactly?"

"No quarrels or anything? No dispute or anything over a game? No Reece-Inman business, for example?"

Britton grinned appreciatively. "Old Mel's all right. Don't you believe all you read, sir. It's bark with 'im, you know. Not bite. *And*, of course, publicity! No—it was all O.K. last night, sir. They were all what you'd call merry and bright. All amicable and good boys together and—" Britton stopped with an abrupt suddenness.

Anthony felt certain that a reminiscence had come to him. "Well—what's the matter?" he asked. "Thought of anything?"

Britton shook his head as though in explanation. "Well, I *have* just thought of one thing, sir, to tell you the truth. It hadn't struck me before. Your question about them being all friendly like brought it into my mind. I'll tell you what I did notice. Mr. Wells and the Honourable Mr. Griggs never spoke a word to each other for the whole time they were in the room. I did notice that, now you've come to speak of these things. Nothink in it, of course. Strangers to each other. Didn't know each other and 'adn't met before. No reason why they should 'old converse, was there? All the same, in a billiard-room—the hatmosphere's usually what you'd call amicable." He again stressed the second syllable of the word.

Anthony turned to Inspector Sutton. "Wells! Satisfied with him?"

Sir Austin intervened explosively. "What did I tell you directly we came in? Didn't I tell you that I didn't care for the sound of him? Look at the facts for yourself, Bathurst. This man Wells turns up here almost at the identical time that Griggs himself did. Why? Why should he? Who is he? Why the coincidence? Must be something in it. Get to work on the Wells end at once, Inspector.

Get at the truth of him and I'll lay ten to one you'll find that he had a motive for killing Griggs. Thank goodness, the case is going to work out satisfactorily after all. I was afraid at the beginning that it was going to present unusual difficulties."

"You may be right, sir," declared Anthony, "but there's a lot yet that we don't know. Working on the billiard line, we find that Griggs played with Searle, Basil Palliser, the actor, and a stranger whom so far, Inspector, you say that you haven't been able to trace. I should certainly like to see some of these other people. Any of 'em round and about at the moment, Inspector Sutton?"

"Yes, sir. Mr. Palliser is, for one. Mornings and evenings are the times when you can't catch him."

"Good," returned Anthony quietly. "Fetch Mr. Palliser, will you?"

Chapter VII
"JEUNE PREMIÈRE"

Basil Palliser timed his entrance to the lounge of the Lansdowne Hotel with his usual aplomb. Although he regarded the position as somewhat humiliating, there was an absence of applause, for instance, the fact that Sir Austin Kemble, the Commissioner of Police himself, was in the cast of interrogation mollified him considerably.

Inspector Sutton received him and made the convenient introductions. Anthony Bathurst at once questioned him.

"You were aware, of course, Mr. Palliser, that the Home Secretary, Mr. Griggs, was in the hotel?"

"Oh, quite. I met him here in this very lounge after dinner, just before I went to the theatre, and afterwards, I regret to say, encountered him in the billiard-room. Appallin' feller. Dead now—which I suppose makes a certain amount of difference. But—er—well—a poisonous-lookin' blighter and—appallin'."

"Were you in the hotel during the afternoon?"

"Yes. I had no matinée. Same as to-day. Loose afternoon. But Griggs wasn't here then. Believe somebody told me that he went for a car ride or something."

"So your acquaintance with the murdered man may be said to have been strictly limited, Mr. Palliser?"

"Oh—absolutely. His society was far more to be avoided than sought after, believe me. I deplore his death, of course. One does. One has to. It's conventionally right. We're taught to do these things. Like keeping clean—and fit."

Sir Austin Kemble intervened. Palliser received the question that the Commissioner put to him with that lazy-eyed indifference and nonchalant carelessness that invariably distinguished his performances before provincial audiences.

"My movements are very easily remembered and quite explainable. I left for the theatre at about twenty to eight. I'm not on until the middle of the first act. I stayed at the 'Orphic' until the rag fell, cleared off, and took my own time in strolling back to the Lansdowne. Came part of the way with my *jeune premiére*. She's digging in Swynford Street. Always does when she plays Lokingham. I got here about twenty to eleven, I should think. Had a 'spot' and went into the billiard-room. Played a hundred up with Griggs and then another with a bloke named Ellis. Quite a decent feller, Ellis. Staying in the hotel. On the road, I fancy. I don't know what in."

"What time did Griggs himself leave the billiard-room?"

"H'm. Let me think. I should say about a quarter past eleven."

"Thank you, Mr. Palliser. Didn't hear anything in the night, I suppose?"

Palliser shook his head. "Not a murmur. Still—that doesn't mean a thing. I sleep like the dead when I'm tired. And when I'm not tired—well, that's about every alternate Coronation day."

Anthony smiled. He tried another attack. "Did you notice the other people who were playing in the billiard-room, Mr. Palliser? At all? Besides Searle and Ellis, the two commercials, there were two others playing, weren't there?"

"There were. But I don't know that I noticed them particularly. There was nothing to make me do so. Neither of 'em was what you'd call a conversationalist. The chap that's staying here—Wells, I think his name is, is definitely not a gentleman. The other bloke was a dour, silent customer. Hard-bitten. Good billiards player, though. Came in the room, I should say, specially for a game. While he was playing, drank scarcely anything. Judging by his form probably plays billiards every night of his life. I never saw finer close cannons from an amateur. Presume that he *was* an amateur. Occasionally, you know, you run across a pro. having a busman's holiday, and pay for the experience." Palliser extended his long arms lazily and stifled a yawn. "Anything more that you want of me, gentlemen?"

"Yes," said Sir Austin Kemble, "there is just one point that has struck me. It's quite a small one. Had you ever met the Home Secretary before, Mr. Palliser, or was he a complete stranger to you?"

Palliser struck an attitude. "Up to now, Sir Austin, God has been very good to me. The Home Secretary and I were unknown to each other. I knew *of* him—that was all. I had met him—but had never spoken to him."

He looked round—expectant for further questions, but none came. "I may go?" asked Basil Palliser.

The Commissioner nodded and dismissed him.

"Well," said Mr. Bathurst, "have we made any advance do you think?"

Sir Austin wagged a sapient head. "Oh—he's all right. Like most of those actor chaps. Doesn't hate himself, you know. It's the life that does it. Crowds of gaping women in the theatre queues always. Seven in ten for most plays and nine in ten for the 'sexy' stuff. These chaps get swelled heads—and half of it's not their fault. It's the blasted women that cause the trouble."

Anthony smiled. An indignant Sir Austin always amused him. Inspector Sutton gazed discreetly out of the window. From his point of view there were some things that needed no answer.

"What's the show at the 'Orphic'? Palliser's, I mean?" The question came from Anthony.

"The manager did tell me," returned Sutton, "but I can't think of it at the moment. Two words. The title, I mean. Something to do with a tea-pot, I fancy."

Anthony walked over and picked up a copy of the *Lokingham Echo* that lay on the divan. "This will tell us," he said, as he sat down. "The local paper always features the local shows. Now—where are we?"

Anthony turned the pages in his search. He found the column he wanted. "Here we are. 'Orphic Theatre, Traquair Road, Lokingham. Special engagement of Howard Baluster's Number One Company. *Strained Relations*—no tea-pots, Sutton, though I get your association. 'With Basil Palliser and—'" Anthony uttered a sharp exclamation and sprang from the divan to his feet. "Sir Austin—look here—please—and you, Inspector! Amazing!"

Sir Austin and the Inspector went to the paper and followed the direction of Anthony Bathurst's pointing finger. Anthony repeated the words aloud.

"With Basil Palliser and Phillida Fortescue."

Phillida Fortescue! The name on one of the visiting-cards found in the dead man's bed-room! Sir Austin let go a low whistle. The cat, by now, was well among the pigeons.

A slight noise caused the three men to turn.

CHAPTER VIII
THE TWO TRAVELLERS

A MAN had stuck his head round the door of the lounge.

"Mr. Staniforth tells me that I'm wanted again. Who wants me this time? Anybody above an Inspector, or is it—"

Inspector Sutton beckoned to the speaker. "Come in, Mr. Searle, if you please."

The man entered and closed the door behind him. The Inspector explained the position in detail.

"I see," remarked Searle. "Well, fire away. I'm at your service, gentlemen. Ask me all you want. That'll be O.K. with me."

Anthony's first questions were of a general nature. There was one point, however, that he quickly elicited. Like Basil Palliser before him, Searle had had little time for the man who had been murdered.

"Candidly," he remarked, "he gave me the idea that he had something on his mind. Seemed to want to keep himself to himself as much as possible. When I think that's the case with anybody, I'm the last person in the world to want to force myself upon a bloke. I should never have gone on the road. When I did so, I must have been the world's craziest optimist! I told Inspector Sutton here the very same thing."

"But you played billiards with Griggs? That implies a certain amount of social approach, surely?"

"That's true," Searle conceded, "but only up to a point. Neither of us was garrulous while we played. I heard Griggs mutter 'bloody fluke' several times under his breath, but beyond that—well . . ."

Searle shrugged his shoulders.

"Pretty late, your game, wasn't it?"

"Towards the end of the evening."

"What time would you say?"

"I told Inspector Sutton about ten past ten. That wouldn't be much out."

"You were playing billiards the whole of the evening?"

"I suppose I was—more or less. Chiefly more. I was in the billiard-room all the time . . . except when I came out to order drinks. I'll tell you what, though, if my opinion's any good to you, Inspector . . ." Searle swung round on to Inspector Sutton.

The latter faced him unsmilingly. "Don't know that it is. Anyhow, spill it to Mr. Bathurst here."

Searle grinned. His good temper showed on his face, and he disregarded Sutton's thrust. "Well—what I *was* going to say was this: Have any of you gentlemen considered the possibility of this crime having a political significance?"

Searle paused. As nobody spoke, he went on again. "These Cabinet Minister johnnies, you know, are often mixed up in things that the ordinary man in the street's got no idea of. Diplomacy and secret treaties and things of that kind. They make many enemies and precious few friends. For instance, Griggs has upset several of the U.S.A. people. I happen to know that for a fact. You hear a lot on the road."

Inspector Sutton and Mr. Bathurst heard him out without interruption, and when he had finished there was silence for a while. Eventually Sir Austin Kemble broke that silence. Searle's suggestion seemed to be ignored.

"What time did you go to bed, Mr. Searle?"

"A little after midnight. Say ten minutes to twelve. Ellis and I have room number fifty-five. Next to the room where Griggs was." Searle spoke quite simply.

Anthony deliberated. He was uncertain as to the exact form of his next question. Searle, however, solved his difficulty by volunteering the information.

"After I finished playing billiards with Griggs, I played another hundred up with Ellis. Wells, the other man in the billiard-room, had gone upstairs some time before that. I think I heard him say that he was tired. Then, when Ellis and I had finished, we both went to bed. Say about a quarter to twelve. It's only five minutes. But it might be nearer."

Anthony intervened. "Did Wells and Griggs have much conversation? Did you notice?"

Searle shook his head. "Very little, I should say, from what I saw of them."

Anthony thrust. "Now—with regard to Palliser, the actor who came in after the theatre was over."

"Yes, know him well. Met him here before. Two or three times. Jolly nice chap. One of the best, in fact."

"No doubt. He had a game with the Home Secretary, didn't he?"

"Yes. Didn't last long. Palliser's pretty hot with a cue, I can tell you. Ran out, I fancy, with an unfinished forty-six or thereabouts. Following a twenty-two. Griggs couldn't go that pace. Palliser had him stone-cold soon after they'd started."

"Palliser all right? With Griggs, I mean? No unpleasantness of any kind—that you noticed?"

"Good Lord—no! How could there be?" Searle was emphatic in the denial.

"Now," continued Mr. Bathurst, "I want you to tell me something else. There was another player in the billiard-room about this time. A stranger. Is that right?"

"Quite right. Came into the hotel for a drink, I should say, and strolled into the billiard-room for a game. Big chap . . . with a determined jaw. He was a thunderin' good player, too. If he had played Palliser level, shouldn't like to bet. Just a matter of how the balls rolled."

Anthony eyed him intently. "Tell me this, Mr. Searle, if you can. What time did this chap clear out? If you can't tell me for certain—don't guess. A guess might complicate matters for me."

"Couldn't say exactly, Mr. Bathurst. But 'Chick' Ellis might be able to tell you. He was with the chap more than I was." Searle glanced at his watch. "He's probably knocking about somewhere—Ellis, I mean. Said he'd be back about this time. Old 'Chick's' nearly always pretty reliable. On time and things like that."

Inspector Sutton caught Anthony's eye. "I'll get Ellis, Mr. Bathurst, if he's about. I think I know where I can find him."

"Good—get him, will you?"

Sutton was back with Ellis in a matter of minutes. "Chick" Ellis was tall and slim and fair. But he looked, nevertheless, like a man who always knew his own mind and where it was taking him.

On the general question concerning Griggs's movements Ellis told much the same story as Searle, which threw little light on the main problem. When, however, Mr. Bathurst came to the point of the time of the departure of the unknown billiard player, he was able to supply the information which had not been forthcoming from his friend.

"I can answer that," he said emphatically, "because I happened to notice particularly. The big fellow went out of the room within a few seconds of Griggs going. It looked to me, almost, as though he'd followed him out. It was less than a couple of minutes."

"Sure of that?" commented Anthony. He forced on Ellis the importance of the question and its subsequent answer.

"Absolutely positive."

"You didn't hear anything, I suppose, after the two men went out?"

"Not a word. Not a sound. There wasn't anything in the nature of an altercation, if that's what you mean. As far as I know, Griggs went to bed soon after he left the billiard-room, and the other bloke cleared off."

"The Home Secretary's room was number fifty-four."

"Yes. That's so. Searle and I were in fifty-five—next door to him—so that had there been a rough house in there after we got upstairs we should have heard. Although the walls are pretty substantial, I should say. I've slept in the hotel many times in the past and can't remember ever having been disturbed by anything from adjoining bedrooms. Just as well, I suppose. Still, you never know—you fall asleep—dead to the world—and while you're like that, anything can happen."

"Thank you, Mr. Ellis," said Anthony. "That's all very clear. I don't think that I need detain you any longer."

Ellis, surprisingly, flushed to the roots of his fair hair. The flush, Sir Austin recognized, was a flush of relief. Ellis was inordinately self-conscious, and now that the job that he had to do was over, his qualities of nervousness and self-consciousness returned to him. He was of the type that only eliminates consciousness of self when the mind is removed from the contemplation of that self to the execution of a particular piece of work. He bowed to the men whom he was on the point of leaving, left the lounge, and closed the door quietly behind him.

"Nothing more in all that," declared the Commissioner. "After all, why shouldn't one man go out of a room just after another? Most natural thing in the world. They'd had a game, and the game was over. Nothing to remain there for. Good Lord—just what you'd expect to happen."

Inspector Sutton nodded his discreetly subordinate approval.

Anthony contented himself with a generality. "Very likely, Sir Austin. On the other hand, it might bear looking into. We can't shut our eyes to one thing. Somebody killed Griggs."

He rose and stood for a moment, deep in thought. Then he turned to the Commissioner and Inspector Sutton.

"I'm going back to that number fifty-four bedroom, sir. I don't know exactly why. But I've a feeling that I may have missed something. One gets a hunch that way sometimes."

The three men went upstairs. Anthony went to the floor on his knees.

"Pity the maid crashed the early morning cup of tea tray and messed up the carpet. Complicated things a bit." He gradually worked his way round the room. "Nothing here that I can see," he remarked on rising.

He walked across and looked again at the bed. The body of the Home Secretary had been removed, but the bed-clothes were as they had been before.

"That book that was found," declared Anthony, "let me have another look at that. My idea concerns that book."

Sutton took the book from the dressing-table and handed it to Anthony Bathurst. Anthony took it and turned it over carefully.

"I've learned to suspect books," he said, with a smile. "More than once in my chequered career I have discovered important significances between the pages of a book. There was that bizarre case of the 'Black Twenty-Two', embracing the memoirs of Réné de St. Maure; there was the puppetry case of Ewart Kenriston, with the mauve Edna, and there was also the more recent affair of the 'Sussex Cuckoo', where a dead man's sheets of manuscript held a vital document."

Anthony fluttered the pages of the book towards the floor. To the surprise of the Commissioner and Inspector Sutton three flimsy little objects dropped from between the pages and fell to the carpet.

"Good gracious!" cried Sir Austin. "What the blazes are they?"

Anthony stooped down and picked up the three objects. Sir Austin and Sutton crowded round him.

"Melon seeds," said Anthony quietly. "Three of 'em."

"Melon seeds," echoed the Inspector. "What on earth are they doing there? Melon seeds in a book?"

"They may mean nothing," replied Mr. Bathurst, "but, on the contrary, they may mean a lot. Surely, Inspector, you don't need me to remind you of the Ku-Klux-Klan?"

"What—those night-shirt people—do you mean?"

"You may call them that, if you choose," returned Anthony quietly, "but the fact remains, my dear Inspector, that the

Ku-Klux-Klan is perhaps the most powerful secret society in the world."

"You don't say," said Inspector Sutton excitedly.

Anthony did, however, and spoke at length upon the habits and activities of the Ku-Klux-Klan. Inspector Sutton was suitable impressed.

CHAPTER IX
SIR AUSTIN BRINGS UP THE PAST

Sir Austin Kemble sat with Anthony Bathurst and Inspector Sutton. He was in genuinely high feather. The Commissioner had been in communication with the Yard that morning and as a result thereof he felt extremely satisfied with himself. He had brought off what he considered to be a triumph of memory. Up to now he had kept the information from Mr. Bathurst, but he felt now that the time was ripe for confidence. He toyed with certain papers on his lap until he felt that the time had matured to strike. Suddenly he looked up and spoke.

"Bathurst," he said quietly, "something has given me a new angle on this case of ours. Do you recall the death of an actress on St. Aidans pier? The case of Daphne Arbuthnot?"

The name sounded familiar to Anthony. "Let me see. Yes . . . I do. Vaguely. I didn't study it to any great extent. I was in Ireland at the time. On that affair of the tortoise-shell cigarette-case. The murder of that doctor in Donegal. Girl died on the stage, didn't she? Drug affair, was it?"

"H'm!" replied Sir Austin. "Well—I'll tell you something—I'm beginning to wonder."

Anthony stared at him interestedly. "Why, sir, what have you got for me?"

"I don't know that I . . ." Sir Austin fumbled with his papers and adjusted his glasses. "Listen to this, then. This is a résumé of the case that I have had specially prepared for your observations."

Anthony stared at him in wonderment. Sir Austin began his account.

"St. Aidans, as you know—and nearly everybody else—is the adjoining seaside town to Spearings, and if you walk along the sea-front from the latter place you will come, in time, and probably without realizing it, to the sister resort of St. Aidans. The girl, Daphne Arbuthnot, died in most extraordinary circumstances.

"She was an actress attached to a touring company controlled by the Howard Baluster circuit. The show was a revival of Dearden and Pertwee's *Interference* and Miss Arbuthnot had been cast for 'Deborah Kane', covering the usual spring and summer tour of the South Coast. They were playing St. Aidans in the early part of May. There, at that particular time of the year, they have come, I may say, to be regarded as a hardy annual." The Commissioner paused.

"The early part of May?" This from Anthony.

"A-ha," said Sir Austin, "but I'll go on. I'll read now from the report that MacMorran has sent down. If I do that, it may help you to understand."

He coughed. "It must be understood that St. Aidans possesses no theatre. That is to say in the usual acceptance of the word. Such performances as it enjoys from week to week take place in the wooden pavilion at the end of the pier. Towards the close of the season, the wash and murmur of the waves of the sea have been known to give certain productions a 'noises off' accompaniment that is entirely unrehearsed and which seems to the audience to border on the bizarre."

"MacMorran likes to spread himself a bit," interjected Sir Austin, "when he gets a fair chance."

"MacMorran's a good scout," said Anthony. "I won't hear a word said against him. Go on."

Sir Austin hummed and hawed. "The intimation that the performance had been abandoned was given to the waiting audience some twenty minutes after the curtain had fallen on the second scene of the second act. The S.M. made it from the front of the drop-curtain."

Anthony leant forward. "Where's all this leading to?"

"You'll hear in a minute. You've often kept me in suspense. Now it's my turn."

"I know the play," said Anthony with a smile. "I saw the original production at the St. James's—Du Maurier, dark-haired Hilda Moore, and Bart Marshall. What was the stage manager's name by the way?"

"It's all here, if you're patient. Let me see now—where is it? Here you are. Roger Langley."

Anthony nodded. "Thought as much. Right-o."

"As you've raised the question, I'll read you what Langley said. MacMorran's got it all here—verbatim." Sir Austin turned a page.

"'Ladies and gentlemen,' said Langley, 'I regret to inform you that a most serious accident has occurred to a member of the company. A doctor has been sent for and he has been behind for over ten minutes. As a result of what has happened, it is with the utmost regret that I tell you, of course, it is necessary that to-night's performance be abandoned. Believe me, the management are left with no option. Miss Arbuthnot, the lady concerned, is seriously ill and doubts are entertained of her recovery. If you inquire at the box office at the entrance to the pier, passes will be issued for the performance of the same play which we hope to give here to-morrow evening, commencing at the usual time.'"

The Commissioner looked over his glasses. "Later on, of course, you may remember, the play was abandoned for the remainder of the week, and the pavilion so far has not been re-opened." He cleared his throat. "The Inspector who took over the case at this stage was your old friend, Inspector Baddeley, of the Sussex Constabulary."

"No!" said Anthony delightedly. "You don't say so? Jolly good! I'm all ears."

"Well, first of all then, listen to the statement that was volunteered by a certain gentleman who happened to be sitting in the audience—in the centre of the stalls—second row from the front. He's a J.P. living at Spearings. Name of Finlayson. James Carly Finlayson. I'll follow MacMorran and read that to you. Just a moment." Sir Austin fumbled for another document.

"Finlayson's statement ran as follows. 'I was in the audience. Stalls—second row—centre. I formed certain conclusions from what I saw on the stage itself and from what I heard the stage manager say in front of the curtain. I should like to say that I had the glasses on Miss Arbuthnot for best part of the second scene of the second act. When she was *supposed* to be lying dead on the divan. When she "died" (in the play, that is), she fell on to a divan arrangement up stage left. That is to say, on the audience's right.

"'Well, I had the glasses on her very carefully and what I took to be a particularly fine piece of acting on her part I am absolutely convinced now wasn't acting at all! She was actually dead, in my opinion, all the time that she lay there. And I'll tell you what makes me say so. *Because she never breathed once during the whole of the scene.* I can make that statement very confidently.'"

Sir Austin put away the piece of paper from which he had been reading. He spoke quietly.

"Dr. McFarlane, the doctor who was called to the girl, afterwards stated that Miss Arbuthnot had been poisoned by prussic acid."

Bathurst's interruption was abrupt and to the point. "Which happens to be the very poison designated in the play, Sir Austin. I feared as much." He shook his head gravely and gestured to the Commissioner. "Well—what happened after that—after the Finlayson chap had had his say?"

"The various members of the cast were then sent for, one by one, and questioned. Would you like to hear what each of them had to say?"

"When you come to Palliser, I shall."

Sir Austin Kemble wagged his head sagely. "You wait a bit, my boy. I've a surprise in store for you. In a minute, I'm going to make you sit up sharply and take notice. The part of the dead girl's lover—'Voaze'—the man who poisons her in the play—was played by . . ." Sir Austin paused a moment, "a fellow called Rodney Fenwick. He swore all the way that he was absolutely innocent. That he gave Miss Arbuthnot ordinary brandy . . . nothing else . . . and nothing more. In short, he knew nothing whatever about it."

"H'm—after him—who came next?"

"The man who had played the lead—the part of Sir John Marlay. His name was—er—Basil Palliser. Now his position was rather peculiar. I mean in relation to the play."

"I know what you mean," said Anthony. "Go on."

"You must remember in this connection," continued the Commissioner, "that Miss Arbuthnot was alive just before the fall of the curtain of the first scene of the second act—several people saw her and spoke to her. *Therefore*, unless she left the stage during the 'black-out' somebody poisoned her on the stage between the fall of the curtain on Scene One and the fall of the curtain on Scene Two. That's elementary, isn't it, my dear boy?"

Inspector Sutton groped for enlightenment. His brows were knitted in some measure of bewilderment.

"'Black-out'?" he repeated. "I think I know what you mean—but if you were to—"

Sir Austin assumed the voice of instruction. "The entire stage is in darkness. That's what is meant by the term."

"Yes. I see, sir. I thought I'd got the idea. And the curtain, of course, is down all that time."

"No," replied Bathurst sharply. "The interval between the two scenes of the play that comprise the second act is very short and the curtain ascends on a dark stage. The lights don't go up for a matter of some little time and one man enters and has the stage to himself during that time—save of course for 'Deborah Kane'—that is to say, Miss Arbuthnot."

"And that man was? . . ." queried Sutton softly.

"Basil Palliser, in the part of the eminent physician, 'Sir John Marlay'."

"You said just now, 'the lights don't go up for some little time'. How long—actually?"

"How long did he have the stage to himself, do you mean?"

Sutton nodded, and Sir Austin listened carefully.

Bathurst made a mental calculation. "I'm not sure from memory; put it at about two minutes and you won't be far out."

"H'm! Not what you'd call long for a job of murder."

"And part of those two minutes, Sutton, to be exact, for about two-thirds of them, I should think Basil Palliser's movements are plainly visible to the audience. But we're digressing—please continue your story, sir."

"I will now read to you," said Sir Austin Kemble, "various statements made by the other members of the cast. First of all,

I will deal with that made by Roger Langley, the man who was acting as stage manager. Here are the questions that were put to him and his answers to these questions. The questions were addressed to him by Inspector Baddeley. I have them here, reproduced verbatim.

"*Inspector Baddeley*: 'What are you in the company, Mr. Langley? What are your exact duties? You're not actually in this cast, are you?'

"*Roger Langley*: 'No, I'm S.M.—stage manager, you know. You may take it that I am, as it were, in charge of all the boys and girls. Get all the kicks and none of the ha'pence. My wife, of course, helps me. Also, I see to most of the odd jobs.'

"*Inspector Baddeley*: 'Such as? . . .'

"*Roger Langley*: 'Well—I've even done a "spot" of prompting on occasion. Must have somebody on the book. On tour, you know—especially when we're playing the provinces—it isn't frantically like starring in the West End. One has to be pretty versatile and to be prepared to take on most things at a second or so's notice.'

"*Inspector Baddeley*: 'Have you any suggestion to make with regard to this evening's affair?'

"*Roger Langley*: 'Not the foggiest! Haven't a glimmer. As a matter of fact, I was just saying the same thing to my wife as you arrived. It's positively amazing. As far as I know, dear old Daphne hadn't an enemy in the whole world.'"

Sir Austin looked up. "Here follows a note by Baddeley: 'It was evident that the tragedy had hit him hard. He thrust his right hand into his trouser pocket and kept it there as he embarked on his further explanation.'

"*Langley (continued)*: 'My wife's Stella Gresham, you know— she was playing Miss Arbuthnot's maid. They're on together in the first scene of Act Two. According to Stella, to whom I spoke at once, Daphne was as right as rain all through their show. Never put a foot wrong. You see, Daphne's been a bit "peaky" lately and a little slow on the beat, but Stella says she timed beautifully and never fluffed once to-night.'

"*Inspector Baddeley*: 'Properties—Mr. Langley? May I see the property poison-bottle, the liqueur-brandy-bottle, and the glass used by Rodney Fenwick, the man playing "Voaze", during the stage poisoning scene?'

"*Roger Langley*: 'With pleasure, Inspector. I have them all here for you. I guessed that you would want to examine them. So I kept my eye on them for you. I know what you Police johnnies are at a time like this.'"

"The props were examined," explained the Commissioner, lowering the paper from which he had been reading. "And Langley then went on to say:

"'Ordinary ginger-wine. Used in the show for liqueur brandy. It's one of the usual stage substitutes for spirits. Cold tea froths too much—gets a proper "head" on it and looks from the front far too much like beer to be really effective. As a slice of banana is to a cutlet, so is ginger wine to the genuine alcoholic article. That stuff's as safe as houses. Fenwick himself has swallowed several doses of it. Besides, I can prove that Fenwick's as innocent as I am. I choose the word "prove" deliberately. Now listen, Inspector. Miss Arbuthnot was alive just before the curtain went up for the second scene in Act Two. I know that for a positive fact—because I heard her speak to Palliser. Which proves conclusively that Fenwick *couldn't* have done it. Basil Palliser used to arrange for a bag, which it was necessary for him to pick up from the floor, to be in an *exact position—down right*—and he'd made a point of nipping on to the stage each show before we rang up for the second scene, to see that this bag was O.K. Palliser's a man who doesn't care about trusting other people. Well, I heard Daphne speak to him, and more than that, I heard Palliser answer. Then I saw him come off, immediately and go to the men's dressing-room. You understand—*immediately*.'

"*Inspector Baddeley*: 'Where were you at that time, Mr. Langley?'

"*Roger Langley*: 'Behind, of course. Everything was pretty slick, the beginners had been warned, and shortly afterwards I rang up.'

"*Inspector Baddeley*: 'I see. That certainly seems to eliminate Fenwick.'

"*Roger Langley*: 'Yes—and we're all very pleased to think that we know it. Old Rodney's one of the whitest and best.'

"*Inspector Baddeley*: 'Thank you, Mr. Langley. You've helped me considerably. I only hope that your company weathers the present storm and that no great financial loss ensues.'"

Sir Austin put down the paper. "I think that I may as well stop there. The Inspector said some more, but it's irrelevant and I won't worry you with it now. Now listen to Basil Palliser's statement, to which I'll turn next. I'll read that to you.

"After he had replied to a question concerning his entrance as 'Sir John Marlay' to 'Deborah Kane's' flat at the commencement of the second scene of the second act, Palliser gave vent to an opinion.

"'It's an absolute mystery to me, Inspector, and perhaps to me more than anybody. Daphne was alive just before that last curtain went up. She spoke to me and I spoke to her. If she'd have taken the fatal dose when Fenwick gave her the supposedly poisoned brandy in the play, she'd have been dead long before that. It's common knowledge that prussic acid acts almost instantaneously.'"

"'Miss Arbuthnot hadn't been too fit recently, had she?' Baddeley put this question diffidently.

"Palliser shook his head. 'No—she hadn't. In fact, we'd all been rather worried about it. Her heart had been a little "dicky", she told me, and that scene when she had to lie motionless for so long had taxed her strength more than once recently. So much so, that she told me she had felt properly exhausted at the end of her show.'

"'Thank you, Mr. Palliser.'

"That concludes Palliser's interview. I don't think that you need hear any more for the time being."

A faint smile flickered in Sir Austin's eyes as he asked the question. Anthony felt some surprise at seeing it there.

"Why do you suggest that, sir?" asked Mr. Bathurst. "Got something more up your sleeve?"

"Why not?" countered the Commissioner.

"You mean, I suppose, that our interest in the case begins and ends with Basil Palliser? He's the Alpha and the Omega of the business—eh?"

"No," said Sir Austin whimsically. "I don't altogether mean that. Like the bridegroom of the wedding feast at Cana, I've kept my good wine until the last—at least, I think that's what the beggar did."

Anthony eyed him curiously. This mood of Sir Austin's was new to him. "Well, sir, what have you got for me? Put me out of my misery."

"Well—just this. You'll rejoice to hear it. Amongst the audience, on the evening in question, was a distinguished personage."

Anthony stared at him. "Who?"

"The Home Secretary," replied Sir Austin gravely, "the Rt. Hon. A.S. Griggs, M.P. You know the name. I believe. He went behind the scenes during Act Two. Act Two—mark you. Invited, of course."

Anthony's face was set. Not a muscle moved. "Thank you very much. Now *I* want information, Sir Austin. The St. Aidans case didn't come under my notice at all. As I told you, I was in Ireland at the time. On the Helen Bryan case. What was the final result of it?"

"In the end the Police got nothing on anybody. 'Wilful Murder Against Some Person or Persons Unknown.' That was the verdict of the Coroner's jury. All the same, my dear Bathurst, it has left me wondering."

"Me, too," returned Anthony curtly.

He thrust his hands deeply into his pockets and began to pace the room. Sir Austin watched him. He knew his Bathurst . . . and when, also, to leave that Bathurst alone.

CHAPTER X
MISS FORTESCUE REMEMBERS

ANTHONY Bathurst, taking three quick strides, rang the bell of an unpretentious-looking dwelling house, designated in the rate-book of the Urban district of Lokingham as Number 22, Swynford Street. A woman with much bosom and more dirt opened the door to him. The look in her eyes was sullen.

"Good morning," said Anthony sweetly. "Is Miss Fortescue in, can you tell me?"

The woman glared at him. "Yes," she said, "she is. Who is it wants her?"

"Would you be good enough to give her my card and ask her if she would favour me with a few minutes' conversation?"

The woman, wiping her hands upon an apron, took the card somewhat after the manner of a curate handling a dilapidated copy of *Ruff's Guide*.

Anthony remained, meanwhile, in the doorway. The woman quickly returned.

"Come this way, if you please, sir. Miss Fortescue says that she won't keep you very long. In here, sir, if you don't mind." The woman pointed.

Anthony entered a room of stiff chairs and an uncompromising sofa, and there awaited the entrance of Phillida Fortescue.

When she came, he saw a tall, slim, fair girl. Her appearance agreeably surprised him. She had grace and poise and style.

"You want to speak to me?" she said simply. "What is it about?"

"I'll be frank with you, Miss Fortescue. I'm connected with Scotland Yard. But regard that connection at the moment as more unofficial than otherwise. A woman died recently on the pier at St. Aidans, and a man died yesterday in his bed at the Lansdowne Hotel, Lokingham. The former was poisoned. The latter was shot."

The girl's eyes showed fear. "I know. And I am sorry. But how do you suggest that I can help you?"

Anthony was direct. "You were in the *Interference* company and . . ." He paused.

"And what, Mr. Bathurst?"

"A card of yours was found in the Home Secretary's wallet—the man who was shot in his bed."

She smiled rather wearily. "That isn't a crime, surely. About my card, I mean?"

"Not at all, Miss Fortescue. But could you . . . help me?"

"Explain—do you mean?" She coloured.

Anthony nodded.

The girl looked away from him. "Mr. Griggs was favouring me with his attentions. That's all. There isn't any more. His attentions were just . . . unwelcome. His feelings were neither encouraged nor reciprocated."

"I see. There was no assignation here, then?"

Her eyes blazed. "Assignation? Not on my part, Mr. Bathurst. But he was at St. Aidans when we were there and it's quite possible that he had come here . . . for the same reason." She crimsoned again.

"I see. He came behind at St. Aidans . . . didn't he? Just before the death of Daphne Arbuthnot?"

"He did. I believe that he had a drink and a sandwich in the men's dressing-room. But that wasn't the room in which he . . . wanted to be." Phillida dropped her eyes.

"Tell me what you can of the St. Aidans affair, will you, Miss Fortescue, please?"

She hesitated. "I was cast as 'Barbara' in the play—the doctor's niece. I wasn't on in the second scene of Act Two. There are four people then, who go near Daphne. But each is in full view of the audience. I think . . ." She hesitated again.

"Tell me, Miss Fortescue, please—I promise you that I won't use anything that you may tell me without further reference to you."

She shook her head at his statement. "It isn't that, Mr. Bathurst. I want to be *sure* of everything, that's all. I *think* that Daphne was poisoned as she lay on the divan arrangement. And not before. Langley spoke the truth. The Police discovered that some of the fatal drink was actually spilt on the divan. There was a slight patch on it. The glass was passed to her in the dark, remember. Now what you have to decide is—who could have been in a position to induce a girl like Daphne to drink in the dark like that? To me the answer is plain. Somebody she must have had absolutely implicit confidence in, Mr. Bathurst. The police should find out who it is that fills that bill."

"Her lover, Miss Fortescue? Do you mean that? That's the only answer to your question of which I can think."

Miss Fortescue's chin tilted determinedly. "I agree with you. But I can give you no information as to who that was. Quite frankly—because I don't know. I really didn't know a thing. Daphne was an oyster when she liked."

"Any feeling against her in the company? Jealousy?"

She shook her head. "None at all. The whole affair was an absolute mystery to me. I can't think seriously that anybody in the world would have wanted to harm her. She was such a thoroughly good sort. In every way warm-hearted, generous, and never the least bit 'catty' if anybody had the fat. I am absolutely puzzled by it."

"Did she speak to Griggs at all when he went behind?"

Again she shook her head. "I didn't see it, if she did. I don't know that she even knew him."

Anthony had drawn blank.

Phillida went on. "I don't want to seem callous about it, but his death means nothing to me. As regards my sex—his tastes . . . were . . . catholic and he seems to have been generally disliked. Funny thing, when I went to the theatre last night one of the electricians was speaking to me about him and the murder. Said he was going to have an extra pint after the show to celebrate Griggs's passing." She shuddered. "Dreadful, isn't it? It appears that this man had seen him only the night before. It must have been only a few hours before he was murdered."

When he heard this, Anthony turned to her sharply. "Where was this?"

"In the billiard-room of the Lansdowne Hotel. This man said that he went in there for a game and Griggs was in there. I won't tell you what he called him . . . but I'm quite sure that he won't send any flowers to the funeral."

Anthony stared at her in amazement. "Tell me, Miss Fortescue—what's this man of yours like? What's his name?"

"Fowles. He's tall. Big nose. Strong jaw. A forbidding sort of expression. Why? As a matter of fact, I can't tell you much about him—because he's new. Hasn't been with us very long. Came to the company somewhere about April, I should think. Or perhaps towards the end of March."

Anthony's thoughts were racing through his brain. Here were complications. Palliser! Why the merry hell hadn't Palliser been frank about this man who had played billiards and whom he had described to them as a complete stranger! Anthony turned again to Phillida Fortescue.

"How many of the St. Aidans company are playing here in *Strained Relations*, Miss Fortescue?"

"Only Basil Palliser and I. Roger Langley's S.M. still and naturally his wife's with us too. But she's not in the cast here. She doesn't do a lot of acting. You see—the company was considerably altered after Daphne died. That was inevitable."

Anthony thought hard over what she had told him. He saw that he must have one more question answered.

"Tell me, Miss Fortescue. Was this electrician of yours, who plays billiards o' nights, with you at St. Aidans?"

She nodded affirmation at once. "Yes. I'm sure of that. I remember seeing him in the crowd when the police-inspector who came to the case was asking us all the questions. But why on earth do you ask me that?" Her eyes held wonderment.

Anthony shook his head. "I don't know quite why I asked you . . . and I don't know either, what it all means . . . but . . . to-morrow is also a day, Miss Fortescue."

When he had gone from her, Miss Fortescue burnt two letters.

CHAPTER XI
THE DISAPPOINTED MAN

Upon his return to the Lansdowne Hotel, Mr. Bathurst found a caller awaiting him. Anthony examined the card that the porter Roberts handed to him, with a strong degree of interest. For it so happened that he had seen the counterpart previously. The inscription on the card was, "Harold L. Oakley, Principal, Maxwell House Academy of Elocution and Dramatic Art, Malplaquet Street, Erlegh, Berkshire."

"I'll see Mr. Oakley, Roberts," said Mr. Bathurst. "I shall be very pleased to see him, in fact. It seems that I am drawn at home.

If he hadn't come to me I should most certainly have gone to see him. Arrange that we aren't disturbed, Roberts."

"I will, sir. In the smoke-room, sir. Thank you, sir."

Roberts smiled appreciatively. Under Mr. Staniforth's régime wages were not too high for the staff at the Lansdowne Hotel.

Anthony found a tall, thin man standing by the mantelpiece in the smoke-room. A man whom he judged to be either in the early forties or the late thirties. The man was hungry and lean, but gave Anthony at the same time the impression that he was a bundle of nervous energy. A man of undoubted force of personality. The photograph of him in his book on elocution did not do him justice.

His long fingers were working with excitement as Anthony approached him. He rose. "You are Mr. Anthony Bathurst?" he asked eagerly.

"I am, Mr. Oakley. Don't get up. Stay just where you were. I find your visit very welcome. I take it that you are here to see me in connection with the Griggs murder."

Oakley nodded quickly. "Yes. Yes. Is it . . . murder . . . for certain, I mean?"

"I'm afraid so. Little doubt of it, I fear. You've seen the papers, of course."

"Naturally, Mr. Bathurst. That's really why I'm here—because of the papers." Oakley paused abruptly.

"Go on," said Anthony encouragingly. "We know, of course, that you and Griggs were not unacquainted."

"Really? Oh . . . my card, I suppose?" His face, which had clouded, as suddenly cleared. "Yes, my card—no doubt. I gave him one when he called at my place the other day. On the afternoon of the day that he was killed, I suppose it would be."

"Do I understand that Griggs called on you, Mr. Oakley?"

"He did. And that's why I'm here, Mr. Bathurst. The point is that I'm the unluckiest man in the world. Always have been where money's concerned and always will be, I suppose, till they take me out feet first."

The chagrin and disappointment on Oakley's face were plain to see. Anthony watched him and the play of his emotions, but made no comment.

"I'll explain myself more clearly," said Oakley. "I've come for a book that belongs to me. Griggs got it from me but didn't pay for it. And honestly, Mr. Bathurst, things aren't so good with me that I can afford to lose the value of it. Just as I was *made*, too. Sitting on velvet! Griggs alive and Griggs dead are two vastly different propositions from my point of view, I can tell you."

"Tell me," smiled Anthony, "everything that you want to tell me. Then perhaps I shall understand better."

Oakley smiled back at him, but the smile was rueful in the extreme. "I'm an elocution teacher, Mr. Bathurst, working for myself and just beginning to make appreciable headway. I mean by that expression that my little school is my own. I'm not on the staff of a technical school or institute, for example. After two or three years of hard struggling, I'm just beginning to hold my own. More than that, as I said, I'm making headway. My methods are original and one or two of my side-lines are catching on. 'Elocution in business', for one. Well—imagine my delight, therefore, when a couple of afternoons ago a slap-up car stopped outside my little place and a man got out, came striding up my humble path, gave a sharp look around, and rang the bell. I answered the call and let him in . . . and . . . well—to cut a long story short—he told me he was A.S. Griggs, the Home Secretary . . . that he was interested in the question of 'Speech Training' generally . . . and eventually he took my breath away when he told me that he wanted me to give him a course of elocution lessons. Me—Harold Oakley. Said, too, which meant a tremendous lot to me—I'll be perfectly frank—that he didn't mind what he paid. In the end he agreed to pay me fifty guineas for my special private course. I positively jumped at the offer. You would have no difficulty in understanding that, Mr. Bathurst, if you realized what it meant to me.

"I gave him my book to read and look at, prior to his first lesson from me, which was to have been yesterday, and he arranged to pay both for the course and for the book when he came along to my place for the first lesson. My wife and I dreamed dreams. Little things that mean nothing to others—but a great deal to her and me. New clothes. A new settee in the better room." Oakley's voice broke in concentrated bitterness. "Those dreams of ours were short-lived. Somebody chose to murder him. It would be so." Oakley sat down and put his face in his hands.

Anthony respected his attitude. At length, Oakley spoke again.

"Damned bad luck for me, wasn't it, Mr. Bathurst? It's my wife that I worry about. She saw—not a cheque for fifty guineas—but a ray of light and comfort. Saw success for me not very far ahead. Taken up by a Cabinet Minister, you know the idea, a big honour for an obscure country teacher—Harold Oakley, the elocutionist who taught the Rt. Hon. A.S. Griggs, the Home Secretary. You know what wives are. Or—don't you?"

"Some," replied Anthony laconically.

"Well, mine's like that, Mr. Bathurst, bless her heart, and her pluck often keeps me going when I'm inclined to be a bit down in the mouth. I wouldn't change her for any other woman in the world. Can I have my book or does the law—"

Anthony shook his head. "The law does. You can't have the book, Mr. Oakley—that's a certainty as things are—but I will see that you are paid for it. I'll give you my own personal assurance on that."

Oakley flushed at the words. "I must seem horribly mercenary. But you're right. I shall be satisfied with the money."

"Render an account. Send it to me. Date it the day that Griggs took the book from you. I'll see that it's cleared up all right."

Oakley's face seemed a trifle brighter. "Oh—thanks awfully. That's good of you." He looked hard at Anthony. "I don't want you to get me all wrong, Mr. Bathurst. But perhaps you don't realise what that fifty guineas meant to me. I've had to scratch along with my money for years. Ever since I married. No margin, you know. This chance that I had was a God-send. I saw relief in front of me. Freedom, for a time at least, from care, worry—anxiety. Release from that wearing, tiring condition that spoils so much of Life for you. Then the doors were banged in my face again. See? Well—that's all I wanted to say." His pride halted him awkwardly. The man was embarrassed.

"Don't worry about anything," said Anthony Bathurst kindly. "I understand how you feel, perfectly. I understand and I sympathize as well. But tell me this, Mr. Oakley, if you can. Have you any definite idea as to why Griggs wanted these elocution lessons so *suddenly*?"

"Oh—yes. You needn't worry over that. He told me the reason when he first came into my place. Made it quite clear to me. It was because of his broadcasting activities—his recent wireless talks."

"Had he been criticized, then?"

"I fancy so, from what I could gather. He didn't say so in as many words, but that was my undoubted impression. That was the gist of it."

"He was a poorish speaker, I suppose?"

"Oh—absolutely hopeless. Almost everything he said was an offence to the trained elocutionist's ear. A vowel properly shaped in the mouth should be a resonant sound, but, my God, you should have heard his! And not the faintest idea of accurate consonantal attack. I should have earned my fifty guineas all right, don't you worry. It wouldn't have been altogether plain sailing."

"Could you have done anything with him? Of real benefit?"

"I could have *improved* him. That almost goes without saying. Take the voice, for example. We all can't have good voices—with 'tone—colour' and so on. If we don't happen to be in the front row when voices are given out—well, we don't get a good one. It's like blue eyes or red hair. We either get 'em or we don't. But—proper management of the voice and *knowing* how to use it means so much. Makes all the difference. Consider this point. How many great actors have fine voices? Not many. But you're an elocutionist yourself. I can tell that. There's no need for me to explain things to you."

Anthony smiled. "I was in the O.U.D.S. That ought to mean something, I suppose."

Oakley smiled back at him. "Not always, Mr. Bathurst, if you'll pardon my saying so."

"How many times had Griggs broadcast? I can't remember. Did he tell you?"

Oakley thought over the question. "I'm not quite sure. Let me see. He did talk of them to me. Either two or three times, I fancy."

"Don't mind this question, will you? Don't misunderstand me. Why did he come to *you*? Why do you *think* that he came to you? Because, you will admit—it was unexpected."

Oakley flushed again under the questions, and as he did so, Anthony was sorry that he had asked them.

"As it happens—I can tell you," said Oakley quietly. "He said that he came to me because I was an unknown man. He said that he didn't want other people to know that he was going to take lessons. If he had gone to one of the fashionable people in town it would have become a topic of general news. Quite feasible, I think, don't you—knowing the man?"

"H'm! Yes—I think that the explanation could be reasonably accepted. After all, the whole business touches, in a way, on that constant factor—human vanity. It's strong, I suppose, in all of us. Just as much now as when the preacher made his historic statement."

Oakley nodded. "I suppose you're right. At any rate, I think that it would have been so with this man Griggs. Not a doubt of it. All the same, I wish now that he hadn't picked on me for his tutor. At least, I should have been spared a bitter disappointment."

"Yes. As I told you before, you have my sincere and worthless sympathy, Mr. Oakley. But we can't arrange these things, you know. We're the puppets of Fate. The gods have us on a chain all the time and they continually remind us of the fact. The length of the particular chain varies—that's all."

Oakley rose on the point of departure. "Well—there's no point in my staying any longer. In a way I'm sorry I came. But I'd brooded on the matter and I had the impulse to come—and there you are."

Anthony smiled. "Don't be sorry. For one thing, you've given me certain information that wasn't in my possession before. I'm indebted to you for it. My thanks."

Oakley flushed again, this time with clear justification. "That's jolly decent of you. But I feel—how shall I put it?—well—*humiliated*. Understand me?"

Anthony held out his hand. "Every time. But don't lose any sleep over it."

CHAPTER XII

IN THE DENNET WATER

INSPECTOR Sutton came to Anthony in a state of excitement. Anthony wondered at him.

"News, Mr. Bathurst—news! Hot news! The freshest ever! What do you think?"

"No idea, Inspector. Brains not working to-day. Shoot."

With an air of mystery, Sutton drew his hand from his pocket. "You couldn't have used a better word, Mr. Bathurst. I mean it. Take a look at that."

With a quick turn of the wrist, Sutton put something on the table. It was a revolver. Regulation Army pattern.

Anthony left his lethargy and his eyes gleamed. "Good news, Sutton? Where did you get it? In a raffle?"

Sutton smiled triumphantly. "Where do you think?"

"Not the foggiest. Have a heart, Inspector. Tell me all."

"I wanted that weapon badly, Mr. Bathurst. Argued it all out with myself. That's a way I have. It wasn't in Griggs's bedroom— was it? Therefore, I said to myself, it must be somewhere else."

"Oh—excellent, Inspector. The epitome of the science of deduction. Nobody believes in that more than I. Well?"

"Well, I worked things out as I thought they might well have happened. See here. I started with the notion that the murderer, after he had killed Griggs, took the weapon away with him . . . with the natural idea of getting rid of it at the first available opportunity. The question then arose in my mind—where best could he have done this? See my idea?"

"Naturally! Go on, Inspector."

"Well—I organized a thorough search of all the likeliest places. Combed all of 'em out. I worked on the route idea. You know what I mean. The various directions that a chap might take after leaving this hotel . . . assuming that he had the weapon with him when he left. Remember the Thompson and Bywaters affair at Ilford in Essex?"

Anthony nodded.

"Very well. Formed strong opinions about it, too. Agree with the late Lord Birkenhead."

Sutton waxed enthusiastic at his reception. "If you remember, the murder took place in a street very close to Ilford station. Late at night. To the best of my memory, the husband and wife were coming home after a visit to the theatre."

"Quite correct, Sutton. They had been to a Ben Travers' play. *The Dippers*, I think. Date—October the third."

"Bywaters met them and stabbed Thompson in the neck. Stabbed him several times. Then—in a panic, no doubt—ran away. But he disposed of his weapon. A sailor's knife. Can you remember what he did with it?"

Anthony smiled. "Yes, Inspector. I can even do that. He threw it down a street drain. The Police discovered it there a short time afterwards. Am I right, Inspector?"

"Quite right, Mr. Bathurst. You seem to have most of the facts. You had nothing to do with the case, I suppose?"

Anthony shook his head. "No, Sutton. Before my time. The first thing that I touched of this kind was the murder in the billiard-room at Sir Charles Considines'. I was dragged into that . . . and since then . . . have paid the penalty."

Sutton nodded approvingly. "I remember the affair. In Sussex. Well—to get back to where we were. I worked on the lines that I've indicated to you. Now, one of the usual ways out of Lokingham, from the Lansdowne Hotel, that is, is over the Dennet Bridge. You've probably stood on the bridge yourself and looked at the little Dennet stream underneath. Picturesque—to say nothing else of it. I had that Dennet water dragged this morning. My men were on the job for some time. Eventually, as you see patience and industry did not go unrewarded. Two of my chaps, Rutherford and Welsh, their names are, fished out this revolver. So we've made one step in the right direction. Well—what have you got to say to me? It's O.K., isn't it?"

"Oh—congratulations—and all that. You've done remarkably well, Inspector. A smart piece of work on your part. But you haven't told me all. You're keeping something up that official sleeve of yours. I'm dead sure of that. Come on—out with it—don't spoil the ship for a ha'porth of tar—finish the story."

Sutton cocked his head to one side. There was no gainsaying the fact that he was extremely pleased with himself. He had scored a definite point. Say what you like—he hadn't allowed the grass to grow under his feet, and he hadn't permitted the Scotland Yard people to walk off with *all* the honours. When Mr. Bathurst heard what else he had to say, he might be still more impressed with the work that he, Sutton, had so far accomplished. The word "Promotion" had a sweet savour.

"Not only have I discovered it . . . but I've traced the ownership of that revolver, Mr. Bathurst. Haven't been long over that—have I?"

"By Jove—no! Good man! Whose is it? Anybody we know?"

"Care to take a guess at it?"

Anthony shook his head with certainty. "I always endeavour not to guess at anything, Inspector. It's so frightfully dangerous. You never know where you'll get. More often than not—*much* more often—'guessing' leads you up the garden. I'll ask you a question, though, if I may. Do you fancy that you've got your hooks in the Home Secretary's murderer?"

Sutton looked a trifle disconsolate at the remark. This was the question which he had been hoping Mr. Bathurst would *not* ask him. However, he had, and that fact conceded, he just perforce be answered.

"No, Mr. Bathurst, I can't, honestly, commit myself as far as that. I'm not exactly a fool, you know."

Anthony was surprised at the terms of Sutton's answer. He had been prepared, it must be confessed, for something a good deal more like certainty on the Inspector's part.

"Oh—why not?"

"For a very good reason, indeed, Mr. Bathurst. Look at it for yourself. That revolver *can't* have belonged to Griggs's murderer."

"It can't! Sure of that?"

"Absolutely. It was a disappointment to me, I'll own, when I found it out. The truth is that this revolver belonged to the Home Secretary himself. And Dr. Wickham hasn't a doubt that the bullet that killed him was fired from it."

This information stung Anthony into an exclamation. "Good Lord, Inspector! Is that a fact? Complicates the situation considerably, doesn't it?"

"I'll say so, Mr. Bathurst. But there's not a doubt about it. I've had it identified by Griggs's chauffeur. He's been down here to-day. As a rule he drove for Griggs, but on this last business Griggs told him when he started out that he wouldn't require him and left him at home. He identified the revolver at once. Never hesitated a second over it."

Anthony frowned. "What's his name?"

"Lester. Horace Lester."

"What exactly did you ask him, Inspector, and how exactly did he answer? I'm interested in this. It may prove important."

"I'll tell you what he told me. One—that Griggs invariably carried the revolver with him. Lester says 'wherever he went'. That was the exact phrase he used. Had an idea that as a prominent politician he was always likely to make enemies and be up against it. And two—this is on all fours with the previous statement—that his master always made a point of taking it with him when he went to bed. What do you make of that?"

Anthony thought over the Inspector's question. "It's hard to say, Sutton. Might be significant and mean a lot. On the other hand—might not. There's this to it. A man in Griggs's position isn't altogether comparable with the man in the street. So very different. He meets so many people . . . of all kinds and classes . . . and makes so many more contacts. Some that this chap made may have been unhealthy for him. One can't tell. Also, there may have been international complications, for instance. If you remember, Inspector, Searle, one of those travellers whom we have interviewed, made a definite suggestion of that kind. It would be interesting to know how long Griggs has carried that revolver. Whether he suddenly took to the habit or has done so for years. That information might help us a lot."

Sutton made a mental note. "I'll tackle friend Lester on the point. He might know."

"Decent bloke, this Lester?"

"Seems so. The usual chauffeur to a man who thought himself no end important. A bit on the common side. Plenty of what the cat cleans itself with. Suited his guv'nor, no doubt. If I knew him—Griggs wouldn't want a man all B.B.C."

"I think that you're right, Inspector. Dr. Wickham's sure of his ground, you say, concerning the bullet that killed our man?"

As he spoke, Anthony Bathurst picked up the revolver that had been taken from the Dennet waters.

Sutton replied. "Absolutely, Mr. Bathurst. When Welsh fished it out of the river it was loaded in five chambers. One had been discharged. Dr. Wickham has the bullet that killed Griggs and he thereupon went into matters. Everything tallies and everything fits."

Anthony nodded. "There's this to it, then, Sutton. That fact seems to me a strong indication in itself that the crime was not premeditated."

Sutton shook his head in opposition. "Not altogether, sir—if I may say so. Not premeditated with a revolver. No more than that. I can't go any further. The murderer may have taken a knife with him."

"What happened then, do you think, if that were so? Reconstruct the crime for me."

Sutton, having considered, delivered himself of the following. "Griggs may have been too quick for him. May have dodged the attack and, in self-defence, grabbed his revolver. Remember, that according to the chauffeur, Lester, he always kept it handy. Then, no doubt, there would be a struggle. You can visualize it. One man against the other. Knife, let us say, against revolver."

"Griggs was in bed—remember. It's a vital point in the issue. That fact alone would place him at a big disadvantage."

"On the other hand, the possession of the revolver would be an advantage to him. Compared with the knife in the hands of his assailant. Agreed on that, sir?"

"Yes. That's a point, certainly. I'll concede it. Go on, Sutton."

"Well, there was a struggle, as I said. The murderer realized that with his knife or whatever the weapon that he carried was, he had no chance against Griggs's revolver. So he struggled, got possession of it, and then shot Griggs with his own gun."

"What was Griggs doing all this time?"

"Struggling."

"Yes—but why didn't he shoot first of all, on your assumption that he held the revolver?"

"Well—I can't supply all the details. That's asking too much of me. Perhaps he didn't get the chance. You can't tell what happens in a scrap of that kind. You don't know the relative positions for one thing. But there's this. Griggs, being in bed, would be, as it were, the under-dog."

"H'm. Here's something else, Inspector, that you can ask Lester. Why, if Griggs always carried a revolver, did he *also* always take it to bed with him? Psychologically, I find it an extreme precaution."

"I can answer that question *now*," retorted Inspector Sutton triumphantly, "because I asked him it myself. It was because Griggs was afraid of a man hiding under the bed. Terribly scared of it. We've all got something that gives us the 'willies,' you know, Mr. Bathurst. Personally, I'm windy of cats. Can't bear their soft, slinky ways. Sometimes the sight of a cat'll give me the shivers for no end of a time. Can you believe that?"

"Easily," returned Anthony Bathurst. "Because I, in my case, detest sheer heights. To look from the edge into space—well, Inspector"—Anthony shrugged his shoulders—"I'd always rather be excused. So Griggs feared a crouching man—eh? Interesting."

Chapter XIII
GLADYS GREENE LOOKS FOR A BRUSH

STANIFORTH, the manager of the Lansdowne Hotel, turned to the girl who walked with him along the hotel corridor with an air of indulgent proprietorship. His manner was fussy in the extreme.

"I'll take you in," he said, "and I'll introduce you. That will— er—smooth the way for you. You've no occasion to be nervous, because there's nothing whatever for you to be afraid of. Both

Inspector Sutton and the gentleman from London . . . when they hear from me . . . who you are . . . will put you at your ease at once. Come along now."

He tapped at the door and entered at the quick invitation which he received. Inspector Sutton and Mr. Bathurst were on either side of the Commissioner of Police, Sir Austin Kemble.

"Now, Gladys," said the manager, "tell these gentlemen your story as you told it to me. I'll tell them all about you first. You sit down over there."

The girl, very flustered, took the chair that Staniforth indicated.

"This is Miss Greene," said Staniforth—"Miss Gladys Greene. She's on the staff at the hotel here. Been with us for a matter of over two years. She has some important information for you. It's been on her mind, so she tells me, ever since she heard that Griggs had been found shot."

He turned towards the girl. "Now, Gladys, tell these gentlemen everything you have to say. Tell them exactly, word for word, if you can, as you told it to me."

The girl pursed her lips and then suddenly started on her story. The words came from her lips almost torrentially. She was well-spoken and seemed intelligent.

"Well, sir," she said, "it was like this. Careless-like, I left a brush in the bathroom—the bathroom that's on the same floor as the room where the murder was. Room Fifty-Four. As far as I can tell, I must have left the brush there early that morning when I was dusting. You see—it's my job to do the dusting on that floor, and the bath-room's the room right at the end of the corridor. In the evening I remembered it . . . just before I was going to bed . . . as a matter of fact . . . and naturally I went up to the bathroom to get it . . . because I should want it again first thing in the morning. On my way, of course, I had to pass the door of the bedroom that's number fifty-four."

"One minute, Miss Greene," interjected Anthony quietly, "before you go on. What time was this?"

Gladys Greene shook her head dubiously. "I'm not very good at times, sir. I usually rely on other people for that. But . . ." she thought hard . . . "I should say it would have been soon after eleven o'clock. Between eleven-fifteen and eleven-thirty, say. I'm only guessing, just reckoning it out from my usual habits. I generally go to bed about eleven o'clock. I have to be up early in the morning, you know. That time wouldn't be a *lot* out."

"Thank you, Miss Greene. Go on with your story, please."

The girl nodded brightly, as though she were thanking Mr. Bathurst for the permission.

"Well, sir, as I passed the door of bedroom number fifty-four, I heard a man's voice say something in an agitated sort of voice. Perhaps it would be better to describe it as a hoarse, *strained* voice. I caught some of the words—'murder' and 'fowls'. Then I think I heard somebody say, 'they belonged to me and I'm entitled to please myself regarding them—do you see?' That sentence was spoken in a 'nasty' tone. You must understand that it was all said as I was passing and I didn't catch any reply. I wasn't deliberately eavesdropping—I wouldn't do such a thing—I know my place too well—and the voice of the speaker was strange to me. I thought—of course it was silly of me—that somebody's car had run over some poultry and that the owner of the fowls that had been killed was gasping—or grasping—for compensation."

Gladys Greene paused and looked at the four men a trifle shamefacedly. "I would have come and told you before. But it all seemed so silly and—trivial. I was afraid that my story would be laughed at."

"You heard nothing beyond this? No reply of any kind?"

Miss Greene shook her head again. "Not a solitary word. I just passed by the door on my way to the bathroom."

"And you heard no shot? Or noise—just afterwards?"

"No, sir. I went into the bathroom and probably closed the door behind me. I can't be sure if I did. I can't remember. But the chances are that I did. I nearly always do."

Anthony rose and addressed Staniforth. "I don't think we need detain Miss Greene any longer. Thank you for bringing her along, Mr. Staniforth. What she has told us is bound to help us."

The manager bowed and ushered out his protégée.

"*Fowles,*" said Sutton, "with an 'e', not 'fowls'. Think of what that young lady told you, Mr. Bathurst. That you passed on to me. Fowles was the name of the electrician who played billiards with Griggs just before the man was murdered."

Anthony paced the room. "I know all about that, Inspector—but I'm bewildered. It doesn't fit, somehow, as I see things. Why did *Daphne Arbuthnot* die, Sir Austin?"

He paused suddenly in his pacing and swung round to the Commissioner. There was a light in his eye.

"Unless . . ."

Anthony came and sat down, facing Sir Austin and the Inspector. Sir Austin Kemble knew of old that look in Bathurst's eyes, even if Sutton didn't.

"Fowles," repeated Mr. Bathurst quietly. "Let me think, now. There's something close at hand that's eluding me for the moment. Something I hadn't thought of before. Now where have I heard that name pretty recently and in what connection?"

Sir Austin frowned. Curse it—he had an idea, too, but for the life of him couldn't grasp it.

Sutton stared. What was the man after now?

There came a period of silence.

"I've got it," said Anthony Bathurst, suddenly and with easy confidence. "'Fowles' was the name of the two men who were hanged last March up in Yorkshire. Two brothers. I'll tell you their Christian names. Walter Fowles and Harper Fowles. They were burglars, and the case was so cut and dried against them that it attracted comparatively little notice down here in the south. The murder was at Marthwaite. A maid was murdered. When I heard the name 'Fowles' just now, it struck me at once as having been recently familiar and I fished round for the connection. Funny thing—it hadn't occurred to me before."

"If this man's a relation, then, it seems pretty plain, sir. There's the motive there for us—staring us in the face." Sutton was impressed in spite of himself.

"Probably the father of the poor wretches. So I should imagine. Nursed a grudge, I suppose, against Griggs because he was Home Secretary." Sir Austin made the contribution and continued pompously: "At the same time, Inspector, you've got a long way to go to bring it home sufficiently to impress a jury. With the evidence that you have. I can quite see that."

Bathurst rose. "And at the same time also, Sir Austin, there's something I can't understand. I'll put it to you. Take what Miss Greene has just told us. Consider the terms of the sentence that she tells us she overheard. I'll repeat them. 'They belonged to me—and I'm entitled to please myself regarding them.'" Anthony shook his head emphatically. Almost discontentedly. "It doesn't altogether make sense to me. That's the trouble."

"Why doesn't it?" cut in Sir Austin. "Work it out logically. Supposing a petition had been presented to Griggs for a reprieve? As a matter of fact, I believe I remember that this actually *did* happen. Supposing he refused it—as he did—wouldn't it be clearer, then? The two men's lives were his then—in a way. They rested on his decision. When the governor of the prison delivers a man to the hangman, he gets a receipt for the body, you know. Just as he signs one in the first instance when he receives a man into the prison."

Anthony furrowed his brows at the Commissioner's statement. "It's a possibility, I suppose—but, damn it all, sir—it's stretching things a hell of a lot. It's not sound honest-to-goodness common sense—as it appears to me. But at the same time, I—" He stopped abruptly.

Sir Austin Kemble took the opportunity that was presented and pounced on his seeming indecision. "At the same time—you—what?"

Anthony smiled with a certain ruefulness. "Well, sir, I'll concede that it answers the equation better than anything else does. At the moment, that is."

He swung round on Sir Austin again with the fierceness of excitement. "Here's a darned curious thing, Sir Austin. May be nothing in it, but I confess that it puzzles me. Take what we know. This man whom we are calling 'Fowles' was an electrician attached to the Howard Baluster company that's actually playing Lokingham this week. I've interviewed two members of that company. Two of the most important members of the cast. *Jeune premier* and *jeune première*. Basil Palliser and Phillida Fortescue. The lady told me how Fowles had played billiards with Griggs on the night that the man died. *Yet Palliser, who actually had played with both Fowles and Griggs*—been in the same room for some time, mind you—never mentioned the man in any other way *than as a complete stranger to him*. A man—mark you—who is an electrician attached to his own company! Don't I naturally ask myself—what is Palliser's little game? *That's my trouble.*"

Sir Austin twitched his eyebrows. Sutton judged it discreet to be silent. These were higher counsels than were his usually. As he said afterwards, when recounting the details of the affair to the wife of his bosom, "You can always say this about me—I've always known when I'm in the presence of my betters. I knew it all the time that I was in on the Lansdowne Hotel murder . . . and unless I was ever asked to speak my mind . . . I held my blinking tongue, Maria. And more than once I was thunderin' glad that I'd had the sense to."

"You suspect Palliser, Bathurst? Is that what you want me to understand?" Sir Austin, true to tradition, made no bones about the direct question.

"Suspect him of what, sir?"

"The murder of Griggs, of course! Not of killing a few stray Rhode Island Reds or Buff Orpingtons. What did you think I meant?"

Anthony grinned cheerfully. "Wasn't sure, sir. Thought you might be alluding to the Arbuthnot case as well."

Sir Austin waved the reply to one side. "Even now you haven't answered my question. Do you suspect this actor fellow, Palliser, of either crime, if I must say it?"

"Yes. I do suspect him. Hang on a minute, though—let me make it perfectly clear of *what* I suspect him. I suspect him chiefly of a distinct *suppressio veri*. Which has made me ask myself this. Why did he let me think that this fellow Fowles was a stranger to him, when all the time, as I said, the man's an electrician attached to Palliser's own company? Answer me that."

The Commissioner of Police grunted at Anthony Bathurst's reply. Anthony proceeded to enlarge upon his statement.

"The main point about Palliser, it seems to me, is this: By that, I mean the main point of interest. Palliser was close to

Daphne Arbuthnot when she died. The case to which *you* have called my attention, sir. And here, near Griggs when *he* dies, is Palliser again!"

"That point of proximity applies to Griggs too. He was in both places."

"Exactly, Sir Austin. Also a Miss Phillida Fortescue. Also a man named Fowles. Seems a connection somewhere with somebody, doesn't there—if we can but find it?"

"There does, most certainly. That was my reason in informing you of the St. Aidans pier affair. It struck me as such a remarkable coincidence."

"And added to it all—Mr. Basil Palliser, not to put too fine a point on it—seems to have been a little less frank than he reasonably might have been. That's all."

A purring Sir Austin showed signs of approval.

"Yes. I agree with all that you say. The case isn't going to be as simple as it first of all looked. I can see that now."

Sir Austin rose, straightened his back and stood by the mantelpiece. Anthony turned to Inspector Sutton.

"Here's something for you to check up on, Inspector. I intended to mention it to you some time ago. You'll call it a bee in my bonnet, no doubt, but I like to leave nothing to chance."

Sutton looked at him curiously. He wondered what was coming next. What did come, surprised him.

"Those two commercial travellers, Sutton. Searle and Ellis, by name. Find out where they've been during the last few weeks. They get about a bit, you know, these fellows. Pretty well all over the country."

Sutton looked mystified.

"Wondering what I mean, Inspector? What the Christian name and telephone number of the bee are?"

"Well—I was, rather."

"Don't worry. I'll tell you. Don't believe in keeping a man too much in the dark. Unless he's the murderer." Anthony chuckled. "Is it possible that Messrs. Searle and Ellis were at St. Aidans, or in the vicinity of St. Aidans, when Daphne Arbuthnot died?

That's what I'd like to know. There you are, Sutton. I've given it to you on a plate."

"Completing the circle—eh?" interrupted Sir Austin.

Anthony shrugged his shoulders. "If there is a circle, we might as well have all the radii, in preference to some only. That's sound business, isn't it?"

Sutton, although the remark had been addressed to the Commissioner of Police, nodded and made a pencil note in his note-book.

Anthony came to him again. "Oh, by the way, Inspector, while you're on the one thing, I may as well deal, at the same time, with another point. The man, Wells. The other man staying in the hotel here who played billiards on the evening of the murder. Who *might* well have used a cube of billiard-chalk. Get a good line on him, Inspector. It's important. I could bear to know quite a considerable amount concerning him. I've seen Staniforth's notes on him, of course, and also those of yours, Sutton, but I'd like fuller details. Is that O.K., Inspector?"

Sutton nodded and smiled with self-satisfaction. "Very good, sir. Actually speaking, I've already started that particular line of inquiry myself. Still, I'll let you have everything that you want. It may take a day or two to rout out . . . you understand that, sir . . . don't you?"

"Oh yes, these things take time, I know. I make a point of never rushing a man . . . unless, of course, the rush is absolutely imperative and there's nothing else for it."

Sir Austin Kemble turned to them from his position that he had taken up by the mantelpiece. But his right elbow still rested thereon.

"What's *your* next move, Bathurst? Your own."

Anthony smiled. "Do you know, sir, I've been expecting you to ask me that. Because I've been turning it over in my mind myself, I suppose. Mental telepathy. To tell the truth, I'm a bit undecided—and I hate indecision." He paused.

Sir Austin Kemble and the Inspector waited for him to proceed. He eyed them interestedly. Eventually his silence forced Sir Austin to a question. "Undecided as to what?"

"As to one of two courses that are open to me."

"What are they, Bathurst? Tell me."

"One—I'll call it the first—to stay here in Lokingham—and follow up one or two trails that appear at the moment to be on the attractive side. Two—to have a breath of sea-air. Ozone unlimited. Might even walk to the end of the pier, find a deck-chair, and bask in the sunshine thereof. I do like to be beside the seaside."

The Commissioner nodded. "St. Aidans?"

"St. Aidans itself, Sir Austin! None other. A mile or two along the parade from Spearings. 'Tamarisk Town'. On mature thoughts, Sir Austin, the second course shall be placed first. St. Aidans it shall be. For a day or so. I have made up my mind. Sutton can keep this end going." He smiled at the Inspector.

"Take my advice then, put up at the 'Angel'," volunteered the Commissioner. "The 'Angel' in Trumpeter Street. I always do when I'm in St. Aidans. Damn' good grub right through the day, from breakfast to dinner—and reasonable too. In fact, I shouldn't dream of going anywhere else in the place. I can thoroughly recommend it. The 'Angel'—the street by the fountain."

"In that case, Sir Austin," said Mr. Bathurst whimsically, "I'll string along with you."

Chapter XIV
ST. AIDANS PIER

As Sir Austin Kemble had predicted so confidently, Anthony found comfortable quarters at the "Angel", St. Aidans, drank from ancient-looking pewter tankards, ate from generously proportioned plates, and, in due season, made his way to the pier.

Photographs of the cast, hung on the pier's prominent parts at annoying angles, announced to him and to the public generally that the performance this week to re-open the Pier Pavilion was of the latest West-end success—by the renowned playwright, Bliss Campion, entitled *Winnowed Chaff*. Prices, it stated, were "as usual".

Anthony paid the customary iniquitous toll to the piermaster and made his way to the pavilion at the end of the pier where the performances took place. He knew this particular pavilion well. Many a time, as a boy, he had been in the audience and had always thoroughly enjoyed the afternoon's or evening's entertainment. Oh for those days of Pennington Gush! As he walked down the pier, he found himself wishing that he had had the luck to have been in the audience on the night that Daphne Arbuthnot had died. Had been murdered—he felt certain! But conditions such as those of his desire seldom fall to the lot of an investigator. There had been but two occasions in his career as a crime expert when he had been lying handy in the front line when the tapes had gone up.

The first of these occasions had happened to be, also, his initiation into matters criminal—the now famous "Billiard-Room Mystery" that had been staged at Considine Manor in Sussex when he had been staying there. The second had been the strange affair of the "Sussex Cuckoo", when James Wynyard Frith, the well-known philosopher and the owner of the much-coveted "Jacobite Collection", had been found dead on the lawn behind his house . . . with an inflamed toe.

At all other times during his career the scent had been comparatively cold upon his arrival, and these circumstances were prevailing again at the present time.

Possessed by these thoughts, Anthony walked steadily on until he came to the door of the Pier Theatre. Here a man was standing. Anthony, seeing him, quickened his pace and advanced towards him with outstretched hand. This man whom Mr. Bathurst approached merits certain details of description.

He was of medium height, several inches shorter than Anthony, and of soldierly bearing. He had dark hair, cut closely to his quickly turning head. His small moustache was neatly trimmed. His face bore the lines of intelligence. His eyes were blue and steady, but they occasionally lit into the friendliest of smiles. His general manner was alert and eminently business-like.

Thus was Inspector Baddeley of the Sussex Constabulary and thus he had been eight years before at Considine Manor when he had encountered Anthony Bathurst for the first time. The fingers of Time had, indeed, touched him but lightly.

He saw Anthony coming towards him, and the blue eyes smiled in welcome. "Mr. Bathurst, say—this is great! I got your wire, and, you bet, came over at once—as you knew I would when you sent it." He stopped, grinned, and held his head back—to survey Anthony, as it were, from a distance. "And what is it this time—eh? What's stirring in the forest of crime? Still the same old wizard?"

Anthony grasped his hand and shook it warmly. "Baddeley, you dear old scout—I'm delighted to see you again. What do you say to another spot of double-harness? Because, if I tell the truth, I badly want your advice."

The Inspector cocked a shrewd eye and fingered his trim moustache. "Even money I can tell you what you're after."

"Drinks—Baddeley. Make it drinks. That's a bet."

"The Arbuthnot case. The girl who was poisoned on this pier here."

Anthony grinned. "I have but one reply, O best of Baddeleys. What will you have and when will you be having it?"

"Come and sit down over here, Mr. Bathurst, and then we can sort things out properly. What price a couple of deck-chairs together before we go inside?"

"Probably, my dear Baddeley, if I know anything—a matter of fourpence. Each chair. Four *denarii*. Still, your suggestion's a damn' good one and we'll act on it. Collar those two over there. They seem to all appearances a trifle drier than the others."

The Inspector obeyed the instruction, appropriated the two chairs, and the two men sat down. Cigarettes going, Anthony talked. Baddeley listened attentively.

Anthony described the various details of the Lansdowne Hotel murder. He then, without preliminary warning, came to Sir Austin Kemble's contribution concerning the death of Daphne Arbuthnot at St. Aidans. He spoke of Basil Palliser and the girl who called herself Phillida Fortescue.

Baddeley nodded sympathetically. At the first mention of the name of Griggs he whistled. He thought he saw where Anthony Bathurst's ideas were inclining.

He brought him back, therefore, to the actual facts of the St. Aidans pier affair.

"You've seen a copy of my notes, you say, Mr. Bathurst?"

"Yes, Inspector, my luck's been in. Sir Austin Kemble read them to me."

Baddeley smiled ruefully. "I was right up against it, you know. There wasn't a shred of evidence against anybody, Mr. Bathurst. Every turning that I took brought me up against a blank wall."

"The girl was poisoned, I suppose?"

"Without a doubt, I'm afraid. But as to who poisoned her—search me." The Inspector shrugged his smart shoulders.

Anthony took up the parable. "I know the play in question well. Saw Du Maurier in it up West. 'Deborah Kane', that's the part played by the dead girl, is cheated by her former lover into drinking poisoned brandy. When she dies, she lies on a sort of divan arrangement up stage left. Is that correct? Now think of this St. Aidans set. Can you remember from what you saw of the stage setting yourself?"

"Yes—you're all right, Mr. Bathurst. Go on."

"I will. Now take the statement that was volunteered by the man in the audience: Finlayson—James Finlayson, the J.P. living at Spearings. If I mistake not, he said something like this. They may not be the exact words but they'll do to make my point clear. 'I had my glasses on her for the best part of Act Two, Scene Two. And I'll swear that the girl was dead all the time that she lay there on the divan. For she never breathed once during the whole of that scene.' Mark that, Baddeley. It *times* matters so conveniently for us. Did you realise that?"

Baddeley seemed a little uneasy at Anthony's analysis.

"Let me explain further, then," proceeded Anthony. "Daphne Arbuthnot is alive at the end of Act Two, Scene One. Fenwick gave her the brandy (as 'Deborah Kane'), and Langley—that's the man who was the stage manager—*heard* Daphne speak to Palliser 'just before we rang up for Act Two, Scene Two'. While the 'black-out' was on. Now, inasmuch as she was dead as mutton at the conclusion of this scene, and taking into account the full and exact nature of Finlayson's statement—she must have been poisoned just *before* the curtain rang up on the 'black-out'. That is to say, just *after* she was heard to speak to Basil Palliser. I'm damned if you can shake the sense of that, Baddeley."

Baddeley nodded his head and scratched his cheek. "Seems O.K. with me. But all the same—and with all that established—you haven't any proof to pin on to anybody."

Anthony shook his head. "You're telling me, Baddeley. Now tell me this. Did you ever find for certain the glass that had held the poison?"

Baddeley was despondent. "Not that we could be sure of. The doctor said that he couldn't say. None of 'em had that bitter almonds smell."

Anthony nodded. "Too clever for all of you. Ten to one it was disposed of by the murderer and in an unexpected manner, I'll lay a wager."

Again Baddeley nodded. "Every wine-glass that we could find was tested."

"The doctor who came along—McFarlane was his name, I fancy—you say that he was *certain* that the poison used was prussic acid?"

"Absolutely. He knelt down at the side of the divan, he said, and sniffed at the girl's lips. He said that there was no mistaking it."

"H'm. I was afraid that you'd tell me that. It's so extraordinary, you know, Baddeley. Prussic acid is the poison used to kill the girl in the play. Coincidence or deliberately conjured? Once again, it seems, Inspector, that 'the play's the thing'. I wonder!" Anthony pulled thoughtfully at his upper lip. "Where were the various members of the cast when you arrived, Baddeley, roughly? Just after Miss Arbuthnot's death was discovered. Can you remember?"

Baddeley considered the question with his usual care. "All of 'em were crowded in the men's dressing-room, Mr. Bathurst. Chattering like a chapel bazaar committee. It took me some minutes, I can tell you, to get anything like coherence amongst 'em."

"I can believe you, Baddeley. Did you examine *all* the hand props? *All* the wine-glasses *particularly*?"

"Everything, Mr. Bathurst. The Sergeant of Police, who was there when I arrived, did the same thing. Neither of us found anything at all suspicious. The curtain, you know, is *up* during the 'black-out' that takes place in the play."

"I know. The interval between the two scenes of the act is very short. The curtain ascends on an unlighted stage. The lights don't go on for a matter of some little time. A man enters and holds the stage to himself during the whole of that time—save, of course, for the fact that Miss Arbuthnot is there."

"Yes," replied Baddeley tersely. "I know all that—and that man was Basil Palliser. Now, look here, Mr. Bathurst, there's something that I'd like to be more sure of. How long *exactly* would be covered by your phrase 'a matter of some little time'?"

"Do you mean how long does Palliser have the stage to himself?"

Baddeley nodded. "That's the very idea itself."

Anthony Bathurst made a mental calculation. "Put it at two to three minutes, Baddeley, and you won't be very far out."

Baddeley frowned at the information. "H'm! Not what you'd call long."

"And for the greater part of those two to three minutes, Baddeley, to be exact for about seventy-five per cent of them, Palliser's movements are plainly visible to the people in the audience. So make what you can of that."

"But, dash it all, Mr. Bathurst, there was the young lady dead right enough—somebody must have—"

"Exactly, Baddeley. I won't contradict you for a moment over that. We *know* that somebody did! To the best of my memory, during the second scene of Act Two, four people besides Palliser approach the body of the dead girl very closely. They are respectively, the porter, the Inspector of Police, the Divisional Surgeon, and 'Helder' the young reporter. But in every one of these four instances, mind you, Baddeley—*it is done in full view of the audience.* Which fact *must* acquit all of them of the crime. No—it all comes back to what I said to you just now. She was poisoned just *before* the curtain went up on the 'black-out' and just after she was heard to reply to Palliser."

"Maybe. But it's a big field, sir. Don't forget that. Dark stage. Curtain down. Plenty of people dashing about behind. Anybody might easily have—"

"Exactly, Baddeley. And that's where the difficulty lies. I know that full well. You see it now in exactly the same way as I do. But, although it's difficult, you must admit that it's clarified just a bit."

"I suppose you're right. I can help, perhaps, over one thing. I interviewed Langley, the stage manager chap. The man who said that he had heard the dead girl speak to Palliser. He told me something else, Mr. Bathurst . . . and you may not be aware of it. When I tell it to you, you'll realize the importance of it. Langley told me that Palliser came off the stage, *immediately* afterwards. Now mark what that means; precisely. Immediately *after she had spoken to him*. If you were inclined to suspect him, that would be vitally in his favour, you know."

"Yes. I agree with you. Did you arrange about inside—as I asked you?" Anthony jerked his head towards the doors.

"I did, Mr. Bathurst. It's all O.K. whenever you like."

Anthony rose. "Right, then. I'm going to have a look at the stage. Come along with me, will you?"

"You're lucky—in a way. I'll tell you why. The company that's playing here now is the first one to appear since the tragedy. There's been a cloud over everything. Owing to the death of the actress the place has been closed for weeks."

"Good! That means considerably less disturbance, possibly, than there might have been. Come along. We'll go in."

The two men walked down the hall towards the stage. They used the right-hand aisle. Anthony put a question to the Inspector.

"Men's dressing-room this side, Baddeley—or the other?"

"The other side, Mr. Bathurst. Ladies this side."

Anthony Bathurst pushed a door open and saw a smallish room almost facing them. The door of this room was open. "Come on in, Baddeley."

Anthony saw chairs, a table arrangement hard by the wall, and a long mirror above it on the eye-level as one sat there. Beyond the furniture there was nothing in the room at all.

"H'm," remarked Anthony. "Now let me see. I must get the hang of things, generally." He looked round and then turned to Inspector Baddeley. "I'm going up on the stage, Baddeley. Come with me, will you?"

Baddeley followed Bathurst up the short flight of steps that led to the stage.

"Not too much room behind," muttered Bathurst; "there's never much on piers, I know, but this is a bit more cramped even than most. Changing scenery must be a deuce of a job. No room for stage furniture. Is there any quick access to the sea, Baddeley—from anywhere behind here—do you know?"

The Inspector shook his head at the question. He found himself wondering what lay behind it. "No, Mr. Bathurst. Not that I can see. You've got to get out at the side here and go round. Take time, it would. What are you thinking of?"

"The glass that was used to hold the poison for Miss Arbuthnot. Because—according to your story—you never saw it, Baddeley, and remember—*the killer had to be quick*. Very quick. Oh, *là là*! So quick that . . ."

Anthony Bathurst paused on the uncompleted sentence—lost in thought. Baddeley watched him steadfastly. He had worked with Mr. Bathurst before and, like Sir Austin Kemble, knew what this look in the eyes of him signified.

There were several seconds of silence. Inspector Baddeley broke it by shuffling his right foot.

CHAPTER XV
THE WINE-GLASS

ANTHONY turned again towards Inspector Baddeley. But before he could say what he had been about to say, the sound of a step behind them arrested the two men's attention. Baddeley jerked his head round in the direction of the sound, and he and Anthony Bathurst saw a man approaching them. He advanced towards them. Neither of them could have stated definitely from where the man had come. There was a look of inquiry in his eyes. Anthony found himself immediately wondering what it was that made this man so eagerly curious. Then Baddeley's opening words put him on his guard.

"Hallo, Mr. Meredith," declared the Inspector; "pleased to meet you again. This is an unexpected pleasure for me. I'll wager that you didn't expect to see me here again so soon."

"No, I don't think that I did," said the newcomer. "What brings you along again? Picked up something fresh?"

Baddeley shrugged his shoulders. He evaded the question and, to cover the hiatus, produced Anthony.

"I was forgetting. Let me introduce you, Mr. Meredith. Mr. William Meredith—Mr. Anthony Bathurst."

Anthony smiled. "Most ancient of all warriors! With a name like that, you should always carry a tooth-pick. Pleased to meet you."

Baddeley embarked upon explanation for Anthony's benefit. "Mr. Meredith played in *Interference* the night that Miss Arbuthnot died. I met him then, as you may guess."

Anthony's face lighted. "Now that's most interesting. What were you playing, Mr. Meredith?"

"The Divisional-Surgeon, Mr. Bathurst. 'Puttock'. When the company broke up, and some of them went into the *Strained Relations* cast, I stayed on here. I'm playing in *Winnowed Chaff* this evening."

Anthony looked him over. He found him easy to place. Meredith was an obvious "character" man. Round-faced, twinkling-eyed, jovially morose and yet despondently jovial. Stock "character". He was inclined to be fussy, perhaps, and Bathurst formed the opinion that the man was still under the cloud that the tragedy of Daphne Arbuthnot had brought to this sea-beaten pier of St. Aidans.

"If you've no objection, I should like to ask you a question then, Mr. Meredith," said Bathurst, after Inspector Baddeley had had a further say. "And that, although an excessively simple one, is, nevertheless, a question of paramount importance. I may as well tell you at once that Scotland Yard is making an inquiry into Miss Arbuthnot's death. When you approached Miss Arbuthnot's body, in your part of 'Dr. Puttock', the Divisional-Surgeon, on the night that she died, did it or did it not strike you that Miss

Arbuthnot had been poisoned? That is to say, before you had a definite statement on the matter from Dr. McFarlane?"

Meredith looked very grave and shifted his feet awkwardly on the ground. He had not anticipated this when he had come to the pier a few moments previously. "It did, Mr. Bathurst—and that's a fact. I won't beat about the bush. Although it may perhaps place me in a peculiar position, I may as well admit it. When I smelt her lips and that horrible bitter almonds smell that hung around them and saw how still she lay, I felt convinced that there was something wrong and, as a result, I nearly 'dried-up' for the moment. I didn't know what to do for the best, honour-bright, I didn't! Let the show run till the end of the act or get the rag rung down there and then. Eventually I decided on the former—it avoided the bigger sensation, you see. Perhaps it was as well that I did—considering everything. Well, when we came to the end of the act, I got off stage and told Palliser and Langley about it at once. They were the two first people whom I met." He mopped his brow in his agitation. "The discovery that I had made must have got on my nerves and showed in my face, for directly I'd finished with Langley and Palliser, I ran into the electrician. Fowles was the bloke's name, I fancy." Baddeley glanced at Anthony significantly. Meredith went on. "'Lord, Mr. Meredith,' Fowles says to me, 'whatever's the matter with you? You're as white as a bloody ghost, you are, and no error!'"

"Altogether an astounding condition," murmured Mr. Bathurst. "I congratulate you on the effect. What did you do then?"

"Butted right into Fenwick and blurted out to him what I thought was the matter."

"What did he say when you told him? Think clearly. Did he seem upset—surprised?"

"No. On the whole—no! Fenwick's remarks were rather surprising. He said he'd been waiting for something of the sort to happen, and that it served Dunbar right for 'tagging' at the second rehearsal. Fenwick's traditionally superstitious. Dunbar was the man playing the part of 'Childers'—'Sir John Marlay's' butler." He stopped, and Bathurst nodded to him.

Baddeley intervened. "Mr. Meredith told me at the time what he has just said, Mr. Bathurst. I can vouch for that."

"Good! I'm pleased. This electrician that you mentioned, Mr. Meredith, Fowles, I think you called him. Where, behind the stage, did you run into him exactly? Was it near the set? You used the phrase 'directly I got off'."

Meredith frowned at the question. "Now where was it that I bumped into Fowles? Let's see if I can remember. Not far from the backcloth."

"Nearer the set than his strict duties would normally take him?"

"A bit, possibly. It's hard to say. You see—conditions vary so. There's so little room behind here—as you can see for yourself."

Anthony took a few steps away. "Come and show me the actual spot, Mr. Meredith, where you encountered this Fowles, the electrician."

Meredith looked round and measured distances with his eyes. Then he pointed. "It would be just about there, I think."

Anthony also measured the distance mentally. "H'm! Not too far from the lighting gadgets—is it?"

"Langley spoke the truth." This came from Baddeley. "Some of the fatal drink that was handed to Miss Arbuthnot was spilt on the divan. There was a discoloration on one of the cushions. I smelt it. The drink of brandy, or whatever it was, was passed to her in the dark. Don't see how Fowles, an electrician, could have pulled a job like that."

Anthony took Meredith by the arm and pointed upwards. "The flats directly behind Miss Arbuthnot's divan would be about there? Yes?"

"Yes. Almost exactly, I should say. The divan that she lay on and the two flats behind it formed a space that was almost a triangle."

Anthony Bathurst nodded in corroboration. Then he moved quickly to a position behind the point where Meredith had indicated. He had come to the sudden determination to test a theory.

Seconds passed. Meredith and Inspector Baddeley, watching intently, heard him whistle softly. Queer words followed the whistle. Anthony Bathurst was in action.

"You will observe, gentlemen," he said, "that we're right over towards the O.P. side. 'Opposite prompt', Inspector, if you're puzzled. More or less significant, eh?" Anthony cocked his head at them.

Baddeley expressed his doubt. "How do you mean, Mr. Bathurst? I don't know that I—"

"*No prompter this side, Baddeley.* Less vigilance—therefore. Also, as a logical consequence, less risk for anybody indulging in a spot of dirty work. Get me?"

"Yes. I'm with you."

Anthony walked briskly towards the wings. Came back again. Walked to the wings once more with quick comprehensive glances from side to side.

"How far to the pier-side from here, Mr. Meredith? You know the place pretty well. If you like me to put it more plainly—from the sea?"

"Distance or in terms of time, Mr. Bathurst?"

Anthony looked at him critically. "In terms of time, say."

Meredith considered. "H'm. To get to the absolute pier-rail—overlooking the water—well, three minutes. Quite that, I should think. You can't get there absolutely direct, you see. You've got to go through the dressing-room, then out through a lavatory, and across a fairly wide stretch of pier. I'd put it at three minutes at least. There are three doors to negotiate—you know what doors mean—that all takes time."

Anthony nodded—almost absent-mindedly. Again he looked round. Considered carefully the general appointments and relative topography. His eye followed the lines of guy-ropes and the ropes by which the heavy drop curtain was operated. He ascended the ladder to the limes platform with rapid steps.

The two men still watched him with keen interest. They saw him look carefully round the platform, run his finger along a line of dust, and then descend to them.

"I'm late on the scene, I know, but I can't help that . . . and there's always the bare chance that the gods may have mercy on you, if you show persistence, and help you." He swung round to address Meredith. "You said that there had been no performance here since Miss Arbuthnot's death—didn't you?"

"To-night's the first. The company that was here with *Interference* was divided up. Some went on the Thames Valley circuit. Others waited to be fixed elsewhere. As I told you, I was one of the latter." Meredith smiled. "To tell the absolute truth," he continued, "I wasn't sorry for the interval for resting. I felt that I could very well do with it."

Anthony Bathurst's brow was furrowed. Meredith's words were significant. Anthony looked again in each obvious direction.

Baddeley, for his part, found himself endeavouring to follow Anthony's line of reasoning. That there was a definite one, active at the moment, he felt certain. His eyes followed Anthony's. They came to rest eventually upon a line of heavy red fire-buckets ranged in a row along the wall on the O.P. side of the stage. Half a dozen of them. They looked to have been fairly recently painted. The red on them was bright, arresting, and vividly distinctive.

Anthony suddenly walked over to them. He stood in front of them and looked at them.

"Baddeley," he said, after an interval of a minute or so, "I want to move these six buckets—there are six, I think—yes—give me a hand, do you mind? Perhaps you would be good enough to help us too, Mr. Meredith. The more the merrier."

Meredith nodded and went over with the Inspector. Anthony issued directions.

"We'll take a couple each, shall we? We'll put them on the floor here in front of us. You'll find them moderately heavy, I'm afraid."

Each man moved towards the line of buckets. They found that, in the opinion expressed, Anthony Bathurst was right. Filled with water, as the buckets were, it took Baddeley all his time to lift the two that were left for him. Meredith's arms wavered and shook as he lowered the buckets to the floor in front of him. From one of them the water slopped to the floor.

"What do we do now?" queried Baddeley. "Follow up the true Jack and Jill tradition?"

Anthony's eye gleamed as he heard the question. "I want to find out if there's anything unusual in any one of them. In any one of the six. That's all."

He regarded the line of buckets as it held the floor. "Try that first one of yours, Mr. Meredith, will you? It's a long shot—but it's the long shot that comes off sometimes, you know."

Meredith looked startled at his words and seemed uncertain as to what to do.

"Don't be afraid. There's nothing to buy. Put your hand in the water," urged Anthony.

Meredith stepped forward and thrust his right hand into the bucket that Anthony had selected for the experiment. Anthony Bathurst and Inspector Baddeley saw a look of astonishment take possession of his face. He withdrew his hand from the water and they saw that it grasped something. Baddeley gasped. Meredith's mouth was open wide. The something was a wine-glass!

Anthony took it from him and held it up in triumph. "Behold. A wine-glass, gentlemen! Or rather *the* wine-glass. The wine-glass that held the poison that killed Daphne Arbuthnot! I am open to receive your congratulations."

CHAPTER XVI
MR. BATHURST DEMONSTRATES

As ANTHONY's voice rang out in triumph, Meredith shuffled uneasy feet. It appeared, too, that words were trembling on his tongue. But doubt and hesitation showed plainly on his features. He took a stumbling sort of step forwards, towards Anthony Bathurst.

"There's something I'm going to tell you," he blurted. "Something that, perhaps, I ought to have made it my business to have told you before."

"We are listening, Mr. Meredith," said Anthony gravely.

"It's this. I remember that the suggestion was, at the first inquiry, that the glass was passed to Daphne in the dark. The question that people asked was, 'who could have been in a position to induce her to drink anything *in the dark*?' Remember, Inspector?"

Baddeley nodded. "Quite so, Mr. Meredith."

"Well, I'll tell you something. Daphne had been off colour from a few days before the show. Felt anyhow, she said. Made no secret of it. Told me so herself. She told me that she had felt so bad at times that she had asked Palliser to get her something each show and that he had given it to her between the scenes—when the 'black out' was on." He paused and then continued. "I hate saying it to you fellows, it makes it look so black for Palliser, but there you are." Meredith stuck out a determined jaw.

Anthony scratched his cheek. "Whoever it was killed her was a clever devil. The murder was planned with an immense amount of cunning. I'll confess that at the moment I'm completely bewildered. Where's the common factor in it all, Baddeley? Tell me that."

"You mean—St. Aidans and then Lokingham?"

"I do. You've got it. This pier here and then that bedroom at the Lansdowne Hotel." He turned again to Meredith. "Cast your mind back again to the night of Daphne Arbuthnot's death, Mr. Meredith. To the visit of the Home Secretary, the Rt. Hon. A.S. Griggs. The *late* Mr. Griggs. *Why* was your company so signally honoured? Any idea?"

Meredith shrugged contemptuous shoulders. "Honoured! That's a euphemism, if ever there were one. Griggs had a crush on Phil Fortescue. He'd been chasin' her for weeks. It was common knowledge in the cast. You know what our line is from that point of view. Our girls have to put up with a rare lot of it."

"It's the romantic atmosphere," grinned Anthony. "Even amateur societies make splendid matrimonial agencies. Mercenary mothers constantly urge eligible daughters to pay homage to Thespis and join the local club. A perennial marriage market and weddings weekly! So that's why Griggs came behind—eh?"

"That is. Phil probably asked him. Or, on the other hand, the blighter may have shoved his nose in on his own. Don't know for certain either way, so I won't say. I never spoke to him. Poisonous merchant, I believe. Couldn't stick the sight of him at any price. To all accounts his society, believe me, was much more to be avoided than cherished."

"When he came behind, where did he go?"

"Came in the men's dressing-room and, I believe, had several drinks. They sounded good, too. Only wanted a lemon in his mouth for the perfect picture."

Anthony began to pace the boards. "Did he actually speak to Miss Fortescue? Did you notice?"

Meredith made an impatient gesture. "No—I didn't exactly notice. But I haven't the slightest doubt that he did. He wouldn't miss any chances."

"The ladies were all in one room?"

"Rather. You don't get private dressing-rooms in places like these."

"I suppose not. I know what it's like myself, to some extent. I've done a bit at the game in my time. Here's another question I want to ask you, Mr. Meredith. Re Griggs, and his pursuit of Miss Fortescue. Did it arouse any ill-feeling in any special quarter?"

"Amongst the members of the company—do you mean?"

"That's it. That's just what I *do* mean."

On this occasion Meredith took an appreciable time over his answer. "Well—I'd say 'no' to that. But don't misunderstand me. I mean by my answer that I never *saw* or *heard* any ill-feeling exhibited. On the surface, that is. But all the same . . ." He paused abruptly.

Anthony prompted him. "Well, Mr. Meredith?"

"There isn't the slightest doubt that Basil Palliser didn't like it. I'd assert that without hesitation. You see, he and Phil have been pals for years. I don't say that they had a definite understanding. I don't know—but they may have had. Nobody would have been surprised to have heard of it. Palliser's a bit of a close bird when he likes—and he usually does like." Baddeley fingered his trim moustache. "What made you fix on that one particular fire-bucket, Mr. Bathurst? You've got me guessing."

Anthony looked grave. "Well, I just chanced an arm, Baddeley, and the shot happened to come off. Reconstruct! Picture the scene for yourself as it was on the night of the murder. The murderer, whoever it was, hands the glass with the poison in it to Daphne Arbuthnot. In the dark. At some time during the 'blackout', remember. She had had the drink, don't forget, two or three times before, handed to her in the same fashion. I suggest fairly confidently that one of the flats just behind Daphne's divan was moved to one side and the hand that held the glass pushed through the space thus made. Not a word spoken, I expect. There was no need for either the giver or the receiver to speak, as far as I can judge. In this way she was handed the glass of poisoned spirits. Daphne took it that it had come in the manner of its predecessors, and, quite unsuspectingly, drank it. That accomplished, she put the glass back in the hand that had held it out to her. Then the murderer, assuming that it was a man, made the mistake that will, I hope, hang him. He knew that he must dispose of the glass *at once*. This was *imperative*. There were, naturally, several stage-hands and members of the cast drifting round in various directions during the change, and in the light of the discovery that he knew was inevitable at the end of the act, nobody must be able to give evidence that they had seen him with such a thing as a wine-glass in his hand. Follow me, gentlemen?"

Meredith and the Inspector nodded.

"I thought you would. There was our killer, then, with his glass, and there also on the O.P. side was that line of fire-buckets. All ready to hand. Beautifully ready. It was the work of a moment to slip along, reach up and drop the wine-glass in one of them. Obviously in the one nearest to him, which was the end one that I selected for Meredith's experiment. Nobody would dream of looking in a fire-bucket for a wine-glass. There it could lie during the first investigation, and when that was over it could be retrieved quietly and dropped into the sea. Question now is—why wasn't it? That makes me wonder."

Baddeley nodded. "None of the property glasses that we tested contained traces of poison. I know that for certain."

"I thought, first of all, that the glass used must have been flung into the sea . . . until I realized that the pier-side was rather too far away. So I looked round for a more convenient hiding-place.

All convenient to the criminal's hand. When my eyes came to rest on that line of fire-buckets against that wall, I felt that I was within sight of home. Quite elementary, my dear Baddeley. When you come to size it all up."

Baddeley smiled at the old familiar quip. "And you say that you reckoned that the murderer chose the bucket nearest to his line of flight—eh? Was that it?"

"Obviously, Inspector. Think of his position. He had no time to waste in picking and choosing. So he dropped the glass in the first one to hand. I want no bouquets for that, Baddeley."

Meredith stood there, open-mouthed. Recent events had administered a severe shock to him.

"Keep that glass, Baddeley. You'll want it. At some future date, perhaps, it may even figure as 'Exhibit A'. At any rate, here's hoping so."

"Feel confident, then?" grinned Baddeley.

Anthony shrugged his shoulders. "Not exactly confident, Baddeley. I wouldn't go as far as to say that. Attracted. Distinctly attracted by as pretty a little problem as one could wish to meet. Consider all that we know. Griggs comes to St. Aidans to see Phillida Fortescue, and Daphne Arbuthnot dies. Griggs goes to Lokingham, where Phillida is again, and dies there himself. Question—connection? Tell me the whys and the wherefores of that, Baddeley, and you'll tell me a hell of a lot." Anthony stopped abruptly and his eyes held a far-away look.

"Might be pure coincidence—after all," remarked Meredith, "the two murders are so different in every way. Might be nothing more than pure chance."

"Might be," returned Mr. Bathurst, "but believe me, Mr. Meredith—it wasn't. Oh, dear no!"

Meredith stared at him wonderingly. Then he harked back. "Funny," he said, "that nobody missed a glass."

But Anthony Bathurst heeded him not. His thoughts were far away. Many a time, subsequently, he was to wish that they hadn't been!

ANTHONY'S first step, upon his return to Lokingham, was to interview Basil Palliser again. This step, it may be said, was taken deliberately. He felt that there was a missing link in the chain of the case somewhere, and that Palliser was the man who could best supply it.

Palliser came to him within a few minutes of being invited. He appeared to be eminently frank and candid. "As a matter of fact, Mr. Bathurst," he opened, "I'm no end glad that you asked me to come and see you again. For the reason that I had something to say to you."

He paused—in Anthony's opinion—somewhat awkwardly.

"In that case, mine can wait, then. First of all, let's have yours, Mr. Palliser."

"Well, I'm afraid that in the first place I owe you an apology. In a way I've an uneasy feeling that I've rather let you down. But 'pon my honour, I didn't do it deliberately, or from malice afore-thought." He flashed a row of white teeth as he spoke.

"That's very decent of you," said Anthony, "but firstly, let's hear what it's all about. Then we can judge. Patience was never my long suit. I hate being kept in suspense."

"Well, it's like this. It really gets back to the night that I played billiards here with Griggs and the others."

He stopped, and Anthony Bathurst knew at once what was coming. Palliser started again.

"You remember that I told you about a bloke that came into the billiard-room pretty late? I said that he was a hard-bitten sort of customer who wielded a pretty snappy cue. Remember? I thought when I had seen him play that he might have even been a pro. at the game. Well—I know this is going to sound a feeble effort—I've found out since that I knew the man all the time. Yes—*actually knew him*—and also his name." Palliser concluded his sentence lamely.

"Explain, Mr. Palliser, please," prompted Anthony softly.

"I'll do my best, and I hope that you'll believe me. But I've a perfectly putrid memory for faces—been like it all my life—and that's the only decent thing that I can urge in my defence. I can remember words or facts, but never faces. You'll probably despise me for it and think me all sorts of a silly ass, but that man was actually an electrician attached to my own company. It's a solemn fact. Whatever must you think of me?"

"Go on, Mr. Palliser. It may perhaps be less peculiar than you think. These things do happen sometimes with people, I know. Even to the best regulated memories. We simply can't explain these things."

Palliser brightened a little at the remark. "I had an idea all the time that I had seen the fellow's mug before somewhere, but simply couldn't place him. I thought that my imagination must be playing tricks with me. Wouldn't have been the first time that that had happened. Result was that I discarded the idea as thoroughly loopy. Judge of my astonishment then, when I walked straight into the bloke at the theatre the very night after our little chat together. When I saw him you could have counted me out. But it's right enough. He's an electrician by the name of Fowles—or rather he was."

The last word stung Anthony into greater activity. "*Was?* What do you mean by that, Mr. Palliser?"

"Simply this, my dear fellow. The beggar's gone. Scrammed. Done an elegant bunk, in other words. Hasn't shown up at the theatre since the night I ran into him as I said."

Anthony's comparative complacence was now thoroughly disturbed. These facts might be extremely significant. He had understood from Inspector Sutton that everybody concerned in the case was being well looked after. Still, there was little cause for alarm. Modern resources have put a heavy handicap upon fugitive criminals. He turned to Palliser, therefore, with a question.

"Looks fishy, doesn't it?" commented the latter. "Especially as there's a spot of cash owing to the beggar. A matter of three quid odd. His sort don't usually do the disappearing act *before* Treasury. At least, I've never known one do it. Usually it's well the other way with 'em—want a 'sub' at the beginning of the week to tide them over—"

Anthony cut in quickly. "You've explained one thing, Mr. Palliser. But I don't think that you've explained another. I'm so curious about it that I suggest that this omission be remedied."

"What's that? You have only to tell me." Palliser tapped a cigarette on his case before offering it to Anthony.

"Why you didn't come to tell me all this before. Surely you should have done? You see what it means. We have not only lost this fellow Fowles—but temporarily, I hope—but we have also lost much valuable time. And that matters a dickens of a lot. Time is a tremendously important factor in an investigation of this kind."

"I know. None knows it better. And I'm profoundly sorry that I've behaved so foolishly. I feel, Bathurst, that I've cut a most inglorious figure all the way through. My only excuses are that I've been busy and didn't perhaps attach the importance to the matter that I should have done. Am I absolved?"

"I suppose that we shall have to make the concession," remarked Anthony, "for what it's worth."

"Thank you. Now can I tell you something else?"

"My dear Palliser—I'm hoping that you will tell me quite a lot. Go on."

"What I'm going to say now I've picked up more or less from hearsay. That is to say, from the various hands attached to the company. You know whom I mean—electricians, stage carpenters, et cetera—the usual fellows that we employ in a company of our kind to work behind. In the course of my work I had very little to do with Fowles, as you may imagine. Scarcely ever ran up against him and actually can't ever remember having spoken to him. But one of the electricians, whose job it was to work with this man Fowles, has told me a most remarkable thing."

"About Fowles—do you mean?"

"Yes. A most extraordinary thing, too. You wouldn't guess what it was if you kept on guessing till midnight."

"I'm not much of a guesser at the best of times. What was it?"

Palliser leant towards him and spoke with the utmost deliberation. "This is what I have been told on the very best authority.

Everywhere that this man Fowles went *he carried a rope with him*. That's what I've been told."

Anthony stared at him in astonishment. "A rope! How do you mean—a rope?"

"A coil of rope. Used to wear it at odd times coiled round his body, or something." Palliser paused to proceed again. "There's no argument about it. There's evidence to support the story. The best evidence that you could possibly get. He's left the coil of rope behind him. I've seen it myself. The man who told me all about it—the other electrician—has shown it to me."

Anthony paced the room. "You used the right adjective when you said 'extraordinary'. This is a new line in hobbies and no mistake." He stopped and thought hard. "If this rope were his inseparable companion," he said, "as you suggested, he has either gone away in a hurry and forgotten it, or he has left it behind him deliberately. If the latter—the question arises—why? Possible answer is that he doesn't require it any longer. Again—why? That last question raises all sorts of interesting possibilities. Do you follow me?"

Palliser nodded. "Every time. I see things as you see them. That's pretty much how I worked things out."

Anthony's next question, however, surprised him. Mr. Bathurst intended that it should.

"What do you want to tell me about St. Aidans?"

"St. Aidans?" A spot of colour showed on each of Palliser's cheeks. For a second his self-possession deserted him.

Mr. Bathurst nodded slowly. "St. Aidans pier—and the death of Daphne Arbuthnot."

"I wasn't going to tell you anything. What gave you the idea that I was? Why . . . you don't think that the two affairs are in any way connected, do you?"

"Don't know. Trying to find out. May be a mere coincidence, of course. But there you are—on the other hand, it may not. Look at the people who impinge on both affairs. Most extraordinary. You yourself, Miss Fortescue, Fowles, our friend of the rope, Griggs himself . . . and possibly others whom I don't know well enough to describe. At any rate, with the four people definitely named the prospect is certainly interesting."

Palliser frowned at Mr. Bathurst's statement. "Yes . . . but hang it all, Daphne Arbuthnot's death was very different from this murder of Griggs. It may well have been accidental death . . . there was no real evidence that the Police could get against anyone."

Anthony answered him curtly. "Don't deceive yourself. Miss Arbuthnot was murdered. Murdered just as deliberately as Griggs was shot in his bed. You can take that from me."

Palliser went paler. "Is that absolutely on the level?"

"It is. I wouldn't deceive you over a thing like that."

"But who would wish to kill *her* . . . *and* Griggs? It's not feasible. They had nothing in common."

"They're both dead, Palliser. They share that distinction. You can't get away from that fact. As to who killed them, I regret that at the moment I can't supply the answer. But to-morrow I may be in a different position."

Palliser shook his head. "Well, I'm sorry, but it doesn't make sense to me—any of it."

"Now, listen. I've been to St. Aidans. Just returned from there, as a matter of fact. Had a conference while I was there with an old Police ally of mine, and went on the pier with him to have a look at the general conditions surrounding the Arbuthnot death. Met an old colleague of yours there, by the way."

Palliser started. Anthony was sure of it. "Oh—who was that?"

"A man named Meredith. A member of the *Interference* company."

"Oh, yes. Of course. I should have remembered. He stayed on there when we came away. Well, what did he have to tell you?"

Anthony described the various points of his conversation with Meredith and then turned to Palliser with a question. "Are those facts substantially correct?"

"Yes. I wouldn't alter anything. Your details of the 'black-out', for instance, are quite accurate. An improbable melodrama—*Interference*—but excellent 'theatre' from beginning to end. At the beginning of the second scene of the second act I don't speak a word for nearly ten minutes. Over five. I move about the room.

Damned trying scene it is, I give you my word. Replace an object here and an object there. Put gloves on. Wipe the rim of the glass—the 'prop' glass that was supposed to have contained the poison. Pour the dregs of the prussic acid into a vase. Then, after that, I have to place the empty poison-bottle between the dead girl's fingers. Little did I think that poor old Daphne was really dead." Palliser looked at his companion.

Anthony's gaze was far away. "Ah—the bottle of poison. I had forgotten that. I've thought all the time in the terms of the glasses. Scent, of course, cold when I got there."

Palliser shook his head again. "The bottle was O.K. It was tested by several people. There had been no poison in that. That fact was absolutely established."

"By the way, Meredith told me something else. It concerned you."

Anthony watched Palliser's face. But Palliser, by now, had it well under control.

"Well, out with it. What did he tell you?"

"That it was your habit to hand Miss Arbuthnot a stimulant— after she 'died' in the play."

Palliser made no answer. Anthony thrust.

"Is that true?"

"Yes." Palliser now was very pale. "Why should I attempt to deny it? There was nothing secret about it. Nearly all the cast knew of it. It was done quite openly, at Daphne's own request. You aren't accusing me of anything, I suppose?" Palliser spoke with dogged determination.

"So that you handed her a drink a few moments before she died?"

"I did, Mr. Bathurst. I usually handed her a brandy-and-soda. Sometimes a whisky-and-soda. The glass that contained the brandy-and-soda contained nothing else. That I'll swear."

"How did you give it to her?"

Palliser hesitated but eventually again replied doggedly. "In the dark, while the 'black-out' was on. After I'd seen that a bag on the stage was O.K. I used to shift one of the flats behind her divan just a little to one side and hand the glass through the aperture."

Anthony looked grave. "Why the hell didn't you make a clean breast of this to Inspector Baddeley when he came to you at St. Aidans? Don't you see what a difference it makes?"

Palliser looked sheepishly at him. "I was windy. I should have done. I know now that I should have done. One doesn't always realize relative importances. I suppose you think that it looks black for me—eh?"

Anthony shook his head. "*You* think that, I imagine, more than I."

Palliser seemed puzzled at Mr. Bathurst's reply. "I don't know that I understand you."

"Yet you should be able to, if you work things out for yourself."

Palliser shook his head uncertainly. "I should be? Why? How do you mean?"

Anthony faced him and eyed him deliberately. "I'll be really magnanimous and give myself away to you, Mr. Palliser. Because I see things like this. If you had intended to murder Miss Arbuthnot by giving her poisoned spirits when she was on the stage—I don't think that you would have called attention to yourself by making a practice of giving her brandy several times beforehand. I may be wrong but that is how it strikes me." Anthony turned away with a shrug of his shoulder.

Palliser's eyes narrowed. Here were comfort and—something else. What that something else was he found it impossible to say. Although he knew that it was definitely there. The result was that he found temporary refuge in words.

"It may be foolish of me to say so; but it's my habit to say what I think irrespective of circumstances. I agree with you. Believe me, Mr. Bathurst, I should never have been so clumsy. Besides—what motive had I to kill Daphne Arbuthnot? All these things must come down to a question of motive in the end."

"That means little. A motive may be there—and yet one may not see it. One may not have the *knowledge* to enable one to see it. Again, I'm wondering something else."

"*What?*" Palliser's question came eagerly. The man was still a little shaken.

Anthony Bathurst chose the words of his reply deliberately. "I am wondering this, Mr. Palliser. I am wondering whether the murder of Miss Arbuthnot took place exactly as it was *meant* to take place. That is to say, whether everything went off—*according to plan*. I'm inclined at the moment to hope that it didn't."

This time it was Palliser's turn to shrug his shoulders. "Bit cryptic that, for me. Don't know that I quite get you."

Anthony smiled. "It doesn't matter a great deal. Don't know that I get myself. Griggs on the horizon too, you know. *And* Miss Fortescue. Can't forget that."

Palliser's lips parted as though he were about to speak, but he checked the words whatever they were. Anthony waited for possible revelation. But vainly—it came not. He tried again, therefore.

"You knew Miss Arbuthnot pretty well. Were playing in the same show with her. That should mean a lot. Going from place to place . . . day after day . . . and all that sort of thing. Mutual companionship, etcetera. Those conditions help understanding. The sharing of the common experience. Would you say, from what you knew of her . . . that she might have killed herself? Disappointment over a love affair, possibly? You know what the over-wrought, highly strung girl is capable of doing when she's at high tension and something snaps suddenly?"

Palliser bit his lip. "That question's difficult to answer. You see—it's so acutely personal. How *can* one answer it? How can one ever know another person thoroughly—so all round and inside-out—to assert one way or the other? Suicide? Seems to me, I have often thought so, that there might come a time when any one of us might succumb to the temptation."

"That's true, possibly, but within limits only. Tendencies and inclinations are usually easily recognizable. One says to oneself when one knows a person pretty well—'he might do this . . . he certainly wouldn't do that'. That assessment of other people may at times be faulty . . . but in the long run, I think, those values that we apportion would turn out to be fairly sound."

"You can't measure things of that kind." Palliser seemed obstinate on the point. He paused for a moment or so and then continued his explanation. "Let me put it like this. You might be right on ninety-nine occasions . . . and on the hundredth . . . the one that *counted* . . . in all probability . . . quite wrong. There's always the unknown factor."

Anthony looked at him. "You haven't really answered my question, you know. I shall be glad if you will."

Palliser smiled a trifle ruefully. "You'd pin me down, would you?"

"Not exactly."

"Well . . . if I must answer you . . . I think that Daphne *might* have killed herself. You see—I can't say . . . honestly . . . that if that piece of news had ever come to me . . . I should have been tremendously surprised at it. There you are . . . you have the answer that you were so keen to get . . . and I'm afraid that now you've got it—it will be of little use to you."

"You never can tell," returned Mr. Bathurst. "It's the little thing that so often turns the scale. Straws and camels, you know."

Palliser nodded, lit a cigarette, and lounged out.

Anthony watched him go. A puzzling case indeed. St. Aidans was a longish way from Lokingham, but the murder that had lurked in a man's heart had brought them together. Anthony Bathurst was as certain of this as he was that night followed day. He took his pen and began to write.

Inspector Sutton removed his hat, wiped his brow, and carefully placed the hat on the chair beside him. Then he pulled the chair on which he was seated nearer to Anthony Bathurst's table. He coughed painstakingly. Mr. Bathurst looked across at him, and there was weariness in Anthony's eyes.

"Good evening, Inspector. You come as a boon and a blessing to men, no doubt, but at the present moment I don't know that I'm exactly overjoyed to see you. It's damn' bad manners on my part, I agree, but you've interrupted a train of thought." Anthony shed his mood and grinned cheerfully, and the grin, at birth, took the censure from the words.

Sutton, reassured, felt more comfortable than he had done. He took out his note-book, placed it in front of him, and flicked the pages with an air of supreme confidence.

"Here's the stuff that you wanted, Mr. Bathurst. What you asked me to get the other day, you know. First of all, we'll deal with Messrs. Searle and Ellis, the two commercial travellers." He paused—expectantly—pencil poised in air.

"Ah," said Anthony, "that's just what I want. That's good of you. Searle and Ellis! Well, what have you got for me?"

"Nothing to please you, I'm afraid."

"Say that you don't know, Sutton! *De gustibus*—etcetera. Let's have it, Lestrade. Don't spare me."

"I beg your pardon, sir?"

"That's all right, Sutton. Searle and Ellis, you said. Fire away."

Sutton cleared his official throat. "From inquiries made, Mr. Bathurst, I have established the fact that neither Searle nor Ellis was at St. Aidans on the same night or even round about the time that Daphne Arbuthnot was killed. That's your first point cleared up."

Anthony held up his hand. "Half a minute, Inspector. Don't rush me. Hang on a bit if you don't mind. That refers to the town of St. Aidans itself. How about the vicinity of St. Aidans? Did you check up on that?"

Sutton shook his head. "Sorry, Mr. Bathurst. Not there either. You draw another blank. The nearest points touched within a week on either side of the date of the murder were the towns of Mariner and Roome—that was by Searle—three days before the murder. Mariner is twenty-two miles from Spearings, and Roome farther away still."

Anthony nodded acquiescence. "Go on, Inspector. That's Searle. Let's have Ellis now."

Sutton turned a page of his note-book. "Ellis comes out even better from the inquiry than Searle. Or worse, perhaps. Depends on the point of view that you take, of course. Ellis's nearest point of contact with St. Aidans was a day after the murder. At that time he was at Chalke. You've a rough idea how far away that is.

Chalke is over fifty miles from Spearings. Fifty-eight to be exact. He arrived in Chalke by way of Thistleton."

Anthony pulled at his upper lip. "Easy distances by car, each of 'em, you know, Sutton. Don't know that I'm as chock-full satisfied as you appear to be. You've checked up on them thoroughly, I suppose? Hotels and everything?"

"Quite, Mr. Bathurst. The man that I sent round is a thoroughly reliable fellow in every way. I picked him out for the job specially. He's examined hotel registers and found that both Searle and Ellis have independent evidence to support the account of their movements that they have given to us. He even went a step further than all that. He asked various people, in the hotels he went to, to describe the two men. Farrington, that's my man's name, says that the descriptions that he collected leave no room for doubt. They were of Ellis and Searle to a *T*. Good enough, Mr. Bathurst, don't you think?"

Anthony looked thoughtful. He stared into space above Sutton's head. "Seems so, I must admit."

"You don't appear to me to be too convinced, Mr. Bathurst?"

Anthony smiled. "I suppose that I'm suffering from the results of my experience. It has taught me so consistently to distrust the obvious. I've made more mistakes than I care to remember through having placed too much faith in it."

Sutton argued stubbornly. "All the same, you can't get away from *facts*. Facts are facts, all the world over, and if we refuse to accept what they tell us, we've only got ourselves to blame. And a man can't be in two places at once. Science is clever enough these days, I know—but even science can't manage to bring that about."

Anthony made no answer. Sutton, doubtless, was entitled to his point of view, and that was all there was to it. The Inspector interpreted Mr. Bathurst's silence as a victorious concession to himself. He thereupon proceeded to finish the mission that had brought him there.

"All of which brings me to the man Wells. You remember Wells? We decided—and Sir Austin Kemble himself, if you remember, insisted on it—that we should keep him well in line."

"Completely, Inspector! Well, what have you got for me in that direction?"

Sutton finessed. He was hoping that he would enjoy this part of the interview better than the part which had preceded it. It is impossible, as it was his habit to say, to make bricks without straw, and in this last instance the straw was already in his hands.

"I am of the opinion, Mr. Bathurst, that you will find Wells to be a much more interesting proposition than either Searle or Ellis has proved to be." Sutton paused.

Anthony detected the note of difference in his voice. "Oh . . . Inspector? I'll bet you've a sound reason for saying that. What about friend Wells?"

"I have something more than a reason, Mr. Bathurst. You'd win that bet all right." Sutton shifted in his seat. "Now, I took over this side of the inquiry myself. It landed me amongst other places in the place where Griggs used to live. In Kent it is."

Anthony nodded agreement. "That's so. At Great Astill. I've seen his house. Ostentatious-looking show. An indignant-looking wyvern sits in malicious state on either side of the gate."

"Quite correct, sir. So they're wyverns, are they? I called 'em gargoyles. Horrible-looking creatures. Well, I got inside the place, and that brought me very quickly to an acquaintance with the late Mr. Griggs's butler. Imposing gentleman by the name of Jayne."

"Plain Jayne?" queried Anthony.

Sutton smiled. "By no means, sir. The real thing, I can tell you, with a lovely stiff neck. Must have been a come-down for him, I should think, to hitch up with Griggs."

"Treason, Sutton. A Cabinet Minister indeed! Go on."

"My time with Jayne, Mr. Bathurst, was well spent. After judicious questioning, I learned that a short time before the murder a man had called on Griggs at Great Astill late one evening. According to Jayne's story, it was some time after dinner."

Anthony looked up. He scented interest. He wondered what was coming.

"This caller, so Jayne told me over the top of his collar, called Griggs a few choice names, and generally speaking also—where he got off. Eventually Jayne was called into the room by Griggs and ordered to put the man out. But not before the chap had threatened Griggs very distinctly. The actual threat was, in the words of Jayne, 'to let daylight into his ugly carcase'."

"Jayne was listening outside, of course?"

Sutton nodded. "I imagine that's what happened, although I didn't actually suggest it. Still, I haven't finished yet. After a persistent piece of inquiring on my part, I managed to extract from Jayne some more details of the interview. All this that I'm about to tell you, Jayne claims to have heard. I fancy that he possessed little illusion concerning his late master's morals."

Anthony whistled. "Like that, was it?"

"Afraid so, Mr. Bathurst. This is what I gathered. This bloke who was out to get Griggs accused him of playing around with his daughter. Called him, amongst other things, 'a bloody old Mormon'."

"Dear, dear, Sutton! That's really too bad. A libel on Brigham Young, Jefferson Hope, and on all the other shining lights of Salt Lake City." Anthony grinned.

Sutton, non-understanding, paid no heed. Mr. Bathurst's allusions had fallen on stony ground.

"Then he went on to say that if Griggs didn't lay off, there'd be—"

"Merry hell, eh, Sutton?"

"That's about the size of it, sir. I couldn't have put it better. But wait a minute, listen to this."

"I know what you're going to say, Inspector. Still, I'll let you say it."

"I expect you do, sir. The man's name was Wells. C.D. Wells. Jayne swears that he remembers the initials . . . and he lives at a village called Hansford, near Brook . . . in Kent. Which all corresponds absolutely with the Wells who was staying at this hotel."

Anthony looked grave. "And who was also in the billiard-room with Griggs before he died—eh? No wonder the conversation between them didn't sparkle. No wonder there was no feast of reason or flow of soul. Remember what the marker, Britton, told us?"

"About 'em not speaking to each other, do you mean?"

Anthony nodded. "That's it. Britton said that not a word passed between Griggs and Wells all the time that they were playing. We remarked on the fact at the time . . ." Anthony paused. "You know, Sutton, this is all exceedingly strange, say what you like about it. Griggs must have recognised Wells. There can be no two opinions about that. If Wells had put the fear of God in him before, according to the gospel of St. Jayne . . . why did he stay there in Wells's company?"

Sutton shook his head. "You can't tell. It's hard to say. All these things come down to the question of a man's temperament . . . like that suicide matter of yours the other day. Griggs may have put a bold face on the matter and openly defied the man. Griggs had a certain strength of character, you know, Mr. Bathurst. All the people that I've tackled about him agree on that score."

"H'm. Well, I'll accept it for the time being. Tell me this. Where's Wells now?"

"Not far away. I've got a line on him all right. Don't worry."

"This news'll suit Sir Austin Kemble down to the ground. He wanted to put a rope round Wells's neck right from the word 'go'. Fairly itched for it. I had the hardest job in the world to hold him back." Anthony paused and reflected. "Well, Sutton, where are we now? Very little advanced, I fear. Seems to me it's a case of confusion worse confounded."

Sutton rubbed his cheek. "I think I know what you mean, sir, but I'd be glad if you explained it more fully."

"I'm referring to the Griggs murder in the main. We'll let the Arbuthnot case run away and play by itself for the time being. Let us take the Griggs case on its own. As though it were self-contained. You'll find, or we have found, let us say, a definite motive for harming Griggs present in the minds of two people. This man Wells—and Fowles the electrician attached to the Baluster company. Which fact alone, oh, curse it, I don't know!" Anthony broke off precipitately with a gesture of impatience.

"What's the trouble, sir?"

Anthony smiled. "Well, don't you see, Sutton, I start by saying that we'll keep off the Arbuthnot end, and almost immediately I find myself playing the giddy goat and coming in contact with it. Through the direct line of Fowles. There he is, you see, both sides of the wretched equation."

Sutton assented gloomily. "I see what you mean, Mr. Bathurst. Yes, it's a fair puzzler, and no mistake."

Anthony turned to him decisively. "I'll tell you what's indicated, Sutton. Pointing the sky for us. Showing the way for us. You must bring in both Fowles and Wells. We can't afford to miss them. You must round 'em up—both of 'em—without delay. Take the case of Wells, now. Let me have another look at those notes *re* Wells that you made, those that you made at your first interview with him. Before I arrived in Lokingham. Got 'em here with you, Inspector?"

Sutton nodded. His hand went to his pocket.

"Good! Pass 'em over, will you?"

Sutton obeyed. Anthony looked carefully through the notes.

"H'm. Charles Dutton Wells, Ransford, Kent. Retired market-gardener. Staying in Lokingham on a holiday." Anthony looked up. "Looks a trifle fishy—what? Beautiful piece of work. Times his arrival to coincide with that of Griggs, eh? Had the latter under observation, perhaps, for some time. Knew where he could pick him up within a little. Motive—revenge? That's why he may have worked the melon-seeds off on to him. To make the affair look more mysterious for poor beggars like us who come a-prying. And then chalked the dead man's shoes. Yes . . . yes . . . all emanating from a distinct personality. I think, Sutton, that *perhaps* the finger of suspicion points more directly towards him than it does towards Fowles. Fowles at least was here in Lokingham in the ordinary course of his daily duty. Mr. C.D. Wells very definitely was not."

Sutton nodded as Anthony Bathurst made each point to him. "It may interest you to know that Sir Austin Kemble thought very much the same about Wells, when he first came down here with you, Mr. Bathurst. He suspected him almost at once."

Anthony made no reply. He was engrossed in an examination of Sutton's further notes. "I say, Inspector. There's something here, Sutton, that strikes me as being strongly significant. Perhaps you've noticed it yourself by now?"

"What's that, sir?" Sutton rose and went over to him.

Anthony tapped Sutton's page of notes. "Why this fact in itself. We're up against another piece of distinct suppression."

"In what way, sir?"

"Why—in this way. Take the various questions that you put to Wells and the answers that he gave you. Here they are. Read them again. Are they frank? Are they open? Is there the slightest suggestion in any one of them that he had never met Griggs before? Now I ask you, Sutton—wouldn't a naturally straightforward man, caught in the clutch of these circumstances, have made a clean breast of the fact that he already had an acquaintanceship with Griggs? Wouldn't you yourself have done—in Wells's place?"

"If I had threatened him just before his death?" queried Sutton pertinently. "You must not overlook that."

"Who knew that?"

"Jayne! The butler. There was Jayne, you know."

"Yes . . . there was Jayne," repeated Anthony Bathurst; "but I question whether Wells ever considered him. I very much question it."

"Wouldn't like to say. Jayne knew things. Things of importance, too. Jayne knew that Wells had threatened his master. Jayne knew what Griggs was. Griggs had yelled for Jayne to come in to him and throw Wells out. Ten to one that's why Wells kept his mouth shut when I questioned him. He took a chance. Which *might* have come off. As it happened, it didn't, but he wasn't to know that. You always get factors like that at work in cases of this kind." Anthony handed back the notes to the Inspector. "It's all very interesting and, at the same time, semi-disturbing. As I said, Sutton, you'll have to get hold of Wells and ask him for a supplementary statement. Make him open his mouth a good deal more than he has done so far. And the sooner the better, or we shall have the Commissioner dropping along and asking you and me some damned awkward questions. We can't put up with that, Sutton! Life will lose its savour and all will be glitter and froth."

"And Fowles—do you think?"

"Yes . . . and Fowles, too. It's no good having one without the other. And, since confidence begets confidence, I'll pass on some information to you regarding friend Fowles. I picked this up from

Palliser. What do you think Fowles carried about with him? As a household pet? All day and every day. Close to his bosom and nestling near his heart?"

"Search me!" said Sutton.

"A coil of rope! Neither more nor less. The hangman's regalia. Good hempen-spun. Remember the words of Wilde, Sutton, that lord of language? Concerning the lineal descendants of Jack Ketch, Billington and Co.? 'He did not pass in purple pomp, Nor ride a moon-white steed. Three yards of cord and a sliding-board, Are all the gallows need. So with rope of shame the Herald came, To do the secret deed.'"

Anthony rubbed his hands. "Three yards of cord, Sutton. Nine blessed feet. And friend Fowles carried it with him. Why, Sutton? Why—oh, why—oh, why?"

"For . . . Griggs?" almost whispered Inspector Sutton.

"Griggs," replied Anthony deliberately, "was killed with a bullet fired from a revolver. The revolver belonged to Griggs himself. The rope was wasted . . . that is to say, if it were intended for Griggs . . . which we're justified in thinking might have been the case. It's a bizarre thought that, you know, Sutton. Picture the avenging Fowles stalking Griggs with the rope coiled round his waist . . . relentlessly . . . inexorably . . . waiting for the moment to wreak his rough justice on him . . . and then letting all his plans go by the board and shooting him in bed, like a lawn-tennis-playing bank-manager might be shot because he had a disinclination to disgorge the family plate when Bill Sikes appeared in front of him and demanded it. What a transformation! From a terrific figure . . . first cousin to Nemesis stalking down the corridors of vengeance . . . Fowles becomes quite an ordinary and prosaic one. Visualize the tremendous possibilities. Supposing you had come upon Griggs hanging from a hook in the ceiling! That sight would have burnt pretty deep into your imagination . . . I'll lay a wager that you would have remembered it for the rest of your natural life! Whereas finding him in bye-byes with a cube of chalk in his pyjamas and a nice bedtime story near him makes you treat the whole thing as bordering upon the commonplace. Thus are opportunities lost and the normal comes into its own."

Anthony grinned at his sally.

Sutton nodded. "I know what you mean, Mr. Bathurst . . . but I don't accept your word 'commonplace'. It's far from that."

"Relative terms, my dear Sutton. Just that and nothing more. All things are relative. Now I've another job for you. Be a good scout and get along to the theatre, the local one, where the Palliser crowd is, and get your hooks into that coil of rope that was part and parcel of Fowles's daily dozen. You'll find that he's left it behind. At least, Palliser says so. I think that we can trust our Palliser."

Sutton cocked his head shrewdly at Anthony's last remark. "Meaning by that?"

"What do *you* mean?"

"It isn't what *I* mean. It's what *you* mean, Mr. Bathurst. Sure you don't mean anything special?"

"No, Sutton. Honour bright. See my finger wet? Nothing cryptic—believe me."

Anthony paused—a far-away look in his eyes. Sutton watched him eagerly. He had the intelligence not to interrupt his companion by speech. He was beginning to understand his Bathurst better.

Anthony came from his day-dream to reality. "I'll tell you something, Inspector. You know that I've been to St. Aidans, don't you? I felt that Sir Austin's story of the Daphne Arbuthnot affair asked for, or rather needed, some little investigation on my part. Well, I've been in touch with the Inspector who had charge of the case—he happened to be an old pal of mine . . . and I've definitely proved . . . to my own satisfaction . . . that Daphne Arbuthnot was deliberately poisoned. But I don't know why . . . Sutton . . . and because I don't know why . . . and can't find out why . . . I'm worried to blazes."

Sutton came to grips. "Does the motive *matter* so much . . . if you're as certain as you say you are?"

"Yes, Sutton, it matters so much that until I'm in possession of it—until I understand perfectly *why* Daphne Arbuthnot died on her divan—I'm floundering in the dark. And I'm blessed if I like floundering, Sutton, one little bit!"

"No, Mr. Bathurst, I can understand that. I don't like it myself. If there's one thing I *do* like in life, it's to know exactly where I am and how I stand."

CHAPTER XIX
ACADEMY

THE Principal of the Maxwell House Academy of Elocution and Dramatic Art sat at his table and moodily opened the correspondence that the morning post had brought him. Almost all of it belonged to one category. Beryl Oakley, his wife, watched him as a mother watches the well-being of the sickly child of her womb. As he tore open envelope after envelope, twinge after twinge pierced her, for she knew the increasing bitterness of his soul and of the iron that had entered therein.

"There you are, Beryl, my dear," he said eventually, tossing documents over to her, "there's what the blessing of the morning post amounts to. Gas, two pounds eight shillings and eightpence; the new linoleum in the hall, four pounds eight; my life Insurance premium, now over-due, they say, one pound fourteen shillings and fourpence; and the bill for books from Scrivener's seven pounds two and ninepence halfpenny. Those damned people never could wait five minutes. Of fees due to me, for tuition given, or books supplied, there seems to be the usual aggregate—nothing, nil, nought and none! I'm one of the world's payers, my dear Beryl—high in the championship class. As a receiver, count me as the most putrid of all the 'also-rans'. Never a snatcher—always a 'snatched-from'."

The bitterness and self-castigation in his voice caused her to writhe inwardly. "If only that dreadful Griggs man hadn't—" She broke off as though the picture that she had conjured up was too distasteful for her to view.

"I know," he said, "that was just my wretched luck, but what's done can't be undone. Griggs is dead and that fact alone, for all we know, may be a misfortune to him. Far worse than it was to me. I merely lost money because of him. There may be Justice somewhere. We don't know, and because we don't know, conjecture is more than idle. It's fatuous."

He rose from the table and looked at his watch. As he moved his hand that held the wrist-watch his wife saw the frayed ends of both shirt and coat sleeves, the sight scorched her. Bricklayers were better off, she thought miserably—and this husband of hers was a clever man. She had a touching faith in him and in his powers. At his own subject, "Spoken English", more than merely competent or ordinarily efficient—an expert with a streak of brilliance. Only a certain quality of fastidiousness that he would have found difficult to diagnose had kept him off the stage in his earlier days. The poverty of his father, a man of brilliant academic attainments—that earned from a grateful Government their inevitable and parsimonious reward—had prevented him from reading for the Bar. At the Grammar School of King John Lackland, he had won the Mortimer Beaufoy prize for Elocution and Dramatic Art four years in succession and his sparkling performance of "Puff" in *The Critic* is still spoken of by many of those who were privileged to see and hear it. What had Irving said to him concerning it? "The finest performance by a boy that I have ever seen."

His "School of Elocution" idea had come to him soon after he had married Beryl Hartley, and the idea had not taken long to become a reality. Urged by her to establish the school first of all in a town area, he had obstinately refused to do so and had started his school in the country district of Erlegh. "We will begin humbly," he had told her, "and rise to higher things." When he had informed Anthony Bathurst how he had fared in this effort, he had spoken the absolute truth. The affair Griggs was *terrific* to him. Thus was he made and thus would he remain, and he found himself hating Griggs for the part that he had played in his life and career.

As he moved to the door of the breakfast-room, a sharp exclamation from his wife recalled him to her side.

"Harold," she said, "look here in this morning's paper. If you could only *do* something about it. And why shouldn't you, my dear? With your brains you might easily succeed where everybody else would fail." She pointed excitedly to the front page of the *Morning Message*. Oakley read the sentences to which she was pointing.

£1,000 Reward. The proprietors of the *Morning Message* offer a reward of £1,000 (one thousand pounds) to any person or persons who will supply information that will lead to the arrest and conviction of the murderer or murderers of the late Hon. A.S. Griggs, M.P., and Secretary of State for Home Affairs, in the Lansdowne Hotel, Lokingham.

Oakley read the announcement. One thousand pounds! El Dorado to him! "Always was a Griggs paper," he said, "though the Lord knows why." He looked at his wife.

"Why don't you try for it?" she said, urging him by voice and gesture. "It would be almost poetic justice if you could bring it off."

"Easier said than done. What could I do? If the police and a man like Anthony Bathurst are baffled, it isn't likely that an impossible amateur such as I am could find out anything."

"Oh, why won't you try? Why won't you believe in yourself more? You never know," replied Beryl Oakley. "You're here on the spot . . . pupils aren't exactly prolific at the moment . . . now—are they? . . . And a thousand pounds isn't four-pence ha'penny. Besides, you're clever! Far cleverer than the average man. Don't I *know* it? Well, then, let other people know it too. You know the Lokingham Hotel . . . and its position . . . you know the whole district round about inside-out. How many people know it as well as you do? Not one in a thousand. Think what a lot we could do with a thousand pounds."

"Yes, or come to that, with a thousand pence. As Reeky Poole said in *The Little Damozel*—'quite a number'. That was a thundering good show—that."

Beryl felt a trifle more hopeful. To have forced a joke from her husband's lips on a morning of this kind, approximated triumph. And her domestic triumphs these days were few and far between. She watched him turn irresolutely to the door again.

"What have you got on this morning?" she asked. "Is there much?"

He fished his daily time-table from his breast-pocket. "Can't tell you for certain—till I've had a look. I'm losing interest so. Let's see." He smoothed out the paper in his diary. "A form for Stage I, 'True Emphasis'. That's from nine-fifteen to ten-fifteen. Then a private pupil, ten-thirty to eleven. What's he got? Stage III, 'Mental Vision'. It's young Hardy from the Vicarage. Better named 'Fool Hardy'. Then from eleven to twelve a form in Stage II, 'The Ethics of Conversation—the Contrast Between Compliment and Flattery'. That's about the bundle before lunch."

"How about after lunch?" she persisted. "Much?"

"Nothing much doing then, worse luck! Two private pupils. That's all. Miss Casson. Young Ruby Casson first . . . she's just starting. Her sister was here a year ago, if you remember, and has done very well since. After Ruby Casson, there's a complete break till a quarter to four. Empty and void. Then comes Miss Worrall. You know her. The one that's stage-struck. So she ought to be! Hard! With every bolt and nut of it. Hopeless! Not an earthly. Mouthful of teeth that hang out to dry and really prize adenoids. Utterly and appallingly hopeless."

"You've a pretty light day, then," urged Beryl Oakley, "taking it all in all."

"You seem almost pleased about it."

"No, I'm not. You know perfectly well what I mean, my dear, so please don't get stuffy. I believe in you, and I believe that you could pull off that one thousand pounds if you seriously put your mind to it. Think it over, Harold. For my sake; for our sakes. I'll leave it at that." She rose and left him.

Oakley stared despondently after her. Women always found talk to be so easy. Their point of view was so different from a man's. Why was it? The light and airy way that they had of removing difficult obstacles with a shrug of the shoulder or breaking down barriers with the gesture of a finger, always annoyed him excessively. Confidence and optimism are all very well in their way—but damn it all—they must be seasoned with sound common sense to be reasonably effective. And yet—he paused. Considering all the circumstances, Beryl's suggestion might not be too bad after all.

One side of it possessed an attractiveness that hadn't occurred to him when she had originally broached it.

If he could do anything there might be publicity for him in it. And publicity of a definite kind would almost certainly be to his personal advantage. For there was no knowing where it might eventually lead. At any rate, there wouldn't be any harm in him having a shot at that reward that was being offered. It would mean that he would probably be in the centre of things. People might hear of his activity and talk about him. He might, for instance, get into touch with Anthony Bathurst again. He might also pick up points from Bathurst that he could turn to good profit. Bathurst had seemed a thoroughly decent chap at that first meeting between them, who might treat him handsomely. Whichever way you look at it—Beryl knew what she was saying—and two intelligences were better than one. It would be a tremendous help, too, if he could find out the directions towards which Bathurst was inclining.

The more he thought over the prospect that the proposition presented, the more roseate it appeared to him. It might well be that it would prove to be a mental tonic in addition, and assist to keep his mind from the too intensive contemplation of his own pecuniary troubles. He took out his pocket-book and referred again to his personal diary. Yes—after he had taken Ethel Worrall, he would be free, if nothing else turned up. And new pupils hadn't been turning up lately. The last had been over a month ago. He'd give Beryl's idea a run—hanged if he wouldn't.

His face brightened perceptibly, and he straightened his tie. He surveyed himself in the glass. Hawkshaw the detective! In other words—"Tip us, the cracksman's crook!"

Anthony Bathurst listened to the man who, but a few hours previously, had been teaching the principles of elocution to two young ladies, one of whom didn't understand it and the other of whom required drastic dental treatment and, most probably also, appendicectomy—judging by her audible signs of digestive derangement. Oakley, strange to say, was less nervous in talking to Anthony than he had been on the previous occasion. He opened the talk in his own way—frankly and disarmingly.

"The mercenary quality is still uppermost, Mr. Bathurst. Have no illusions regarding me. Behold me less humiliated than, in all decency, I should be. But I haven't turned up here to collect the price of a three half-crown book this time. We'll call that the sprat. This time, I've come for the mackerel."

"A tasty fish," said Anthony. "Soused and with a garnish of cloves—I always find it highly delectable. But it should refrain from exposing its head to the sun, I believe. At least, my mother always told me so."

Oakley stared in surprise at the man whom he had come to see. Anthony's mood, however, changed quickly.

"Sorry, Mr. Oakley. It was your mention of mackerel that set my thoughts wandering. Say what you want to say. I promise to listen as intelligently as I can."

Oakley wisely changed his tactics. He decided to discard the lighter note that he had so far adopted and become his own natural self.

"First of all, I will put my cards on the table, Mr. Bathurst. Then we shall know where we are."

Anthony looked quickly up at him. The man was deadly serious, anyway. His eyes showed that—unmistakably. There might be something in this.

He contented himself by saying: "Go on, Mr. Oakley, please."

Oakley accepted the invitation and continued.

"This morning's copy of the *Morning Message* offers a reward of one thousand pounds for information that will lead to the arrest and conviction of Griggs's murderer. Do you happen to have seen the offer yourself?"

"Yes. I've read it. Naturally, I should read it. I was highly interested in it. I read everything that I can read of the Griggs case."

"Good. That will save me making any more preliminary explanation. One thousand pounds is a lot of money, Mr. Bathurst. It may not mean so much to you, but to me it's an almost incredible sum of money. To acquire it, would transform my life. I came to tell you that I'm going to do my best to secure it. Don't laugh at me—preposterous though the idea may seem. The idea wasn't mine in the first place. I won't claim the credit for it, therefore. It emanated from Mrs. Oakley." He smiled whimsically. "You see, Mr. Bathurst—my wife has a quaint and rather touching belief in me. She has a higher opinion of me than anybody else has. A much higher one than I merit. Personally, I don't think that I've the slightest chance of pulling the job off, but there you are, you never know. The tortoise, if you remember, once triumphed over the hare."

Anthony was amused at Oakley's attempt at self-depreciation. "And how does all this affect me, Mr. Oakley? I'm not quite sure where I stand in it. I can assure you that you need not regard me as a rival competitor for the *Morning Message*'s one thousand pounds."

Oakley flushed with discomfiture. Each cheek showed a spot of colour. "Well, I came to you in the hope that you might be able to help me."

"How? To win the reward?"

Oakley's flush became deeper. Was this sarcasm on Bathurst's part? "I fear that I must appear unutterably mercenary. I know that I do. Otherwise you wouldn't put things quite as you do. I hoped when I came that you might be able to give me some information. I am sorry now—I assure you."

Anthony smiled at him. "In what way?"

"With regard to the case generally."

Anthony shook his head. "I'm afraid that I still don't follow you. Do you mean any special piece of information?"

Oakley demurred. "No, not exactly. I thought that you might tell me, for example, how your investigation was faring generally. Then I thought that if *I* were lucky enough to pick up anything, I'd pass it on to you as a *quid pro quo*. An exchange of ideas. See what I mean?"

Anthony grinned at the somewhat naive proposal. "Still harping on the quids?"

Oakley's face twisted painfully.

"Sorry," said Anthony quickly, with genuine regret, "that was too bad of me. I oughtn't to have said it. Get it into your head that I couldn't resist it."

"That's all right. I can't blame you for scourging me. I've asked for all I get."

The man seemed so bereft of strength, personal courage, and independence, that Mr. Bathurst felt suddenly and strangely sympathetic towards him.

"The case moves but slowly, Oakley. If it moves at all. Most of the attacks that I have so far made have ended in either failure or alternately in an impenetrably blank wall. There are two main threads that we have been endeavouring to disentangle. Ever heard of a place called St. Aidans?"

"Of course. Near Tamarisk. The seaside town next to Spearings. But why do you ask? What has St. Aidans to do with the murder of Griggs?"

Anthony shook his head. "If I knew that, my dear Oakley—well, the *Morning Message* wouldn't be offering its one thousand pounds, and you wouldn't be considering winning it. Because I feel certain that the town of St. Aidans has in some way a curious connection with the town of Lokingham. But I don't know why it has, and I feel that I'm perilously close to being the rottenest detective that the world has ever known. Candidly speaking, the headway that I've made in the case would go into a small ice-cream glass and then you could put an ice on top without the slightest difficulty."

Oakley looked at him vaguely. "I'm still in the dark about why St. Aidans is so important," he urged.

"Yes? Well—I'll put you wise to it. Not so very long before our friend Griggs was gathered to his fathers in so unceremonious a fashion, a girl named Daphne Arbuthnot died on St. Aidans pier. She was an actress of sorts . . . playing in a show called *Interference* . . . the main facts of the affair were as follows. . . ."

Anthony gave Oakley a brief résumé of the Arbuthnot case. That is to say, of as much of it as had become public information. Oakley listened to him attentively. Right to the end of Mr. Bathurst's recital.

"There you are," concluded the latter; "now you know as much as I do about all of it. Consider yourself highly honoured."

"I do. It's awfully decent of you to have told me what you have done. But what about the Lokingham end of the tangle . . . have you linked up anything there yet?"

"This, perhaps. Griggs wasn't everybody's white-headed boy. I can tell you that. He didn't exactly sweat popularity."

"I'm not surprised to hear you say that. Between ourselves, I thought as much myself."

Anthony eyed him shrewdly and chose words deliberately. "He may even have incurred the dislike of the Ku-Klux-Klan . . . that's as far as we know."

Oakley looked at him wonderingly. "I . . . er . . . beg your pardon? What was that you said?"

"I'm trying you too highly, perhaps? Ah, well—never mind about that. We'll leave it at this: The Ku-Klux Klan is a secret society that had its origin in the Southern states of America. With the possible exception of the Mafia and the primary Chinese 'Tong', I should describe it as the most powerful secret society in the world."

"Why is it called the Ku-Klux-Klan?"

"The name is supposed to have been taken from the sound made by the cocking of a rifle. An onomatopoeia, Mr. Oakley. Although not so easy to discern as some. Warnings are sent to intended victims, and these warnings take bizarre shape . . . such as dried pips or seeds or even leaves."

Oakley trembled with excitement. "And you associate this society with Griggs?"

"It's on the cards. I may tell you that there is a definite pointer to such a condition."

Oakley's eyes bulged with excitement. Here were happenings! "You interest me tremendously, Mr. Bathurst. I'd been inclined to regard it as an extremely sordid and unromantic murder. Now I find it hedged round with glamorous intrigue. I'm almost glad that I put my novice hand to the detective's plough." Oakley looked round. Then he leant forward and pulled his chair nearer to Anthony. "You've been frightfully decent to me, Mr. Bathurst, since I came to see you. Many men, situated as you were, would have hoofed me in the pants. I'm not unmindful of your kindness. In return for it, I'll pass something on to you. Something I've thought about many times since it happened. You remember how I told you that Griggs had called upon me—just before he was killed—and how brief my little triumph proved to be?"

Anthony nodded. What was coming now?

Oakley continued: "Amongst other things that he said to me he made a peculiar remark. I told you that he confessed to me that he was inclined to be nervous of his broadcasting. That was the real reason why he wanted me to give him the lessons in elocution that he arranged to have. Now listen to something that he told me that afternoon in my house. At the time I don't think that I realized the significance of it. But now, after having heard what you have to say . . . 'I'm not windy of death, Mr. Oakley, never have been and I hope and trust, never will be, and I'm not frightened when devils from hell put their filthy trademark of the seeds on me . . . but I'm scared stiff to have to talk into that "mike." I go all dithery at the very thought of it.' They were Griggs's words, Mr. Bathurst, as nearly as I can remember them. When you mentioned pips and seeds and leaves, I could scarcely believe my ears. You almost took my breath away." Oakley leant forward again towards Anthony, trembling with excitement. "Have I helped you, Mr. Bathurst? I should be no end bucked if I thought I had."

Anthony considered carefully before he replied. Here was the Ku-Klux-Klan again! In what way had Griggs made contact with the Ku-Klux-Klan? Did it all go back to the years that had gone? The case was honey-combed with doubt and difficulty, Anthony shook his head.

"It's difficult to say, Oakley. Because at the moment I'll be candid and confess that I can see very little light indeed. All the same, thanks for coming. I shall certainly remember what you have told me. If you manage to get hold of anything else that you think I ought to know—well—I shall appreciate your telling me. We'll leave it at that, shall we?"

Oakley shook hands. He had begun well. Beryl would be pleased. And to have pleased Beryl . . . !

Chapter XX
AT BAY

INSPECTOR Sutton was seated in his room at Lokingham police-station when the news was 'phoned through that Fowles had been traced and was being brought along to make a statement. To say that the news gave him pleasure is putting it but mildly. Fowles had actually been found in a cheap lodging-house in the neighbouring town of Huntley. Patmore, the constable who had picked him up, told Inspector Sutton that Fowles had been quite open concerning his movements and had agreed quite readily to come over to Lokingham and give any information to the authorities that it lay in his power to give.

As Sutton had listened to the full tenor of Patmore's message his pleasurable optimism was inclined to diminish. But he had quickly recovered his confidence and told himself that a brazen and apparently frank exterior was very often to be found accompanying guilt.

He looked rather impatiently at his watch. According to his reckoning, Patmore should be here with his charge very shortly now. Sutton fidgeted at his desk. He left his chair and paced the room. Went to the window and looked out. He wished now that he had 'phoned to Anthony Bathurst and asked him to be present at this interview with Fowles that was so shortly to take place. At any rate, he would take the greatest care that he missed nothing, so that he could duly report the full details to Bathurst afterwards. There was no knowing what a man like Fowles might attempt to put over . . . if . . .

The telephone bell rang again. This was the signal, no doubt. Sutton lifted the receiver and asked questions. Yes. All to plan. "Bring Mr. Fowles up . . . Patmore. And ask Sergeant Hudson to come along with you. Good! That's O.K. I'm ready right now." Sutton went to his chair again.

The door opened. Sergeant Hudson and Patmore entered with a third man behind them. A man with dark, heavy, brooding eyes . . . thus Fowles.

Fowles sidled into the room, and all Sutton's instincts warned him to watch his step and tread carefully. The man, he saw now more plainly, was big, burly, efficient, distinctly truculent, and certainly not lacking in confidence. He opened the ball, in fact.

"I have been told that you wish to see me. What exactly for, may I ask? Kindly understand, before we start, that I've accompanied your man here purely voluntarily."

Sutton exuded charm. Out of his strength came forth sweetness. He rather fancied his genial suit.

"It's like this, Mr. Fowles," he said. "You've heard, I'm sure, of the sudden and surprising death that took place in the Lansdowne Hotel the other morning. You know, too, that the dead man was a celebrity in his way. None other than the Hon. A.S. Griggs, M.P. The Home Secretary, you know. But the newspapers will have told you all that."

Fowles stuck out a hostile jaw. He glared at the Inspector. "Suppose I have. What's it all got to do with me? I don't happen to be in the talking-shop myself."

"Well—there's this. You were staying in Lokingham at the time, and I thought it was just possible that you might be able to assist me. In fact, I've been in touch with several people and they're all agreed on the point. You see—"

Fowles frowned uncompromisingly. Sutton stopped directly— almost as though he had been commanded.

"That sounds all right—from your point of view. How can I assist you?"

"Well, for one thing, you played billiards with Griggs on the evening before he died, didn't you?"

"I did. Nothing remarkable in that. I had to play with somebody. Wouldn't play with myself very well. What of it?"

Sutton still remained the essence of courtesy. His experience had taught him that men of this type required careful handling. He determined to keep a firm grip of himself.

"You didn't hear him say anything, I suppose, while you were playing, that might throw any light on his death? Any chance remark—or fragment of conversation?"

"Heard a lot after I got between the sheets. Trams—motor-lorries, wireless, a bloody gramophone—"

"Never mind about that. I'm referring to when you were in the billiard-room with Griggs. You heard nothing then to excite your suspicions, eh?"

"Couldn't do. Never had any."

"I see." Sutton shifted his course. Things were going badly. "You had never met the dead man, I presume, Mr. Fowles, before you went into the Lansdowne Hotel billiard-room that night?"

"Never." Fowles was quietly emphatic.

"Ah well, then it couldn't have been you who was overheard talking to him in his room after the billiards were over. You didn't follow him to his bedroom, by any chance?"

Fowles stared. "When? What do you take me for?"

Sutton seemed to relinquish the idea. "Never mind. It's of no consequence. But I'm downright sorry you can't help me, Mr. Fowles."

Fowles lurched forward. There was aggression in the movement. The lurch brought him appreciably nearer to Sutton's desk. Words poured from his lips.

"Look here, Mr. Policeman. This is all very, well as far as it goes. But, as I said, it's all from your point of view. It doesn't cut any ice from mine. True to the blasted Police tradition. You've never put your dirty paws on me yet, not one of you, and I'm going to take damned care that you never do. I know your ways—got good reason to. You're the finest liars in the world. If you haven't got a shred of evidence against the poor wretch that gets in your hands, you soon manufacture some nice juicy stuff against him. I know that. None better. I came along here because this flat-footed hayseed of yours told me it would be better for everybody if I did. What happened? What I was pretty sure would happen when I agreed to come. You ask me a lot of damned silly questions about a man who was a complete stranger to me. What do I care if he *was* murdered? He probably deserved all that went to him. But you're not going to get away with it. I'm askin' myself a question now. What's behind it all? Come on! Play the game with me if you can—although I know it's askin' a hell of a lot to ask you that. Now tell me—what do you really want to know? Be straight and spill it."

Sutton met the verbal onslaught with complete imperturbability. The man was an awkward customer, who required delicate and careful handling.

"Look here, Fowles," he commenced, "there's no earthly reason why you should carry on like this . . ."

At that moment the telephone bell on his desk rang again. Sutton broke off his conversation and answered the call. Directly he spoke his face cleared. The men who watched him wondered at the nature of the interruption.

"Certainly . . . come right along, Mr. Bathurst," they heard him say. "Yes . . . at this very moment . . . Fowles is actually with me now." He replaced the receiver.

As he did so, Fowles tossed his head impatiently. "What's this?" he growled. "A trap for me? Another of your clever frame-ups? Well—let me tell you this . . . before you try any more of your tricks, remember that I came here willingly and now show me your authority to . . ."

Fowles stopped and turned abruptly as the door opened behind him. His dark, brooding eyes sought the eyes of the tall man who entered. They faced each other.

"Good afternoon, gentlemen," said Mr. Bathurst. "Thank you, Inspector, for the privilege that you're according me. I should hate to have thought that I was *de trop*. Go on with what you were doing. Don't mind me. Oh, by the way . . . Mr. Fowles, isn't it? Pleased to meet you."

Fowles spoke from the side of his mouth. "Don't be too sure about that. You seem to have plenty of what the cat cleans itself with, and I'll tell you this—I've no love for 'busys'."

Anthony smiled at his pugnacity. "Don't misunderstand me, my dear sir. I wouldn't have that happen on any account. It may surprise you, but I don't even want you to love me."

Fowles glared. The reply that had come to him was unexpected. Sutton diplomatically intervened.

"Mr. Fowles and I had almost finished, Mr. Bathurst, when you 'phoned just now. I rather fancy, indeed, that he was just going. I don't know whether you would care to ask him anything before he leaves us. That is, of course, if Mr. Fowles is prepared to answer."

"Don't know that I am. Why should I? I know a bit about the law myself. *And* about judges' rules concerning the use of evidence." His lip curled in sarcasm as he fell to quotation—"'then one of them which was a lawyer went unto Him'—it's just the same as it's written in the Good Book. Nineteen hundred years and people haven't changed a bit."

Anthony lounged nonchalantly against the door. "Got a new job, Fowles?"

"That's my business."

"But surely, the old job *used* to be."

"Used to be what?"

"Your business. At any rate, you must admit that you left the old job in a hurry. Didn't even stop to put your things away nicely."

"I leave my jobs when and how I like."

"Good! That's one point we're agreed on, then. Do you make a habit also of leaving your belongings behind?"

Fowles stared at him. There was no doubt that this last question from Mr. Bathurst was a complete surprise to him. He stuck out the same hostile jaw that Sutton had seen close to him but a few minutes previously. But Anthony felt certain that his face registered something beyond surprise. Perhaps not a condition of alarm or fear, but a quality dangerously close to apprehension.

"Belongings? What do you mean by that? I don't understand you."

"No? Yet you should, I think. It's quite an ordinary word, after all, isn't it?"

The man's eyes smouldered angrily. "I know what the word means all right. I don't understand it in this connection. What's more—you knew I meant that, too, so don't play about."

Anthony smiled at him. "Oh, don't split hairs, man. You'll waste the time of both of us, if you do. I'll repeat my question. Do you make a habit of leaving behind, when you leave your various jobs, any of your personal possessions? Or was it, on this occasion, due to mere forgetfulness on your part?"

Fowles looked stolidly in front of him. "Don't know what you're talkin' about, guv'nor. I don't possess much in this world—not being one of the lucky ones—so I'm not likely to leave behind me anything at all valuable. But out with it, man, tell me straight what you're gettin' at."

"You raise the question of value. Values are difficult to assess. There are intrinsic and extrinsic values which in themselves have an ever-changing standard according to prevailing conditions and the adjustment of those conditions. For instance, in order to make my meaning more clear to you, I can imagine a set of circumstances where a knife might be infinitely more valuable to a man than a bag of gold . . . or even another, when a handful of diamonds might be of far less worth—to somebody in personal danger—say, than a coil of rope! See what I mean now, Fowles? Or are you still in doubt as to my question?"

The muscles in Fowles's jaw tightened. A dark flush showed round his temples. All in the room who watched him knew that Mr. Bathurst's thrust had gone home. But Fowles was made of sterner stuff than most. Yorkshire born and Yorkshire bred, he held the fight of George Hirst and Wilfred Rhodes, and because of that he wasn't beaten until the fall of the last wicket. He made a clumsy movement of his strong, square shoulders.

"You're talkin' silly, guv'nor, you are really. What should I want a rope for now, anyway? You know as well as I do—you *must* do from what you just said to me—that I've turned the theatre job in. Got on my nerves it did. Too much hustle and bustle for me. Run here and a hop, skip and a jump there. Surely that don't take much understanding?"

Anthony's voice took on a slightly sharper tone. "Electrician to the company, weren't you? Wanted the rope, I suppose, to harness the electricity? Or to hitch your wagon to the magnetic stars that are greater than those of Hollywood. Sorry, Fowles, and all that, but candidly I don't believe you."

Fowles twisted his face into a grin. "That does upset me. Reckon I'll lose sleep to-night over that. Still, I'll make you a fair offer. Fair and square and all above-board. You can have the rope, guv'nor, for keeps. I'll give it to you . . . and for all I care you can bloody well twist it round your 'bushel' and hang yourself with it!"

Anthony was unperturbed. He smiled again. "Thanks, Fowles . . . and really, I shall hate to disappoint you. I'll have your rope, and to please you I promise you that I'll take a good look at it. It may even have qualities that I hitherto haven't suspected. One never knows. Still . . . I agree with you in one respect . . . *you had no further use for it*. I think . . . that there are some things that I am just beginning to understand."

Fowles stared at Anthony with silent aggression. His eyes flickered and showed the enmity that was harboured by his soul. He felt that he was safer silent than voluble with this man who confronted him.

Anthony turned to Inspector Sutton. "Does he know, Inspector, that Gladys Greene, in the course of her daily duty, went to look for a brush? Or shall we tell him?"

Sutton looked up, a trifle puzzled. Then he understood what Anthony Bathurst meant. "No. That is—not quite."

"Well, I think that we owe it to him to tell him. After all, it's only fair that we should. You know, he's volunteered to come back here and make this statement. Yes, Sutton, we must tell him of Gladys. It is definitely indicated."

All this time, Fowles had been watching Mr. Bathurst from the corner of his eye. Like a dog about to jump one way or another, but temporarily undecided. Something told him that this grey-eyed stranger was playing him as the skilled angler plays the lean-jawed pike. Well, if that were the case, as in the case of the pike, there would be a tremendous struggle before he was landed and gaffed. He made no sign, therefore, but waited for Mr. Bathurst to proceed. He was not kept in suspense long.

"Listen, Fowles. Soon after eleven o'clock on the night of Griggs's death, according to reliable information that has reached us, voices were heard coming from the dead man's bedroom. Voices, the tone and general quality of which hinted at something in the nature of a quarrel between Griggs and the person who was in there with him."

Fowles broke in heatedly. "Don't try that game! You can't put this over on to me. I never went inside the bedroom. I only—" Fowles stopped as abruptly as he had started. His mouth shut like the jaws of a trap.

Anthony pounced on his hesitation. "You only . . . yes . . . what did you do? I could bear to know that, Fowles."

Fowles made a jerky movement of the shoulder. "Played billiards . . . and when that was finished went back to my digs. Call round there now and ask my landlady what time I returned, if you don't believe me."

"I see. You went back to your digs. Still, let me finish what I was about to say when you interrupted me. Regarding these voices that were heard coming from Griggs's bedroom. Number Fifty-Four, wasn't it?"

"Yes."

The reply came before Fowles realized all that it implied. Again Anthony was swift to strike.

"So you knew the number of the bedroom, then?"

Fowles was quick to recover the ground that he had temporarily lost. "Yes. And I can explain how I knew. If you want to know, I heard Griggs mention it in the billiard-room when I was playing billiards in there."

"You didn't set yourself out deliberately to obtain the information?"

"I did not."

"You've remembered the number, though? You have a good memory?"

"For some things. Not for others. Like most of us."

"You don't forget easily . . . or quickly?"

"Depends on what it is."

"You're a Yorkshireman. You would carry a stone in your pocket for years before you threw it at a certain somebody."

Fowles frowned. Again he realized the extent of the implication. "Might do. If it suited my book. Still, get on with your 'mysterious voices'. I shall think I'm at Lourdes next with the happy band of pilgrims."

"Or even windward, possibly. Well, these voices weren't so mysterious as you seem to imagine. They were real. Nothing ghostly about them. Because certain words that were used were heard quite distinctly. One of them was that supremely interesting word 'murder'; and another of them was—as was believed at the time by the person that heard it—'fowls'; you know what I mean. Rhode Island Reds and Buff Orpingtons and White Wyandottes. Yet, in the light of further information that has come our way, that word may well have been, not 'f-o-w-l-s', but 'F-o-w-l-e-s'." Anthony spelt the two words letter by letter.

There was a silence.

Fowles countered him cleverly. Far more adroitly than Anthony had anticipated.

"Funny sort of conversation your pal heard . . . whoever she was. Only two words in it apparently. What was it really—a charade? Working out syllables?"

Anthony's voice became sterner. He would waste no more time with this man in a battle of words.

"You are right, Fowles. The two words *are* inadequate. Other things *were* said. We won't stress them unduly. The man who shot Griggs said, 'They belonged to me and I'm entitled to please myself regarding them.' That gives you a more comprehensive idea, perhaps, of the bedroom conversation that we're discussing."

Fowles made no answer to this. Anthony walked across to him.

"What relation are you, Fowles, to the two men who were hanged at Armley in March last . . . for the murder of a servant girl?"

The sullen smoulder in Fowles's eyes came to a burning blaze, and the man suddenly shed his combative truculence and achieved dignity.

"I *was*," he said, stressing the verb, "their father. Let 'em alone, can't you—and their memory? They're dead. My boys . . . choked black by a bloody rope round their throats . . . and we won't talk about 'em. Their mother's eyes do all that—and more. Well . . . what more do you want of me? My soul . . . to add to their blessed buried bodies?"

The man's voice broke with emotion. He stood there, hands trembling, and with beads of sweat on his brow.

Anthony made a quiet sign to Inspector Sutton. The latter understood and nodded. Mr. Bathurst said no more. He slipped quietly from the room. The honours at the fall of the last wicket had been with Fowles—the father of two dead sons.

Chapter XXI
C.D. WELLS OF RANSFORD

ANTHONY Bathurst looked at the coil of rope that Inspector Sutton put on the table in front of him. He immediately saw significances.

"The coil of Fowles," he said softly.

"That's it, Mr. Bathurst. The rope he left behind in the theatre. Notice this?" An awed Sutton pointed to the looped noose.

"Too true, my dear Sutton. And—do you know—I find myself wishing that it weren't there." Mr. Bathurst ascended to quotation again. "Remember, Sutton? 'He did not pass in purple pomp, Nor ride a moon-white steed. Three yards of cord and a sliding-board, Are all the gallows' need: So with rope of shame the Herald came, To do the secret deed.'"

Sutton lifted his brows.

"Reading Gaol—Inspector. The Ballad thereof. Written by a poor devil who was there. *Reading*, you observe—not Armley. *Not* many miles away."

Sutton grunted at the information.

"I know what you're thinking," continued Anthony.

"What?"

"That this noose of friend Fowles in front of us is both obvious and ominous. That's your idea, isn't it?"

Sutton nodded. "That's about the size of it. What else can I think?"

"Eh, man—I'm not blaming you. How can I? But—now how shall I put it?—my experience has taught me almost always to distrust the glaringly obvious."

"Almost *always*?"

"I won't commit myself entirely. Constantly, let me say, as a rule."

"Well, you can please yourself, Mr. Bathurst, but I'm inclined to go my own way, thank you."

Anthony grinned at Sutton's remark. "Like every other mother's son. Of course you are. As I said, I can't find it in my heart to blame you. And yet, O inestimable Sutton, *I am not satisfied.* Oh no! Indeed I am far from satisfied."

The Inspector pushed his hands through his hair. "But *why,* Mr. Bathurst? Why exactly? I confess that I can't follow you in regard to that."

"Well, I can't get anything to fit. That is to say, to fit *properly.* Fowles and Griggs? Yes! Every time. Nicely packed motive and all that. Fowles and Daphne Arbuthnot? No! No! A thousand times no!"

"Yet Fowles was *there,* Mr. Bathurst. At St. Aidans. On the spot all the time. By Griggs and by Miss Arbuthnot on the pier. You can't shut your eyes to the truth of that."

Anthony Bathurst nodded in agreement. "Yes—Fowles was there. I know he was. But there's a strand missing from the skein somewhere. If I could get hold of it, that vitally coloured strand, Sutton, I feel in my bones that I should grasp the truth of the whole puzzling business. But I *can't.* I feel that I'm running round in circles. An annoying, irritating thought, Sutton, that all you're doing is to grin like a dog and run about through the city."

Sutton contested the point. He brought up a battery of what he considered was common sense. "If you avoid the straight path that stretches out clearly in front of you and deliberately seek the circles, as you call them—well, you must put up with what you get—it's your own fault. At least, that's how it strikes me." Sutton shrugged his shoulders.

Anthony grinned again. "I'm a wandering sheep, Sutton. I do not love the fold. Neither the orthodox fold nor this particular fold. On the other hand, I want to prowl around. Like the troops of Midian. How they prowled, those Midianites. Hymns—Sutton—but not songs of praise—just ordinary ancient and modern. You may find it difficult to believe but I'm a whale on hymns. For a testimonial to that effect take a train to the West Country, change at Polchester and apply to the Rector of Kirve St. Laudus, the Rev. Parry-Probyn."

He grinned amiably at the Inspector. "Well, Sutton, what's your next step? Made up your mind? Sensational headlines and startling placards? Arrest of Fowles?"

Sutton persisted in his point of view.

"I think so," he replied doggedly. "I can't afford to risk letting him loose."

"On what charge will you hold him?"

"Murder—of course."

"Of whom?"

"Why, Griggs. There's motive. He was there on the night. He skipped directly afterwards. That'll be good enough to be getting along with."

Anthony shook his head. "I doubt it, Sutton. I do really. I am a slave of doubt. Even when the glass seems so obviously 'set fair'. Look here, let me persuade you to hold your official hand. Say—for at least a week. I'll guarantee to produce a substantial rabbit from the Bathurst hat within that time. And a good rabbit might be better than a pair of old fowls. Well, is it a bargain?"

Sutton grinned and then pursed his lips. "That's all very well for you, but how about me? This is a pastime for you, but it's my job. Bread and butter to me."

"All the more reason, therefore, why you can't afford to make a mistake. On the other hand, I can. And do very often. But luckily for me, they don't matter. Yours will, Inspector. If you make it. That's the difference. Well, Inspector—what's your decision?"

Sutton looked straight ahead of him. He realized the truth of what Anthony had said. For some seconds he made no reply. Anthony watched him and eventually saw his face change as he crossed the rubicon of decision.

"Very well, Mr. Bathurst. I'll be guided by you. Your reputation is good enough for me. I'll put myself in your hands and chance it."

Anthony gripped him by the hand. "Good man. That's very sporting of you. Now it's up to me. I'll do my level best not to let you down. If Fowles is the murderer, as you're inclined to bank on, we can take him next week as easily as we can take him now.

You know where he is and it won't be a difficult matter to keep your eye on him. Delays, you know, are not always so desperately dangerous. Look before you leap, and discretion is the better part of valour. I know a lot more like that, but I promise to spare you, Sutton."

Sutton smiled amiably, and before the smile had died from his face the 'phone-bell rang on his desk. Anthony watched him interestedly as he answered it. He saw the Inspector nod several times, and then his face change suddenly. At last he spoke.

"O.K. Yes . . . I agree. You've done well, Welsh. Yes . . . I'll see him now . . . as it happens, it couldn't have come at a more opportune moment. Mr. Bathurst happens to be with me now." He replaced the receiver and turned to his companion. "Rather remarkable this, Mr. Bathurst. It's Wells. The other fellow in the billiard-room that evening. I've already had one talk with him. One of my men, Welsh his name is, has brought him along. Like Fowles before him, Wells said that he was quite willing to come along and answer any further questions that we might care to put to him. Welsh says that he seems sound enough to him."

"Mind me staying?" queried Anthony.

"Should say not. My idea that you should. That's why I told the constable I'd see the fellow now. Oh . . . Lord! . . . I wonder where we shall get to before we finish."

"Doesn't matter particularly." Anthony was laconic. He continued, however: "As long as we eventually *do* finish. *Orando— laborando*. With humble, lowly and contrite hearts—you know. Rugby, my dear Inspector. Where a certain William Webb Ellis picked up the ball and ran with it."

Sutton's face expanded into a broad grin. "I've read about that, Mr. Bathurst. In a book one of my boys has got at home. You're alluding to the game of 'Rugger', I take it, sir?"

"Yes . . . but here's your man, Inspector . . . if I mistake not. Let's hear what he has to say to us." The footsteps outside ceased and the door of Inspector Sutton's room opened to admit two men. The man Wells came in quietly—at the side of Constable Welsh. Anthony was a trifle surprised at his appearance. Clean-shaven and fair, his skin had a ruddiness of colour that in some indefinable manner did not seem to belong to him naturally. The face had a certain crudeness of feature—almost an ugliness, and taking him as he stood there, facing Inspector Sutton, Anthony considered that he was not of the sort which he would have expected to find, in the ordinary course of things, signing the reception-book at the Lansdowne Hotel, Lokingham. His general attitude was altogether different from that of his predecessor, Fowles. This Wells fellow had a smugness of sly satisfaction. Fowles had exhibited a hard, unyielding truculence. Oil as to granite.

"Sit down, Mr. Wells," said the Inspector. "I appreciate the fact that once again you're quite willing to give us any information that may prove useful to us. You won't mind us, then, asking you one or two additional questions? You're at perfect liberty, of course, to say what you like—or otherwise."

"He speaks me fair," said Wells rather unctuously.

"You know what it's all about. It's about this death at the Lansdowne Hotel, Lokingham. The late Mr. Griggs—you know, Home Secretary, that was. You remember that I had a few words with you before about it. We thought that as you were staying at the hotel at the same time as he was you might have thought of something or remembered something . . . that might possibly—I only say 'possibly', mind you—have had some bearing on the matter."

Wells shook his head with decision. "No. Can't help you any more than I told you first of all. Sorry. Heard nothing. Saw nothing. Wish I had."

"Why?" intervened Anthony sharply.

Wells shrugged his shoulders. "Why?" he repeated. "So's I could have helped this gentleman, of course. I'd love to help him. Same as he said."

Anthony watched him with close scrutiny, and then took up the thread of conversation again. "That's a pity. You admitted to the Inspector here that you were in the billiard-room with him, I think, during the evening before his death."

"Quite right. Everything was all right in there."

"Did you speak to him at all . . . in the billiard-room?"

"I *might* have exchanged a word or two. But nothing much. Well . . . now . . . I ask you . . . he was the great Griggs . . . I was a mere nobody. Griggs was Griggs and Wells was Wells . . . you know the rest, I expect. No, we certainly weren't Old Chinas together, by any manner of means." Wells smiled happily as he finished what he had to say.

Anthony struck. "You hadn't met before, by any chance?"

But Wells flicked away the missile with the utmost nonchalance. He even allowed himself the luxury of a chuckle. Anthony, as he heard it, felt certain that the man, for some reason, was feeling very pleased with himself.

"Lord—no! What a hope! Whatever put that idea in your head? Didn't I tell you. The likes of me don't associate with the big-heads. Except when it comes about by accident, like gettin' in a train together or putting up at the same hotel. Why, it's enough to make the poor old boy turn in his grave, a suggestion like that. Bad enough for him to get bumped off—without lowering his social status." He grinned openly in the Inspector's face.

Anthony lounged over towards him. He had been speaking to him from a distance. "So you know, Mr. Wells, I find that last statement of yours just a little difficult to fit in."

Wells curled his lips. "No! Do you? To fit in with what?"

"With knowledge."

"Whose knowledge?"

"Ours. The Inspector's and mine."

The face of Wells straightened somewhat. By now he felt slightly out of his depth and a trifle unsure as to where he was eventually being taken. As was his habit, he sought refuge in evasion.

"I don't know what you're talking about. Don't get you at all."

"Explanation is absurdly easy, Mr. Wells. And since you've asked for it, you shall have it. We have information that you were already acquainted with the late Home Secretary when you booked your room at the Lansdowne Hotel."

"Did you say—'acquainted'?" Wells' voice held a ring of defiance. "You're talkin' out of your hat, mister. Hot air. We didn't mix in the same circles."

"I am not suggesting that you did. But I'm suggesting that you knew Griggs sufficiently well to have had certain dealings with him. Now what do you say?"

"That I've never had any dealings with him. That's what I say and that's what I'd swear to."

"H'm. Would you deny also that you had ever called upon him? At his house at Great Astill?" Sutton was watching Wells closely, and saw the man change colour at Anthony's words.

"Come," said Anthony, pressing him. "Would you deny that?"

Wells looked from Anthony Bathurst to the Inspector and then reversed the process. Things had panned out somewhat differently from his anticipation.

"Well? I should think carefully before I answered if I were you. It's important, you know. Griggs was murdered."

Wells chewed nervously at his underlip. "Supposing I admit that I called on him, what then? You can call on a man and not know him, can't you? Where does that get me?"

"Who can say?" returned Anthony. "But if you take my advice, you'll be as frank with us as you can be. And that frankness will certainly pay you."

The attitude of the man to whom he spoke underwent a complete change. "Look here," he said, "you fellows know more than I thought you did. Though it beats me where you picked up the information. I'll come across and tell you what I called to see Griggs about . . . but don't get the bee in your bonnet that I know anything about his mur—his death." He paused to take breath.

Sutton's hand went to his note-book. Careful of correct procedure, he always remembered the judges' rules in relation to the use of evidence. "You don't object, Mr. Wells, to me making notes of what you are about to say, do you?" he inquired.

The reply, when it came, was definitely hostile. "Oh, you can do as you please, it won't worry me. You've got nothing on me, as I told you."

"Thank you, Mr. Wells."

Anthony gestured to Wells to proceed with his statement.

"If you must know, I called on Griggs at his house at Great Astill over a matter connected with—" he paused abruptly.

Anthony felt certain that he was realizing for the first time, probably, the seriousness of the position in which he stood.

"Yes . . ." said Sutton interrogatively, "connected with . . . ?"

"Connected with my daughter."

There came a period of silence.

"Well?"

"Well—what?"

"Did Griggs know your daughter, then?"

"No."

Sutton looked at him hard. "Why did you call on him then?"

More hesitation. "I wanted to interest him in the matter of her employment. In other words, I thought that, in his position and with his influence, he might help her to get a job. Or a better job."

"Why did you pick on him specially? If you didn't know him at all?"

"I was recommended to try him."

"By whom?" questioned Anthony swiftly.

Wells hesitated again—ever so slightly—but noticeably. "By a friend of mine who had known Griggs for some time."

"Name?" queried Sutton laconically.

"Er . . . Jones. George Jones."

"Thank you. Yes?"

Wells screwed up his face. "Well, what else is there?"

"What happened with Griggs when you called upon him? Did he help you?"

"No. He said that he couldn't do anything. That there were far too many people after him and worrying him for the same thing."

"I see. And when he told you that he couldn't do anything for you, you came away, eh?"

"Yes. That was about all, I think."

"No bad feeling between you—on any account? No irritation or soreness?"

"Oh no! Why should there be? Over an ordinary affair like that."

Sutton flicked back the pages of his note-book. "Why didn't you tell me this when I interviewed you the first time? Just after the murder?"

Wells shifted his feet clumsily and looked sullen. "You didn't ask me . . . exactly . . . and I didn't see what it had to do with the death of Griggs, anyway . . . and I didn't want any of my affairs mixed up with this. Was it likely? Sorry, Inspector, and all that, if I've caused you any trouble, but I didn't think it was important."

"You aren't the best judge of the importance of things. And you might have been the cause of my wasting an enormous amount of time."

Anthony hereupon took up the parable. "Did you happen to meet anybody else when you called on Griggs at Great Astill? For instance, did you see anybody else there?"

This time Wells changed colour appreciably. "I don't remember that I did. Why do you ask?"

"Surely, Mr. Wells, you must have done. Who let you in, for instance? I don't suppose for a moment that a man in the position of Griggs would have come to the door himself?"

Wells affected to remember. "Why, yes, of course. There was a manservant chap—sort of butler-bloke. He let me in. I'd clean forgotten all about him. Stupid of me. But I attached so little importance to him that—you know—I didn't keep him in my mind."

"Did this man, this butler, hear any part of your interview with Griggs?"

Wells shook his head, but the look in his eyes told a story. "Not as far as I know. Shouldn't imagine that he did. He certainly didn't come into the room while I was there—if that's what you mean."

"So that if he says that you were on bad terms with Griggs; that you threatened him with violence; that Griggs called him in to protect himself against you—he's not telling the truth or anything like the truth—eh?"

Wells' eyes flashed with the anger of mortification. "Truth!" he exclaimed. "It's a damned lie—if he says any of that—and that's putting it mildly."

"There's just this to it. He supports his story, too, you know," returned Anthony softly. "Gives reasons for his answer—and all that. Those reasons, I should tell you, tend to make his story much stronger. From the point of view of likely acceptance. Almost give it the stamp of truth. At least, that's how ninety-nine people out of a hundred would look at it. Would you care to hear any of them? Oh, but you can't refuse. You *must* hear them."

"Get on with it," cried Wells with sour sullenness. "A few more lies won't make a deal of difference."

"Jayne, that's the name of the man who let you in, and had been in the service of Griggs for some years, states that he heard you accuse his master of philandering with your daughter. Which, of course, *might* be regarded as settling the much-vexed question of *motive*. You never know. I am referring there, of course, to Griggs's murder."

Anthony was still speaking quietly and softly. Wells made no reply. Things were looking far worse for him than he had anticipated when he had agreed to come along to see Sutton. This second interview had proved to be an entirely different affair from the previous one.

Anthony was speaking again. Wells now heard the voice of his accuser as from afar off.

"And then there's also that most remarkable coincidence—of course, it *might* be easily explained—of your turning up at the Lansdowne Hotel just as your daughter's friend Griggs did."

Wells flashed round on this man who was scourging him and pulled a photograph from his pocket. He handed it to Anthony. "You leave my daughter out of it. Look at her. Is she the sort for a man like Griggs to play the fool with?"

"I can't leave her out of it—because *you* did. If you hadn't, I should have done. You have only yourself to blame, you know, for the turn that the affair has taken." Anthony looked at the photograph. The girl was unusually beautiful.

Wells threw up his head. "Very good, then. If that's the line you're going to take, I'm saying no more. You can find out all the rest for yourself. If you think that I killed Griggs"—he laughed harshly—"well, it's your funeral, not mine. Prove it against me. And I shan't have to brief Norman Birkett either. No—nor fix it up with Sir Oliver Lodge to bring Marshall Hall over from the other side. Kill Griggs! Me! You make me laugh. My luck's never been as good as all that."

At this outburst Sutton glanced quickly across to Anthony. The latter understood the significance of the Inspector's glance and slightly shook his head.

"Well," cried Wells aggressively, "make up your mind—are you going to arrest me? Don't forget that I came here voluntarily. It's not everybody who would have been Billy Muggins enough to do a thing like that."

Sutton intervened sharply. "When we arrest you, Mr. Wells, you'll know all about it. We shan't leave you in any doubt as to our intentions. You're a foolish man, all the same. Complete frankness in the first place would have paid you better than anything."

Wells' face twisted into an ugly smile. "You think so—do you? Well, it's just possible that I'm a better judge of that than you are. They won't swing you for the murder—though the world 'ud be a damn' sight healthier place if two-thirds of the 'busys' were bumped off out of it, I'm thinkin'. The air would smell sweeter."

"And perhaps I'm the better judge of that," returned the Inspector coldly.

Anthony grinned at the exchange of compliments. He felt more pleased over this interview than he had felt for a considerable time. For the germ of an idea had entered his brain. A chance remark had helped to put it there. He rose from his chair.

"I'm satisfied. I'll leave you to it, Inspector. I'll come and see you again later. Regard me now as 'the Ball'."

Sutton stared. Wells still looked ugly and menacing. Anthony countered the looks gaily.

"The Ball, Sutton. 'The Ball no question asks of Ayes or Noes—but down the field—as strikes the player—goes.' Behold me, therefore, down the field. I've just been well and truly struck."

Wells nodded knowingly. He thought that he understood what Mr. Bathurst meant. But Inspector Sutton's mind refused to take the risk.

Anthony waved his hand and disappeared.

Chapter XXII
FIRST REPORT (OAKLEY)

ANTHONY Bathurst was not terribly surprised when he was informed that Oakley, the elocution teacher of Erlegh, wanted to speak to him. From what he had already seen of the man at the previous encounter, he had judged him as one who wouldn't allow the grass to grow under his mental feet.

Oakley entered the room effusively and was quick to apologize for what he was pleased to term "his rather selfish intrusion".

"Not a bit of it. Don't you worry yourself on that score. Actually, I was expecting you. Almost a day or two ago, in fact. Well, how are matters shaping? What's in the first report?"

Oakley came to the reply with an excess of eagerness. "I'm on to something, Mr. Bathurst. I am really. I feel sure of it. And, would you believe it, I picked it up in a remarkable way. If I take you into my confidence you'll see that I'm dealt with fairly by the *Morning Message* as regards that thousand pounds reward, won't you?"

Anthony smiled at the man's evident anxiety. "I shan't compete with you, if that's what's worrying you, Mr. Oakley. I've already promised you that much. You need have no fears on that score."

Oakley reddened under the reply. Anthony knew his man and felt sympathy towards him.

"I didn't mean *that*—quite—Mr. Bathurst. Nevertheless, your assurance satisfies me. That is to say, your answer will do."

"Good. Having cleared the air, now, what news have you for me? You promised me a *quid pro quo*, if you remember."

"I remember perfectly, Mr. Bathurst. That's the reason why I'm here now. I've been to your town of St. Aidans to have a look round there. A thousand pounds is a tremendous incentive to a poor man, believe me."

Anthony was interested in spite of himself almost. "Oh, good man! Well—and what said St. Aidans?"

"Not a lot perhaps. But I picked up one thing that I resolved to tell you about as soon as I got back here."

"Go ahead, then."

"Did you find out whether Griggs stayed anywhere at St. Aidans during that week or merely went down there on the day of Miss Arbuthnot's death?"

"No. It didn't occur to me to inquire. But you never know. Did you look into it?"

"Yes, I did. He stayed at the 'Spread Eagle', the big hotel by the rock garden. When I heard that, I resolved to see if I could find anything that might help. I've been there. I followed up an idea that I had—although it came, I'll admit, from *you* in the original instance. You'll hear what I mean in a minute for so. Eventually I ran across a man—a sort of out-door porter who calls at the hotel and who saw to Griggs's luggage when Griggs went away from there. A man by the name of Kennedy. I found out when and where I could get hold of this chap at his lodging. I called on him—went, after him pell-mell, to tell the truth . . . and what do you think he told me, Mr. Bathurst?"

Anthony shook a doubtful head. "If I guess, I shall guess wrong. Spill it, Oakley."

"That the day he cleared Griggs's suit-case from the bedroom, to put it on the car for the station, there were four melon seeds lying on the top of it."

There came a gleam into Anthony's grey eyes. "Yes?" he said softly. "That news suits me all right. There might well have been melon seeds at St. Aidans as we know that there were at Loking-ham. So they followed him from St. Aidans, did they? But why . . . ?" Anthony paused to consider his own question. His voice trailed off into silence.

"Why—what?" demanded Oakley eagerly. "What puzzles you about it? It seemed to me to be perfectly logical and to fit in all right, as you say yourself. You have told me about the Ku-Klux-Klan and their methods . . . I imagined that my news would help you no end. That's why I seized on it so avidly."

"Agreed, my dear Oakley, with all that you have so recently and so admirably said. I can find no fault with it. Or with you. Or with what you have done. In fact, I have only congratulations for you. Heartiest congratulations. My difficulty lies in a completely different direction."

Oakley shook his head vaguely. All this was complex to him. At what was Bathurst hinting? "Where's that?" he questioned.

"Where? Why—just this: If the *melon seeds*—why Daphne Arbuthnot? *Not* Griggs—you observe! Why, in the name of goodness, put the seeds on Griggs and kill a young actress in a touring company?"

Again Oakley shook his head. Almost vacantly—as a child does when asked by a teacher a question that is unanswerable.

"Yes . . . it makes you shake your head, doesn't it?"

"In a way, perhaps," assented Oakley, "but at the same time we're distinctly better off than we were. Your theory of the Ku-Klux-Klan looks like turning out something much more than a mere theory now, doesn't it?"

"Let's have a good look at things. The first poisoned. The second killed by a revolver shot. H'm . . . variation of attack! That, I believe, is consistent with the methods of the dreaded K.K.K." Anthony nodded to himself. Then he looked up and questioned Oakley. "Kennedy, you say, was the name of this porter chap at the 'Spread Eagle'?"

"Yes. Alec Kennedy."

"Reliable, would you say?"

"Struck me as so—from what little I saw of him. I'm not experienced, of course, but that was my impression."

"Tell me this, Oakley. What was his own attitude to those seeds that were put on Griggs?"

"How do you mean exactly?"

"Well, it's difficult to put it into words. Did he seem surprised to have found them there? Seriously surprised, that is—or was he more inclined to treat the matter humorously?"

"The latter, I should say. Let me try to give you some idea of how he told the story. That will help you, better than anything else I can do, to form an opinion. I had asked him one or two questions concerning Griggs and his stay at the 'Spread Eagle'— questions that I imagined you might have asked had you been in my place—see? After this manner. 'Did Griggs seem comfortable?'

'Yes—quite comfortable'. 'Had Kennedy noticed any strange incident occur during Griggs' occupation of the room?' 'No—he hadn't.' 'Had anybody unusual *visited* Griggs while he was up there?' 'Yes—a young lady had called to see him. A knock-out! A fair good-looker.' 'Did he know who she was by any chance—did she give her name?' 'No—he didn't—and she didn't. He wished that she had.'

"Then, just as I was beginning to feel that I had drawn a complete blank and was only wasting my time, he burst out with this. 'I'll tell you what, though, guv'nor—I do remember something now that did strike me as bloomin' funny at the time. It was a new one on me.' I was all ears, of course, when Kennedy said this. He went on. 'When I went up to the bloke's room to put his luggage and stuff in the wagon to shove into the hotel lift for taking downstairs, what do you think I found on his suitcase?' I expressed ignorance—naturally. 'Nothing more nor less, guv'nor, than four perishin' melon seeds. Arranged in a sort of pattern, too, they was.' That was good enough for me, Bathurst. All that you had told me about Griggs here came rushing back into my mind. I tipped him half a dollar and blew back here by the first train that I could jump into. Couldn't get back fast enough."

"How far does Kennedy live from the 'Spread Eagle'?"

"Just a few streets, that's all. In Trafalgar Street. Fifty-five, I think the number was."

"Did he attempt any explanation of the seeds being there? Any explanation of his own?"

"Oh, yes. He's just of the sort that would. He reckoned that Griggs had had a spot of melon in his bedroom, 'on the Q.T.', as he put it, and had amused himself subsequently by spitting the seeds on to his suit-case."

"In that case, then, where were the remaining seeds? I should think, from my experience of melon seeds, that there'd be at least another twenty-two for disposal as shooting practice." Anthony grinned. "What do you say, Oakley? How long since you folded your mouth round a nice juicy melon?"

Oakley returned the grin with a quick shake of the head. "Donkeys' years! I loathe the things. But I agree with you about the number of the seeds. Most melons that I have met in my time certainly had their quiver full. Well, what do you really think about it all? I'm ever so interested."

"Just as I told you. What beats me is the Daphne Arbuthnot business. I continually say to myself that I won't consider it. That I'll ignore it. More than ignore it. That I'll empty my mind of it, as it were. Pour it away from myself. That all my eyes shall be blind to it and I'll devote myself entirely to the dead Griggs. Yet, Oakley, despite all those excellent resolutions that I make, I just as continually find myself coming back to it. As the moth to the candle flame. Now that I've unburdened myself to you, kick me for a confounded ass, Oakley."

"Not a bit of it. Who shall blame you?" Oakley was always dead serious. After all, a thousand pounds was a thousand pounds. "On the contrary, I am all sympathy with you. I don't see how you can very well help doing as you say. I see the difficulty that you're in every bit as plainly as you do yourself. Because there seems such little doubt now that the two murders are connected. I wasn't so sure of it when you first told me."

"I never had any doubt, Oakley. So many of the players appear in the two casts. You can't get away from it. And St. Aidans isn't exactly on the Lokingham doorstep."

"Who are they exactly? Tell me again, will you? These double appearance people, I mean. Remember that I may not know them all."

Anthony gave him the required names. Oakley at once became critical.

"Yes, but several of those come into the two places legitim-ately, don't they? That is, say, through following the course of their ordinary duties. That makes a tremendous difference, you know. Fowles, Miss Fortescue, Palliser—there are three of them that do. That only leaves Wells playing a doubtful part."

"I grant you all that. But there's this to remember, also. Ordin-ary conditions may have been specially utilized for the murders. We can never tell. That is to say, the murderer, having planned his job, may have deliberately taken advantage of the conditions, knowing that they were there, so to speak, to be had for the taking. It's a possibility that must be considered."

Oakley nodded somewhat ruefully. "Yes, I see. That's where your experience scores, compared with mine. I only see the obvious. I never thought of it in the light that you have put it. But I see quite clearly that it *could* have occurred like that."

"I don't know when I have ever felt so uncertain about a case. Or when the light was so long in breaking through. I've made at least five serious mistakes. Lucky for me, they're all reparable. I've chased rainbows and left undone things I ought to have done. For instance, there's one important question that I must ask Palliser. I understand that he'll be in the district until Saturday night of next week."

"What are the others—the mistakes you've made?"

Anthony shook his head. "Chiefly sins of omission. Which are always easier to rectify than those of the other sort. There's this, too, though. I must go and have a look at Griggs's house at Great Astill. Sutton's already given it what he describes as the 'once over', but I want to have a nose round there myself. There's a butler at the house, by the name of Jayne. I fancy that on closer acquaintance he may prove to be more than ordinarily interesting."

"Why particularly?"

"Well, butlers, you know, have been said to see most of the game. They're the expert lookers-on and peepers-through."

Oakley leant towards Anthony Bathurst. "Tell me, Bathurst, if you don't mind. Suppose that you definitely fix this murder on to the Ku-Klux-Klan. Pin it on to them beyond the shadow of a doubt. How will you go on then?"

"How do you mean, Oakley?"

"Well, how will you proceed? From what you've told me, the Ku-Klux-Klan is a toughish proposition to be up against. Mighty different from the local green-grocer."

Anthony smiled at his concern. "The man who supplies the melons compared with the purchasers thereof, eh? Ah, well—your question as to my procedure wants a lot of answering. Yes . . . Oakley . . . as you say, the K.K.K. has a long and powerful arm. But so has Scotland Yard."

"There is little doubt of the Ku-Klux-Klan power, I suppose? It isn't based on mere rumour or fanciful tales?"

Anthony went to the writing-table and picked up a book which he opened. "I have given the K.K.K. some serious attention during the last few days, my dear Oakley. In the light of what you have brought me now, I am glad that I have used my time so profitably." He turned over certain pages. "Listen to this, Oakley, and you'll hear your question answered:

"The Ku-Klux-Klan—a mighty secret society with a tremendously large membership, which strikes absolute terror into the hearts of those who are unfortunate enough to incur its enmity. It is believed to have been formed by a number of ex-Confederate soldiers, in the Southern States of America, soon after the conclusion of the hostilities of the Civil War, and it rapidly formed local branches in different parts of the country, chief amongst which may be noted those in the states of Tennessee, Louisiana, the Carolinas, Georgia, and Florida. Its power was chiefly used for political purposes. The negro voters were completely terrorized by the general campaign of the Society, and many who had the temerity to oppose its views and activities were either murdered or driven from the country in an extremity of fear.

"Now listen to this next piece specially.

"The outrages of the Ku-Klux-Klan were usually preceded by a mysterious warning which was sent to the doomed person in some fantastic but generally recognized shape—for instance, in some districts a sprig of oak leaves would be used for this purpose, in others, orange pips, and in other parts *melon* seeds. On receiving the warning the victim knew what his fate was likely to be. If he chose to stay in the country and brave the matter out, death would unfailingly come upon him almost immediately and usually in a strange and entirely unforeseen manner.

"So perfect was the organization of the Society and so expertly systematic its methods, that there is scarcely a case known to history of any person who succeeded in opposing it with impunity or even in which many of its outrages were traced and definitely brought home to the perpetrators, so that punishment ensued. It was a law unto itself, and brooked no interference or opposition from any source whatever. It wielded its power in the most despotic and tyrannical manner possible and eventually came to be feared, more perhaps, than any other secret society known to history. The Government of the United States and the better classes of the Southern community made strenuous endeavours to stamp it out, but it resisted all these efforts and continued to flourish and did flourish for many years.

"In 1869, however, there came distinct signs that its activities were on the wane, but there is an undoubted basis for the belief that in recent years the Society has shown clear and distinct evidence of its re-organization and subsequent resuscitation, for many reports of its operations have come to the ears of the authorities. In other words, the implacable and vindictive spirits that formed it have been born and live again in future generations."

Anthony closed the book and replaced it on the writing-table. "There, my dear Oakley, you have some short account of that sinister society known sometimes as the Terror of the Treble K. What do you think of the knowledge that you have gained? Do you find it interesting?"

Oakley's face was set and grave. "'Pon my soul, Bathurst, your reading of it has given me the creeps. I had no idea that it was anything like what that account makes it out to be. I seem to have strayed from my own peaceful valley of quiet and tranquillity on to a plain of death and destruction. I am not used to these things. I never thought that they would even approach me. I suppose none of us thinks so until dreadful things actually happen to us. I am almost inclined to shiver."

Anthony Bathurst clapped him on the shoulder.

"Come, come, it's not so bad as all that. England is more or less free of these terrors. You've let your imagination get hold of you. To-morrow morning you'll laugh—at your fears and forebodings."

Oakley shook his head despondently; "No; I'm not used to it. That explains a lot. It's largely my own fault, I suppose. But all my life has been spent in the byways. The translation has been too sudden for me to take in my stride and I'm not anything like acclimatized yet. I've never been a man of action. I've loved beauty, poetry and all . . . the—you know—soft things of life. I've always argued that the faculty of poetic thought is almost invariably antagonistic to action. There's no getting away from it. It's true."

"Perhaps it is, but you're exaggerating your own weakness. You're letting your imagination run riot with you. In the morning you'll feel a different man and won't care two hoots for twenty-two Ku-Klux-Klans."

Oakley smiled ruefully. "It's good of you to try to hearten me. I appreciate it immensely."

"Good man! Try another outlook. Think of that one thousand pounds. There's a splendid spur for you. It will be hard for you to kick against those pricks."

Oakley smiled another feeble smile. "I'm not like you, Bathurst. I lack your guts. It's not a bit of good my shutting my eyes to it. I do! I let things get me down and then let them worry and harass me like hell. Lose sleep over them and very often appetite as well. You're different. You're strong . . . and a fighter . . . and your personality's all vivid and colourful. Mine's weak and emasculate. You don't know what it is to have fears."

"Don't you believe it, Oakley. We're all much of a muchness when it comes to the final test. I have an unholy fear of many things. And I know it. 'And the knowledge of thyself will preserve thee from vanity.' That's always worth remembering, my dear Oakley." Mr. Bathurst, it will be observed, quoted Cervantes, but it is doubtful whether Oakley was convinced.

CHAPTER XXIII
EAST FIFTY-SIXTH STREET

ANTHONY Bathurst drove the eight-cylindered Chrysler hard and fiercely. Time was precious to him. He had two calls to make that afternoon. One at Great Astill, in the county of Kent, and the other at the seaside resort of St. Aidans in the neighbouring county of Sussex. He decided to take first the house where Griggs had lived.

The powerful car travelled with swift, imperious majesty. The speedometer needle went smoothly and certainly to fifty. The car climbed on and up hills and swept along straight broad roads. Anthony came to cross-roads. Here he turned left. Although it was some considerable time since he had travelled that particular road, he felt moderately certain of his locality, and, therefore, of the way that he should take.

The car rounded a corner and purred down a narrow, winding lane intensely typical of the county of Hengist, Horsa, and Frank Woolley. After perhaps a couple of hundred yards, the lane seemed to think better of itself and its serpentine qualities and turned itself into a highly respectable road. From there it mounted an almost imperceptible rise, and after passing three farm-houses unusually close together, emptied itself on to another square of cross-roads where stood in splendid isolation a four-fingered signpost.

Anthony slowed up in order to read its announcements. The road ahead, so said the lonely wooden sign, led to Ruddock and the Reepings. Anthony found no thrill in that. That to the left to Arnoldbury, Buckston and Newdene. Also unsatisfying. The road to the right went, said the signpost, to Trafford, Dempster and Great Astill. Anthony, duly grateful for the information, swung the car to the right. The road now was good, bounded by sound fencing and with a well-made ditch showing on each side. In a matter of about an hour Anthony came to the village of Great Astill.

The house of the late Home Secretary was easy to find. To his surprise, an elderly woman answered his inquiry. He told her his name, and she allowed him to enter immediately. He followed her across a wide passage-way and into a library—the room in which Griggs had sat when he had decided the Fowles case and where Wells had come to him.

The library was lengthy, and to Anthony, as he entered it, seemed to stretch from the front of the house to the back. He noticed that it had a line of french windows. The room was furnished artistically—surprisingly so—Anthony thought, when he remembered what he knew of the man who in life had occupied it. The appointments and general decorations belonged to no set style or period, but nevertheless blended beautifully and therefore became definitely pleasing. There were but two pictures. One, a glorious etching of a gondola on Venetian waters and the other looked like a Birket Foster.

The woman found him a seat, closed the big oak door, and left him there. There was an oppressive silence. Anthony sat in a low chair by one of the french windows. The heavy silence of the room seemed to be taken up and embraced by the entire house. It was an almost tangible silence, which, as it were, folded itself round the house and inexorably squeezed the sounds of life out of it. Suddenly the door opened and a young girl entered and came across to him. Taken somewhat by surprise, Anthony lounged back in his chair, his long legs stuck out across the floor. The girl advanced slowly towards him. He saw at once that she was a girl of the people.

"Mother asked me to come in and see you. What was it that you wanted, sir?"

Anthony rose and thanked her for the attention. "I wanted to see Jayne . . . if it's convenient for me to do so. Jayne, the man that is, who was butler to the late Mr. Griggs."

The girl nodded. "Oh yes, sir. I understand. I know what you want. Mr. Jayne was my uncle. My Uncle Alfred."

Anthony furrowed his brows. This wasn't according to plan. "*Was* your uncle? Do you mean that he's—"

"Yes, sir—he's gone."

"Gone? Good heavens! You don't mean that your uncle is dead?"

The girl smiled rather sweetly. "No, sir. Don't be alarmed. It isn't as bad as that. I mean that Uncle Alfred's left here. He's gone abroad. And Mrs. Griggs and the girls have gone as well. My mother and I are looking after the house here until it's been sold."

The news took Anthony by surprise. "That's a pity. I'm sorry. I mean about your uncle not being here. Because I have come here specially to see him."

"I am sorry, too, sir. I suppose that there's nothing my mother or I could do for you, is there?"

"I'm afraid not . . . Miss—"

"Jayne, sir. My father was Uncle Alfred's brother."

"Do you mind if I ask you a question?"

"No, sir. I'll do my best to answer it."

"Why did your uncle leave here so suddenly?"

"Because of Mr. Griggs dying. That was the reason. He'd always expressed a wish to go abroad, and when his master died there was nothing really left to keep him here. So he took the chance and went. That was all there was to it, sir."

Anthony nodded slowly. "I see. Where's he gone? Can you tell me? I presume that you know?"

"Oh . . . yes, sir. I'll get you his address from Mother if you'll wait here a moment. I know one thing. He's gone to the United States of America."

Anthony looked up at this. The United States of America? This was interesting . . . unusually interesting. "What took him there?" he asked Miss Jayne.

"Oh . . . he'd always wanted to go there. Right from a small boy . . . I've heard Mother say many a time. My grandfather, Uncle Alfred's father, I mean, spent some years out there, and Mr. Griggs, his master that's just been killed, was connected in some way with people out there. I think that's probably where my uncle has gone. He sailed on the *Gigantic*. But if you wait here a little while, I'll see Mother and bring you my uncle's full address." Anthony thanked her and said that he would. When the girl had gone, thoughts ran riot in his brain. America again! The home of the Ku-Klux-Klan! Purveyors of melon seeds. What a labyrinthine chase he had had, to be sure. He owed it to Sutton to pull something off before long. He had advised the Inspector to hold his hand, and he must soon place himself in such a position that he could justify the advice which Sutton had taken. Sir Austin Kemble, too, was growing impatient—according to the telephone message that he had received from him that day. Oakley's chance shot with the luggage-porter at St. Aidans might well prove to be the determining factor in the case. Novice's luck again. Fowles . . . Wells . . . Palliser . . . and now the trail leading *away* from them to the society of the Treble K.

As he mused, the door opened again to admit Miss Jayne. She carried a slip of paper in her hand.

"Here you are, sir," she said. "This is the address to which Uncle has gone. I've copied it word for word off Mother's envelope."

She handed the slip to Mr. Bathurst. "C/o Colonel Colquhoun," he read, "222, East Fifty-Sixth Street, New York, U.S.A."

"If you want to communicate with Uncle, you can now, as soon as you please."

"Yes, I shall be able to. Thank you, Miss Jayne. I'm afraid I'm an awful nuisance, but I wonder if you would do me another favour. Yes?"

The girl nodded. "If I can. What is it?"

"Could I see your uncle's room?"

The girl shook her head doubtfully. "He's taken everything with him. Everything, that is, that belonged to him personally. There's only the furniture left behind. There was no will found, you know, sir, when Mr. Griggs died."

"So I understand. Ah, well—if things are as you say—I won't trouble you then. How long had your uncle been in the service of Mr. Griggs? A long time?"

"Some years, I think, sir. In fact, from what my mother has told me, I think he had stopped in this position longer than he had done in any before." Anthony thanked Miss Jayne again and came away from the house at Great Astill. Was he at last nearing the end of his journey or was he striking off in yet another vain direction?

Anthony entered his car. He would be three hours before he reached St. Aidans. Mr. Bathurst stepped on the gas.

It was hot as he drove. It had been a blazing day. "Summer had looked out from her Brazen Tower, Through the Flashing Bars of July." Insects had hummed drowsily in the air and more than once a bee, more subtly adventurous than his fellows, had precipitated himself with abandoned courage against the windscreen of the car. The Chrysler accomplished the distance to St. Aidans in just under the three hours which Anthony had allotted to himself.

An inquiry of the A.A. man at the cross-roads, just before the main avenue that leads towards the town, put him on the right road to Trafalgar Street. The houses here were of the type that one finds scattered profusely in all the southern seaside towns of England. Anthony pulled up before Number Fifty-Five, descended and knocked at the door.

A man, coatless, with a pipe dangling from his lips, answered the summons. It looked to Anthony that his knock on the door had awakened this gentleman from an exercise of sleep. A quiff of lank hair hung untidily over his forehead and his expression was quaintly humorous.

"Don't tell me I've pulled it off at last, guv'nor! Put me out of me misery quick. What's the figure? A couple of thousand, or two and tuppence ha'penny?"

Anthony smiled at his reception. "Sorry to disappoint you. But you've got me all wrong."

"Ain't you from the *Sunday Signal*?"

"Alas—no! Were you expecting a signalman?" The man spat on the highway with masterly finesse. "When I see your car and you 'op out of it . . . I thought you'd come to tell me that I'd won last week's 'Crossword'. I've been tryin' for over three years. Blimey— you give me a turn and no mistake. Not 'arf you didn't." He wiped his brow with a dirty handkerchief. "Well—what *do* you want?"

"I'm so acutely conscious of representing to you the figure of Supreme Disillusion, that I hardly like to tell you."

"'Ark at 'im," remarked the man, rubbing the tip of his nose. "What a beauty! Talks like a ruddy top-notcher. Take a deep breath, Mussolini, get over your faint-heartedness, and let's 'ave it good and proper. *All* of it! What are you knockin' here for?"

Anthony smiled at him. "I won't keep you wondering any longer. I hoped to have a word with a gentleman who resides here. This is Number Fifty-Five, I believe? A Mr. Kennedy. A Mr. Alec Kennedy, to describe him fully. I believe that he is a porter of luggage."

The man wagged his head sapiently. "You hoped! Well—that's as far as you'll get. You know what they say 'appens to 'ope. It's emptied in delight! Used to be in 'Oly Trinity choir, I did. That's where I learned about 'ope! Got many a tanner from the old trouts in the congregation for the way I sang the solos. 'O for the swings and a shove.' I wasn't bad-lookin' either, in a bad light. Which boiled down, mister, means that as far as you're concerned with Mr. Alec Kennedy, there ain't goin' to be no core. You ain't goin' to have your word you wanted with him. In other words, you're on a non-runner. Which is better than a loser by a long sight. Especially if you've got it doubled up with a winner."

Anthony sought clarity. "Is Kennedy out, do you mean?"

"Is he out? Very much so, guv'nor. He's more than out. He's gone."

"Gone?"

"Yes. Bunked! 'Opped it!"

"Where's he gone, do you know?"

"I do. And if you make it worth my while I'll get his new address for you, if you give me 'arf a cock-linnet. Wait here, guv'nor, and I'll turn up my filing cabinet. Ho, yis—the Kalamazoo. I won't ask you inside, because the fountains ain't playin' yet and dinner ain't served."

The man disappeared like a shot into the interior of the house. Anthony waited patiently for his return.

"'Ere you are, guv'nor," he declared upon his reappearance. "'Ere's our Mr. Kennedy's new abode. Words and music. Seems a bit outlandish to me . . . but there you are. It's in his own handwriting. If it 'ad been in mine, you wouldn't have been able to read it. The wife made 'im write it down for us."

He handed over a slip of paper to Mr. Bathurst, much as Miss Jayne had a few hours previously. Anthony's thoughts were far away as he took it almost mechanically from the man's hand. This porter, Kennedy, must have left St. Aidans almost immediately after Oakley had interviewed him. *Must* have done. Why? What had been the real reason? Had he taken fright at the inquiry and bolted?

Anthony's eyes caught the writing on the slip of paper that the man had handed to him. "Alec Kennedy, c/o Colonel Colquhoun, 222, East Fifty-Sixth Street, New York, U.S.A." Anthony stared at the man who faced him, in undisguised amazement.

"America?" he said weakly, in a voice that seemed more like another's than his own.

"Go on!" said the coatless one mercilessly. "Is that so, now? America, eh? You must have been listening to the wireless! It's wonderful the education that you can pick up if you switch orf intelligently. New York—America—oh, my dear 'Olmes—you don't say!"

He wagged his head, and suddenly Anthony caught the humour of the situation and laughed immoderately.

The man broke into song. "A . . . 'appy birds that sing and fly . . ."

CHAPTER XXIV
SUTTON LEARNS OF COLONEL COLQUHOUN

"Sit down, Sutton," said Anthony. "There you are. Make yourself comfortable. I sent for you because I have information that it isn't healthy to keep to myself. In the first place, I want to talk to you about melon seeds."

Sutton shook his head as though he were humouring him. "You don't mean to tell me that you're coming back to that, Mr. Bathurst? That's where we were almost at the start."

"Don't rub it in, Inspector. Anything less brilliant than my performance throughout I can't imagine. As I told you before, I've run round in circles and got nowhere. But melon seeds are very definitely on the menu this morning, and I want you to listen to me for a little while. I'll make it as snappy as I can."

"That's O.K. with me, Mr. Bathurst. It doesn't matter *how* you arrive, as long as you *do* arrive. I don't always hold with so-called brilliance. Hard work often whacks it in the end."

"That's a nice, forgiving, fatherly Sutton. Now to business. Strict business. My story begins with the Oakley man. The elocution teacher originally—now cast in a new role. Sir Eagerheart in shining armour. During the last week or so, he's got all worked up over the *Morning Message* reward. The thousand quid racket. Mrs. O, I fancy, was the driving force. He came to me the other day, enthusiasm dripping from all pores, and as a result of the interview and various pieces of advice that I passed on to him, he threw himself wholeheartedly into the science of deduction."

Sutton nodded gloomily. "I know all about that. I've seen him dashing about in Lokingham. Much more perspiration than inspiration. Leave him alone. He'll play for hours."

"Very likely he will. But out of the mouths of babes—remember, Inspector? Chance it, he blew down to St. Aidans and while he was there he had a stroke of luck. When I remember my own performance—I should be the last man to say that it was undeserved. Now listen to this."

Anthony told him of the melon seeds in Griggs's room at the hotel at St. Aidans. Sutton whistled at the information.

"So it's Ku-Klux-Klan, you mean, after all?"

"Hold on, Sutton. Wait a minute. I haven't finished yet. I want you to realise exactly where we're getting . . . you'll find the direction singularly illuminating, I fancy. I thought the news over and eventually decided that I'd have a little back-chat with this porter chap who spilled the story of the seeds to Oakley, and then kill two birds with one stone, by having a similar trifling heart-to-heart talk with Jayne. You remember friend Jayne, the butler at Great Astill? Griggs was Uncle Jayne's hero . . . I don't think! You see where I am, don't you?"

"I'm with you all the way, sir—so far. Just knocking at Jayne's door we are. Or did you like to be beside the seaside and go to St. Aidans first?"

"No. As it happened, I repaired first to Great Astill and our Jayne. And when I got there, Sutton, I bumped into a genuine surprise."

"Why—what did he tell you? Was it about Wells?"

"He told me nowt, Sutton. Neither of Wells nor of water-brooks. For the best of reasons. The Jayne bird, let me tell you, had flown. Over the hills and far away."

Sutton whistled and then nodded knowingly. "Destination unknown, I suppose?"

"Oh, no. Nothing secretive about Jayne. Address all fair, square and above board."

"Where?"

"Where had Jayne gone? Back to the shack where the black-eyed Susans grow. Way down in Tennessee—or to the Swanee river, if you like. In other words, Sutton, he had flown to the States. To be precise, Mr. Jayne can now be found at 222, East Fifty-Sixth Street, New York. Care of Colonel Colquhoun—whoever he may be. Ever heard of him, by the way?"

Sutton shook his head. "Never, Mr. Bathurst. Don't see why I should. I'm no Pinkerton man. I'm only a country bobby, you know, stuck away down here by the Dennet."

"There's many a gem that's doomed to blush unseen, Sutton. A lady said that. And your blush is a beauty. Real schoolgirl complexion. Well—so much for Alfred Jayne. When death called to his master, the land of the Blessed Eagle of Freedom called to him—and he answered the call. Willingly—so his niece told me. Keep that fact tucked away in your mind. You'll probably want it again before long. Well, having drawn a blank with Jayne, I hied me to the seaside resort of St. Aidans. Oakley's Kennedy lived in a house a little way from the front. That is to say, my dear Sutton—I hope that you're listening, because here comes the crucial point—he *had* lived there."

Sutton stared at him. "Do you mean that he had flitted too?"

"Undeniably, Sutton. He also had 'moofed'. Told our friend Oakley the tale of the melon seeds and then skipped like a lamb."

"You don't say!"

"I do, Inspector. Every time—and then some! There's nary a doubt of it according to a gentleman I met there who was quite a character in his way. He interviewed me in his shirt-sleeves."

"And where's this fellow Kennedy gone? Did you get his address too?"

"You bet I did, Inspector. And you may be surprised to hear that Alexander Kennedy, one-time porter for luggage at the Spread Eagle, St. Aidans, who found melon-seeds on Griggs's suitcase, has also returned to his old home on the range, where the deer and the antelope play. For *his* address will now be 222, East Fifty-Sixth Street, New York, and he will also reside under the kindly wing of the hospitable Colonel Colquhoun, the kindly Colonel

Colquhoun, of whom you haven't heard." Anthony grinned and pressed the tobacco into the bowl of his pipe.

Sutton was startled into an exclamation. "Holy smoke! The same address. Looks darned fishy, doesn't it?"

"Don't know about 'fishy', but it's darned interesting. There can't be the slightest doubt that there's a link between the two of 'em somewhere, somehow, or somewhen. And we've got to find it. True, the link may be a perfectly legitimate one, and when you strike it, easily understandable. But there's the chance that it may not. As I said, our job is to find out what it is."

Sutton shook his head decisively. "No doubt what the link is, Mr. Bathurst. It sticks out a mile. As I see it, that is."

"Go on, Sutton. Tell me what you're thinking. I'm listening."

"Why, it's to do with your night-shirt secret society, of course, this Ku-Klux-Klan, as you call it. Everything, so it seems to me, points to it. Jayne and this fellow Kennedy were planted on to Griggs. To watch and ultimately get him. One at Great Astill. The other at St. Aidans. Probably he's been dogged by the society everywhere he went. That idea's on all fours with their customary methods, I should say."

Anthony smiled. "I see what you mean. Everywhere that Albert went, the Klan was sure to go, eh? It followed him to an hotel one day—that the idea? Don't forget that neither Jayne nor Kennedy has shown up at Lokingham."

"As far as you know."

"I agree. As far as we know. But I don't think either of 'em did."

"Somebody else may have done so, though. Jayne and Kennedy may not have been the only two. Don't omit that possibility."

"You mean somebody else bearing allegiance to the Treble K?"

"Aye, Mr. Bathurst. That's exactly what I do mean."

"Well, I can't blame you, Inspector. It's feasible, I grant. But— and there's always that big 'but' in the way as far as I'm concerned."

"Which big 'but'?"

"The same one as before, Sutton. The more the case changes, the more there remains the same 'but'. *Semper idem.* I refer to St. Aidans pier and the murder of Daphne Arbuthnot. It's always in front of me. Mocks me to my everlasting discontent. *What*

*connection was there between Griggs and Daphne Arbuth-
not?* Try as I may, I can't find one. The skeleton of one, even."

Sutton stared ahead of him. "Yes, I see the difficulty. And it
beats me—entirely."

"There are two of us, Sutton, so don't grow an inferiority
complex. You see, you can't close your mind to this. Griggs wasn't
everybody's darling. Far from it. Look at what we know about him.
Fowles hated him. Wells didn't love him a little bit. Palliser and
Miss Fortescue were by no means thrilled by him. In addition,
we are now up against the Ku-Klux-Klan line of enmity. More
important, perhaps, from the murder point of view, than all the
others put together. Sift those as you choose, pick here and select
there, winnow the chaff from the true grain . . . and then, after all
that process of refinement and elimination, where are you? You
are still confronted, my dear Inspector, by the body of the girl
who died on the divan during a performance of *Interference*."

At this moment Sutton made what Anthony thought was a
rather surprising contribution. "Have you given much thought
to Glady's Greene's evidence, Mr. Bathurst?"

"The maid who left the brush at the end of the corridor?"

"Yes."

"I haven't entirely overlooked it."

"Well—this is what I'm trying to say—have we made the mistake of paying too little attention to it? Sometimes I think that
we have. That in some way, perhaps, we have missed the real
significance of it. That it may be the crux, as it were, of the whole
situation. Have you ever thought on those lines, Mr. Bathurst?"

"I see your point. You mean that from some points of view it
was the most *indicative* statement that has so far come our way.
Centred all round Griggs, the murdered man, it contained two
vital words. Each with a direct bearing on the case. 'Murder' and
'Fowles'. The Greene girl thought of the word, of course, when she
heard it, as 'f-o-w-l-s'—but that's a trifling matter which makes
no difference to us. Because we know better—for the reason that
we are fortified by more knowledge than she possessed."

The Inspector nodded. "Exactly. And I think, possibly, that
we've been inclined to ignore the obvious."

"And chase the shadows of the moon? Well, you can apply the same argument to the Wells line too, you know. You were itching to put the bracelets on him the other day, but happily you listened to my restraining influence."

Sutton rummaged in his pocket. Eventually he produced a folded newspaper cutting. "Since you told me about the K.K.K., the other day I came across this paragraph in the *Morning Message*. Very interesting. It's a reprint of *The Times*, October the fifth, nineteen twenty-one." He passed the cutting over to Anthony, who read it immediately.

"The Ku-Klux-Klan, a secret society active in the southern states of America, has of late committed a great number of crimes and outrages on the plea of upholding the supremacy of the white race. In particular, it has spread terror in large areas of Texas. A favourite device of this powerful body is to abduct and tar and feather persons who come under its displeasure, or, as an alternative, brand them with the three initials K.K.K. Many terrible murders are also laid to the charge of the Society."

Sutton interposed. "Many murders, Mr. Bathurst! You observe that, don't you?"

Anthony handed back the slip. "I know, Sutton. I *knew*—rather."

"And still you can't get over Daphne Arbuthnot?"

"No. When I do, I fancy, only fancy, mind you, that I shall be in the straight for the solution of the Lokingham affair as well."

"And in the meantime, Mr. Bathurst, what do I do? Sit and kick my heels?"

"I know that I'm trying you, Sutton, and I know I'm asking a hell of a lot of you. Be patient with me. On the whole, the Press hasn't been too bad. Sir Austin's influence has helped, naturally, to muzzle it a bit. I admit, though, that the quiet can't go on for ever. I feel in my bones that I'm on the verge of a discovery. Can't tell you why. Just feel it. Sort of 'Fee-Fie-Fo-Fum' business. Do you know what I'm going to do? I'm going to fill my pipe this evening and settle down to a spot of really intensive thinking. If the gods be kind to me, then I promise you, Sutton, you shall hear all about it in the morning. I can't say fairer than that, can I?" He smiled at Inspector Sutton and extended his hand.

"I'll be waiting at the very edge of the 'phone, Mr. Bathurst. Ears cocked and fingers tingling. Like you—I can't explain it, but something tells me, too, that we're nearing the end of our journey. Let's hope we're both right."

"Inspector," said Mr. Bathurst, "I don't know what I should do without you."

Sutton grinned at him cheerfully.

There was one thing about Bathurst. He did appreciate a chap!

CHAPTER XXV
FLOODLIGHT ON THE PIER

ANTHONY Lotherington Bathurst lay at full length on a settee. That is to say, his legs dangled over one end of that piece of furniture. The position of his head was moderately comfortable. Smoke clouds hung heavily about him. Thus he attempted to find the sovereign mood of Holmes, the master. That great detective to whom he had always sworn eternal fidelity. Analysis. Dissection. The understanding of personal psychology. The science of deduction. The weighing and assessing of motive. *Cui bono?*

Prior to lighting his pipe he had followed his usual practice and committed certain names and facts to paper. Then he had discarded the paper on which the names were and had surveyed them by the other and more intensive process of mental visualization. Through the wraith-like wisps of smoke that floated above his head, both the names and the facts that he had attached to them were all plain to him. He had listed the names in the order of their personal contact with what he described as the main case—that of Griggs—murdered in the bedroom of the hotel at Lokingham.

He considered them in this order. The maid, Ada Cracknell, and the porter, Roberts. Results in relation to both entirely negative. Nothing whatever against either of them. No possible motive in either case; no—not quite that—cut out "possible" and insert "probable". No contact with the pier at St. Aidans. Following them, he came to Staniforth, the hotel manager. Same conditions absolutely. No bad marks, no motive, no St. Aidans connection that had been established or even suggested. Mr. Bathurst dropped Staniforth into the Cracknell and Roberts category.

Then came the two commercial travellers, Ellis and Searle. Anthony lingered some time over them. Different propositions entirely. Their calling, to a certain extent, placed them in a different division from the other members of the cast.

This brought Anthony to what he was inclined to describe to himself as "the inner circle". Number one of this circle—Wells. Here we approached much more closely to the problem of "motive". Revenge? Very likely. Supported by the weight of fact. Griggs's unwelcome attentions to his daughter—against the continuance of which Wells had warned and threatened Griggs at the latter's own house shortly before the murder. Added to which, Wells turns up most conveniently—from some angles—at the Lansdowne Hotel, Lokingham, absolutely coincidentally with Griggs, the man on whom he had recently called and vowed vengeance. Again, there was the additional and undoubted fact that Wells had lied concerning his previous acquaintanceship with Griggs. Anthony, thinking hard, decided to put the name of Wells on one side for the time being, to be ready to be picked up again at a moment's notice should he so desire.

From Wells he travelled, in natural sequence, to Fowles. Somehow or other, he always connected the two men. They were linked in more ways than one. They had each been in the billiard-room with Griggs the night before the murder. As with Wells, there was motive, too, lying in the mind of Fowles. Again—revenge! For two sons who had gone to the gallows when a word from Griggs might have saved them. Thus the sorrowing father might argue. There came too, in the case of Fowles, the first contact with the St. Aidans case. And he had carried a rope with him . . . until Griggs had died . . . which contingency eventuating, he had left the rope behind him. Why? Because he saw no further use for it? Mr. Bathurst's thoughts ran on. Fowles—an electrician in Daphne Arbuthnot's company—who, besides leaving a rope behind him, had left his employment after Griggs had died. Anthony shifted uneasily on his settee and made the cushion for his head more comfortable. He certainly could not dispose of Fowles. Fowles could join Wells in the doubtful division. Who next?

Basil Palliser and Miss Fortescue. St. Aidans *and* Lokingham. Query: affairs of the heart and triangular interference? Griggs, possibly, the apex of the triangle. Query, too, in this connection, Daphne as a likely entanglement. Actor and actresses. Actresses. They have a much better time when they're naughty. . . .

Then, bringing up the rear, came Jayne, Griggs's butler who had gone to live with Colonel Colquhoun in East Fifty-Sixth Street . . . with Kennedy, a luggage porter at St. Aidans, who had entered the cast, very late, because he had seen melon seeds in Griggs's bedroom. There could be no doubt about these melon seeds, because he had seen them himself between the pages of a book found in the bed at Lokingham. Wherein, then, lay the Ku-Klux-Klan activity? In whose personality was it vested?

Anthony shook his head and exhaled smoke that became floating clouds over him. In many respects, he meditated, one of the most remarkable cases with which he had ever been called upon to deal. Thundering good job, in a way, that Oakley had picked up Kennedy's evidence when he did. A few more days and it would have been too late. Anthony put down his pipe. Now where was he?

If Griggs had gone to St. Aidans for the sake of the bright eyes of Phillida Fortescue, which was by far the most reasonable supposition . . . and Basil Palliser were there as well . . . *and* this unknown quantity, presumably representing the Ku-Klux-Klan . . . *and* Fowles were employed as electrician . . . in that particular company . . . *with his rope* . . . there, then, were all the ingredients of the murder mixture ready to hand in one place.

Further to that. Supposing that Daphne Arbuthnot, waiting on the divan during the all-important "black-out", had turned round, as it was her habit to turn round, seen the hand of Palliser holding the fatal glass that contained the poison that was so soon to choke the life out of her . . . well . . . there you were and . . .

Anthony started up from the settee with a cry of amazement. For, at that second, it had been revealed to him and he had seen clearly and vividly *how* and *why* had come about the killing of Daphne Arbuthnot. Thrice muddy-minded fool that he had been! Of course! Of course! How could he have missed such a vital point for so long? It explained everything . . . of the St. Aidans pier mystery. That was where Daphne Arbuthnot came in. But what of Griggs and Lokingham? Never mind for the time being. That could wait. He would get this first murder settled up and tucked away as a beginning.

Where the hell was Sutton? Oh, he remembered with a smile, sitting by the telephone. On the very edge thereof waiting for news. Anthony Bathurst took three mighty strides across the room and picked up the receiver.

"Sutton," he said, when the reply came through, "come up and see me some time, will you? And let that some time be now. Listen, laddie—uncock those ears of yours—we're halfway there!"

"Where?" queried the Inspector dubiously.

"Floodlight on the pier," returned A.L.B. with a chuckle.

"Pier? Why . . . what . . . ?"

"St. Aidans . . . where once a girl died . . . suddenly, Sutton."

"Whisky, Inspector? Help yourself. I shan't watch you as you fill your glass. I'm Irish. Besides, it'll all go down on my bill, whether you drink it or no. Plus a substantial amount for corkage, I expect. That's right, Sutton. Pour yourself out a stiff peg."

Sutton complied, moistened his lips, and raised a glass in Mr. Bathurst's honour.

"Cigarettes? No? Prefer a pipe? Good!"

Sutton settled himself. He was tired and this was something that approximated comfort.

Anthony began to talk. "Scene, Sutton—St. Aidans pier. On the stage of the little theatre that adorns that pier—a Howard Baluster company playing the well-known West End success, *Interference*, before the usual seaside audience. In the cast of the play, as performed, we have three people who interest us. People who have been in our minds now for some considerable time. I will name them: Palliser, Miss Fortescue, and Daphne Arbuthnot. The last-named because she was the first victim in our chain of murder.

Extra to the cast of the play we have, first of all, Griggs. Destined so soon afterwards to play the lead in a tragedy . . . that ran for one night. He is there, at St. Aidans, because his amorous eye has lighted on the fair Phillida. Get that fact into your head, good Sutton. Secondly, we have Fowles, a recently appointed electrician to the Baluster company. Question, *why* was Fowles there?"

Sutton shook his head. "Do you mean why did he take up the job?"

"Put it that way, if you like."

"I'll have a shot. Trailing Griggs?"

"Right—first pop. Friend Fowles is a man with an *idée fixe*—he nurses hatred of Griggs because of the judgment of the law that had been executed upon his two boys. He carries a hangman's rope with him. To remind him . . . *and* Griggs. Well, there are your *dramatis personae*. Nothing happens until the time of the famous 'black-out'—about which you've already heard so much. I've seen Inspector Baddeley, remember, the man who first handled the St. Aidans case. I will endeavour now, Sutton, to the best of my ability, to reconstruct the St. Aidans crime for you. During the *entr'acte*, Griggs, either invited or self-invited, Cabinet Minister, you know, and all that, used to poking his nose into places that didn't concern him, enters the men's dressing-room. He is anxious to find Miss Fortescue, and this is one way of getting appreciably nearer to her without exciting strong comment.

"Now, from one dressing-room to another, you know, was not a great distance, and it would be a comparatively easy matter for Griggs to slip from one to the other. Right. Now think clearly. Put up one of your classic efforts, Sutton. What would happen directly Griggs entered the men's dressing-room?"

Sutton shook his head as though he had failed to understand.

"Easy, Sutton. Dead easy. You'll never have a simpler question than that to answer, if you live to be as old as Methuselah. I'll answer it for you. Somebody said to Griggs, Langley, the S.M., I expect, more likely he than anybody else, 'what'll you have?' Ever heard the expression applied to yourself?"

Sutton nodded with a grin. "Yes. I see what you mean now. Go on, Mr. Bathurst. You're makin' me thirsty. Besides, this is getting interesting."

"Right. Somebody pours Griggs out a Scotch. I say a Scotch because the odds are heavily that way. It's the best thing that Scotland's ever done. What happens? The glass is put on the table direct to his hand. Undoubtedly with others similar to it. But *for some reason*, which we shall never know, he delays picking it up. I think that he either saw Phillida Fortescue or heard her voice. Whatever it was, I suggest, caused him to turn away from the table where the glass was. Perhaps he may even have walked to the door that led across to the ladies' dressing-room. At any rate, I am moderately certain that he walked some distance away from the table. During those few seconds or even perhaps a minute *. . . his glass had been marked down and his drink poisoned by the addition of the prussic acid.*

"Now, Sutton of Suttons, mark the amazing sequel. When our friend, Griggs, on absolutely nodding terms with the last Admiral, returns to the table, *he picks up*—by a most romantic stroke of fate—*the wrong glass!* An excessively simple matter, Sutton, because I'll stake my reputation that there were several there in a row. It's astonishing how glasses accumulate. *Now* where are we?"

"Well there! I know the way now, Mr. Bathurst."

"What's next on the board, then?"

"Palliser," replied Sutton laconically.

"Excellent! Enter Palliser then. In two senses. For what has he come? Again the answer is easy. He has come from the stage, having checked up on his 'props', for the ill-fated Daphne's nightly 'pick-me-up', which it is Palliser's habit to hand to her through the gap between the two flats directly behind the divan where she is lying. Palliser, unknowingly, picks up the glass containing the poison. He had probably cut things rather fine that night and was a little late in going for the glass of spirits. I suggest that the known proximity of Griggs had caused him to keep an unusually vigilant eye on Phillida Fortescue. Jealousy, you know is a most powerful agent. It's a mere suggestion—but I'd bank on its authenticity. Now he knows that it's either brandy or whisky, and the colour's all O.K., so accordingly he takes it along back stage, pushes the movable flat to one side, as he has done regularly for several nights and hands the glass to Daphne Arbuthnot; she drinks, hands it back—and farewell Daphne! But the murderer, watching in the wings, knows by this time that his plan has miscarried. Griggs is still walking about, 'ale and 'earty. Where has the fatal glass gone? He hangs about behind, sees Palliser return with the glass to the men's dressing-room just before the 'rag' goes up again, captures the tell-tale glass without knowing who had drunk from it, and only just has time to dispose of it in the fire-bucket hanging by the wall on the O.P. side. Where it lay until I found it! *Voilà mon cher Sutton*. In that way was encompassed the death of Daphne."

Sutton regarded him intently. When he spoke, he spoke impressively. "You see 'the murderer', Mr. Bathurst. Can't you give him a name?"

"Nothing easier. Meredith, the man I met on St. Aidans pier, encountered him behind the flats, almost immediately after Daphne's death had been discovered. He actually *spoke* to Meredith. Of course he did. His words were prompted and engendered by anxiety. Consider his position. Not only had he missed his quarry, but he had been the means of bringing death to somebody else—an entirely innocent person who had never harmed him in any shape or form. Also he had to start his work, somewhere else, all over again. A succession of nasty jolts those, Sutton."

"I know . . . who it was! You mean . . . *Fowles*?"

"Fowles," returned Anthony simply.

"And Daphne, then, died by accident?"

There came a period of silence. Sutton eventually broke it.

"Which means that Fowles followed Griggs to Lokingham—" He broke off suddenly. "I say, why did he take on that electrician's job, if he wanted to get Griggs so badly? Griggs wasn't always—"

"Why? He knew of the gentleman's desires in the direction of Miss Fortescue, of course. Where *she* was, Griggs would be . . . and he, Fowles, would be also."

"Yes . . . I see. That explains it. I'll go back to what I was about to say just now. Fowles followed his man here to Lokingham . . . and *got* him . . . is that it? I can safely arrest him?"

Anthony made no immediate answer. He started to fill his pipe again . . . slowly and deliberately. "You've got to look at it like this: you'll never prove the Arbuthnot case against him, Sutton. I've been realizing that all the more while I've been telling you the story."

"Perhaps not. But what about the second murder? Surely I can get him on that? Look at the value of the evidence from the point of view of its accumulation. You can't get away from it."

Anthony struck a match and lit the tobacco in his pipe. "Yes. I know all about that, Inspector . . . but—don't forget—there's also one thing that I don't know. And that makes all the difference."

"What don't you know?"

"I don't know . . . yet, my dear Sutton, to be entirely satisfied, that is . . ." Anthony stopped.

Sutton intervened eagerly. "What, Mr. Bathurst?"

"That Fowles *did* kill Griggs after all. Griggs was a different proposition from Daphne Arbuthnot. You see, in his case . . . it's all a question of those melon seeds."

Anthony sat and smoked. Inspector Sutton watched him.

Chapter XXVI
THE CHEF AND THE FRUITERER

It was at twenty-two minutes past two that night, or rather that morning, that Anthony Lotherington Bathurst knew who had killed the Home Secretary. The knowledge came to him in the watches of the night. He had, as far as his memory would stand the test, gone over the whole of the ground again. Data. Incidents. Conversations. He came to the last words that Meredith had spoken to him on the pier at St. Aidans. "Nobody had missed a glass . . ." And the revelation was immediately followed by an acute realization of his own stupidity. What an utterly blind fool he had been, to be sure! On the other hand, though, what an amazing crime he had been called upon to investigate. And how easily he had been misled and missed the vital points and parts of it, all along the line from the inception. *Easily!* The word was inadequate. How *pitiably*, rather!

He communed with his *alter ego* thuswise. "If I ever fear that I like myself too much, put on 'roll', of exult unduly at petty triumphs, whisper to me gently, but firmly, 'Anthony, my boy, what did you do in the Lokingham Hotel murder?' Whisper it again and again—and believe me, I shall hear, pay attention and profit accordingly."

Anthony eventually wooed sleep successfully somewhere in the region of three a.m. The morning found him tired . . . *épuisé*, perhaps . . . but mentally a new man. Anthony sang in his bath that morning, and carolled joyously to the combination of sponge and soap. His breakfast tasted better than it had tasted for some considerable time. The Lansdowne Hotel took on a higher place in his table of estimation. The coffee was excellent . . . the mixed grill tasty and satisfying . . . the marmalade and toast were fit for a king. Better even than Bill Congreve's at Nellen when he had been looking into that strange and bizarre problem that had been handed down to history by his commentator under the title of "The Sussex Cuckoo."

At ten minutes past ten Anthony rose from the breakfast-table. There were two more nails that he must drive home before he could consider his case high and dry for the last stroke to be played. One—and the first in the order of what he called "convenient activity"—could be dealt with, fortunately, almost on the spot. That is to say, the kitchens of the Lansdowne Hotel were comparatively close at hand. He had but to go below and seek the seclusion that the grill would grant. For where the kitchens and the grill were, there would be, too, Adolpe, the chef . . . the all-powerful and puissant emperor of his own culinary domain. Staniforth, the manager, whom Anthony had seen earlier that morning, accompanied him on his journey kitchenwards.

"It's best for *you* to see Adolphe," said Staniforth, "see him yourself. I'm certain that he'd remember what you want to know far more accurately than I should. It's his job and he's frightfully keen on it. I've a thousand and one jobs—besides a rotten memory. If you hate anybody like poison, and feel downright vindictive towards 'em, get 'em a job as an hotel manager. Subtle revenge, Mr. Bathurst. Do I know? Do I? Could I write a book about it?"

"I expect you could, Mr. Staniforth, and a most interesting volume at that—but do you think that when you had written it you could sell it? That's the awkward point about writing books, you know. Selling's much more difficult than writing. Craig, 'the old Surrey poet,' was the first man to bring that to my notice at a place known as Kennington Oval. The bowlers bowl there for run-outs. Ask Charlie Parker."

The smell of the kitchens, now very close to them, tickled Mr. Bathurst's nostrils. He sniffed appreciatively and quoted: "The stag at eve had drunk his fill . . ." when Staniforth intervened.

"Don't suppose Adolphe will be overjoyed to see us at this time in the morning. Rather awkward for him. We shall get in his way. He's a law unto himself, let me tell you, and down here, what he says goes! What do you think of this? I'll tell you something. Seven women in different capitals of Europe regard themselves as his lawful wife! And the old devil writes to 'em all in turn. When any of 'em reply he burns the letter without reading it. In case they want money, he says. Two passions in life for Adolphe. Women and soft roes on toast."

"Glad you said 'two'," remarked Mr. Bathurst, "otherwise I might possibly have misunderstood you and thought that you were referring to a new dish."

"They're a curious breed. Do you know, we had a chef here before him, off the *Minnetonka*, who placed things in this way. He called it his order of merit. One, a poached egg on toast; two, a snowflake; three, a beautiful girl. Yes. They're funny beggars— these chaps. Latin, you know, and that's saying a lot if you ask me."

Staniforth pushed open the door. "Here you are. Come through here."

In the background Anthony caught a glimpse of a white-hatted figure, with a spoon in its hand. He heard dimly certain words spoken. They were familiar, but the accent in which they were delivered was a trifle strange to his ear. Certainly Adolphe swore like an artist. Anthony recognized the master touch.

"You fool," said Adolphe to a tall, thin lad standing next to him—"you little bloodee bastard fool, you forget that it is soup you make—not cats . . ."

Adolpe paused precipitately—certainly the pause was fortunate in its timing. Staniforth went over and spoke to him.

"Adolphe . . . you're more important than ever, this morning. Right in the headlines. This gentleman here is a famous detective. He wants your help."

Adolphe surrendered his spoon to his assistant and twirled a moustache-end. "I am enraptured. But I am not surprised. He has, perhaps, come to interview me? Is it my soft roes on toast . . . or my own famous sauce for . . . ?" He paused expectantly.

"Neither the one, Adolphe, nor the other," said Anthony, "but just a mere matter of mind, memory, and melon seeds."

Adolphe's gallant geniality vanished as snow under sun. Detective! Was the man, then, a buffoon? Pouf! Melon seeds, indeed! He stiffened himself to a most admirable frigidity.

"Your pardon, monsieur, but . . . frankly . . . I do not understand you. I should have been 'appy to advise you on—"

"On anything but melon seeds, I suppose?" declared Anthony smilingly.

Adolphe shook his head. "I do not understand. What can melon seeds 'ave to do with me? I am Adolphe . . . I 'ave not always been at Lokingham. I served for twenty-two years at the 'Splendide' . . ."

"Let me explain more fully," said Anthony, ". . . then I'm sure we shall be good friends together. Otherwise, I fear—"

Adolphe summoned his dignity. "It shall be as you say, monsieur. Explain, if you please."

"I will. How long, Adolphe, is it since you had melon on your menu here—melon served in any shape or form? For instance, when did you last have such a thing as a melon in the kitchen here?" Anthony gestured round the kitchen.

Adolphe stared at him in undisguised amazement. "Such a thing as a melon?" he repeated after Anthony. "When did I 'ave it in the kitchen 'ere last?"

"That's it, M. Adolphe," remarked A.L.B. "Word for word just as you've said it. The answer's a melon."

Adolphe turned to the tall, thin boy who stood open-mouthed by him and discharged a torrent of spoken words. It was as though the man had been condemned to silence for a term of many years, and that at this moment the length of that term had just expired and there had come a spate of speech. French and Italian terms mingled with each other in such rapid and torrential succession that beyond a snatch of phrase here and there Anthony found it impossible to follow Adolphe's outburst to the extent of understanding.

The boy contented himself with but few words in reply. Anthony noted them. "All right, Mussolini, old cock, keep your hair on." Anthony felt that he could have roared with uncontrollable laughter, but Staniforth's face, as he watched the scene, was clouded by a frown.

The chef turned to Mr. Bathurst. "There is but one thing I ever use for the menu to do with the melon. It is a fruit most insipid. No taste. No delicacy. But sometimes, not very often, I make what is called the 'melon cantaloup'. The fruit, it is put to the bed in ice—oh, for at least 'alf a day. That is most important. Its rind is on—then you cut out the slices and arrange them round a bowl of ice—as in the cantaloup banana. You know, eh, what I mean? But it is certain, monsieur, it is the imperative thing that you should use the Krona pepper. Otherwise—oh, *là, là*—no good. For the perfection of flavour, you understand—*hein*? For the—what you say—discriminating palate. Monsieur, it is many months since I gave my patrons in the hotel upstairs my melon cantaloup. Is it not, Mr. Staniforth—you will bear me out?" He swung round excitedly on the manager. "You can give the testimonial to the truth of that which I speak for this gentleman?"

"It's a long time, I should say, Adolpe. But I can't remember these things like you can, you know, and I couldn't answer in terms of weeks or months. Grub and such like only interests me when it's on the table in front of me—not before and not afterwards."

Anthony tackled Adolphe again. "Do you remember the evening before the gentleman named Griggs was found dead in his bedroom?"

"Oh, very well, monsieur. I will tell you what I sent up for dinner on that evening. A really beautiful flan of Kentish strawberries. The secret with a flan is to remove the rice when three parts baked and then fill up with the strawberries. It was a triumph, monsieur, even for Adolphe, who 'as 'ad thousands of triumphs. It was a triumph! *Magnifique!*"

"No melon, then," said Anthony, "but strawberries, eh?"

"But strawberries, monsieur. There is no comparison between them. I shall never forget the flan that I made that evening. I may even talk of it again."

"I shouldn't be at all surprised," remarked Mr. Bathurst. "But thank you, M. Adolphe, for your kindness, your memory, and the mere description of that classic flan. But tell me this, if you can. If I should desire a really good melon, say, to-day, to quench a most noble and distinguished thirst . . . where, in this district or its immediate vicinity, would you recommend me to buy it? I am a comparative stranger, and I know so little of the shops round here."

Adolphe pursed his lips in consideration of Mr. Bathurst's question. There is little doubt that he was flattered at the confidence that was evidently placed in him. "The best of the fruiterers, you mean? That is a question absurdly easy to answer. You must go where Adolphe purchases. Always! Why, monsieur? I will tell you why. I know *how* to buy. I know *what* to buy. I know *where* to buy. And I know *when* to buy. Perhaps that last one is the importance of them all!"

"That's excellent. I knew that I shouldn't go far wrong if I asked you, Adolphe," murmured Anthony appraisingly; "now tell me the place. Is it near here?"

"Yes. But certainly at no great distance. And I will tell you! There is an old one there who owns the business, the son of 'is father before him, and that old one has forgotten more of the fruit and of the vegetable trade than most men of 'is kind will ever know. I, Adolphe, say so—I know what I am saying—and no one will contradict me." Adolphe struck an attitude.

"Name and address of this paragon of raspberry-sellers, Adolphe, please?" It must be recorded that Anthony had found Adolphe distinctly amusing.

"The shop of which I tell you is in Traquair Road. Only a few doors from the theatre. The 'Orphic'. The name of the old one who keeps the shop is Westwood."

Adolphe pronounced the surname to the best of his limited ability. Anthony noted the information.

"Well—is that all you want, Mr. Bathurst?" inquired Staniforth. "Or do you want—"

"That's a big question. I'll content myself by saying that I hope I shall get what I want *from* it. If I fail I must try something else. But melons, you know, are not such 'fruity' fruit, as, say, cherries and strawberries are! Even grocers and general storekeepers have been known to sell melons . . . whereas they seldom do strawberries or peaches. See my point? Anyhow, we'll thank the gods for the gifts they send us . . . include Adolphe among them . . . and see what the information, duly exploited, brings forth."

Anthony slipped a handsome *pourboire* into Adolphe's hand and made his way from the kitchens of the Lansdowne Hotel. Staniforth followed him. Staniforth's thoughts may be placed on paper. He had started the case by running upstairs at Ada Cracknell's behest—now he had gone below, at this man Bathurst's desire. Strange, he ruminated, what things come to one in life and how unexpectedly. He watched Anthony Bathurst leave the hotel by the front exit, and as soon as he was out of sight walked quickly to the telephone.

Anthony crossed the road and turned down the side street that, he knew, would take him to Traquair Road and the Orphic Theatre. After loitering here for a few minutes, he entered. A short time later he emerged from the theatre and came to Swynford Street. He passed the house where Phillida Fortescue had lodged—was still lodging in all probability. For he remembered that *Strained Relations* was still being played at the theatre. Swynford Street was a turning out of Traquair Road, he recollected. He walked down Swynford Street until it made junction with Traquair Road. The shop bearing the name "Josiah Westwood" was discovered almost immediately in front of him. Undoubtedly, as Adolphe had indicated, a high-class fruiterer and greengrocer.

Anthony entered the shop and found his man, who listened curiously to Mr. Bathurst's statement.

"Well, there's not a big trade in melons, sir, I agree. They're not what you'd call a popular fruit, and there's not a big call for them. And, of course, it's hard to say, but I'd reckon that of all the melons supplied to people in the district—that's to say all round the area of the Dennet Valley—well, nine-tenths of 'em, at least, come from me here. P'raps even a bigger percentage than that. So you see how it is! I really can't say. I might be able to serve your purpose—and I might not. And there you are, guv'nor."

"I agree entirely. I anticipated that you would tell me that. But we'll see how things turn out . . . it's a chance . . . and from my point of view, it's well worth taking. That's why I've come along to see you."

"Right you are, guv'nor. Now, what's your date?"

"June the twenty-second. Or possibly a day or so previously. You have a number of *regular* customers, for instance? People to whom you send a daily order?"

"Oh, yes. Of course. Over two hundred of 'em."

"Well, there's this to it, my inquiry wouldn't relate to a 'regular'—I'm certain of that."

"June the twenty-second, you said. Now, let me turn up my—" Westwood stopped. "I say . . . just a minute, guv'nor . . . wasn't that the date of the day that Griggs, the Home Secretary, was killed over in the Lansdowne Hotel? It seems to strike a chord in my memory."

Anthony looked at him eagerly. "Yes. You're right. That is the date. But why do you mention it? In this connection, I mean?"

"I'll tell you why. And most remarkable too, considering what you've asked me. On the evening of the twenty-second of June, I was in this very shop . . . reading the evening newspaper. You can guess what I was reading about. Local sensation. The Lokingham Hotel murder. Griggs . . . the Home Secretary, that was. Now I'll tell you why I remember it so well. And the more I think of it, the more extraordinary it is."

Westwood's voice grew almost hoarse in his excitement and his hands gripped the edge of the counter. "When I read how Griggs had been found dead in his bed at the hotel, I thought of something that had happened in my shop that same afternoon. Just a little piece of what I'll call 'association of ideas'. No wonder you're asking me about the sale of melons. I should say so."

Westwood turned and eyed Anthony shrewdly. "What are you—Scotland Yard?"

"Almost," smiled Anthony. "You can call me that if you like."

"I see. I feared as much. Listen, then. On the afternoon of the day that the murder took place . . . a lady came into this shop—quite young she was, and attractive, and purchased a melon. And while I was putting it into a bag for her . . . she mentioned to me quite casually that the Home Secretary, Griggs, was stopping at Lokingham at the Lansdowne Hotel. Now, sir, you can see how my mind worked with regard to things. When I read of his death on the next evening, naturally I thought of her . . . and when you mentioned the date just now . . . all the sequence of events came back to me."

Westwood took a handkerchief from his pocket and wiped his brow. The telling of his tale had tried him, and his nerves were all on edge. Such an event as this didn't come his way every day.

Anthony heaved a sigh of relief when Westwood finished his story. Here was fight at last.

"Tell me, Mr. Westwood," he said, "this young lady that bought the melon—when she mentioned the name of Griggs to you—what sort of tone did she use? In her voice? Did she speak . . . well . . . what shall we say . . . with any enthusiasm?" Westwood thought hard over the question. "Well, sir . . . it's some time ago when it happened, and I don't know that I could . . ." He put his two hands over his forehead in an attempt at concentration. "I'm trying to picture it all again. Where she stood. Over there it was. She turned . . . as she put the melon into the shopping-bag that she was carrying. I can see her turning toward me. No . . . *not* enthusiasm in my opinion. I wouldn't call it that. Certainly not enthusiasm."

"Animosity? Vindictiveness? Hatred? Contempt? Any one of those . . . er . . . *major* conditions?"

Westwood's reply this time was more definite. "No. Nothing quite so . . . big . . . as any of those. But . . . now how shall I put it? It's difficult to express a thing like that—in mere words . . . she was, well, sarcastic—cynical, perhaps, would be the best word."

Anthony intervened eagerly. "What was it exactly that gave you that impression?"

"H'm! What was it? Let me think. I know. The details of her conversation are coming back to me. It was the phrase that she used about Griggs being in Lokingham. 'I suppose . . . we ought to feel ourselves highly honoured . . . to-day . . . by the presence of the famous Home Secretary in Lokingham.' You know what I mean, sir. She said it as though she didn't mean it. Much more as though she meant the opposite."

Anthony nodded. "A lady? Socially?"

"Oh, undoubtedly. You could tell that by the way she spoke. Oh—yes . . . every time."

"Good-looker?"

"Pretty, do you mean? Yes . . . a pretty woman—as things go round here."

"Have you seen her before in the district?"

"No. Don't think so. Certainly not a regular customer."

"Well dressed, you say?"

"H'm . . . fairish. Good clothes when she first had 'em—but not too new, I should say. Walked well. Carriage and so on. Held herself well."

Anthony smiled. "Good! So she ought to have done . . . it ought to be part of her job . . . but it isn't always so, unfortunately. Just a minute, though, Mr. Westwood, and perhaps we can clinch the matter. There's nothing like making certain of things." Anthony fumbled in his pocket for a second. Eventually he found what he wanted. "There you are, Mr. Westwood, I've been able to get hold of that. Have a look at it."

Westwood took the photograph and held it up.

"Is that the girl who bought melon on a cold and frosty morning?"

Westwood looked hard at the photograph and whistled softly at what he saw. "Yes, sir. This is certainly the lady who bought the melon on a June afternoon. Not a doubt of it. There's no mistaking her."

"Thank you, Mr. Westwood. That's splendid! Send that basket of peaches to the Lokingham General Hospital for me, will you? I rather fancy that my case is complete."

Chapter XXVII
NEARING THE END

ANTHONY Lotherington Bathurst sat in conference with Inspector Sutton. He had previously spoken on the telephone to Sir Austin Kemble, Commissioner of Police at New Scotland Yard. Sir Austin had been intensely relieved to hear what Mr. Bathurst had to tell him and had not hesitated to express that relief.

"Good!" had been his rejoinder to Anthony's statement. "That's all splendid, Bathurst. And distinctly opportune. To tell you the truth, I'd been getting more than a little uneasy. You know what these things are. As a matter of fact, the Premier's been on my collar only this week. I shoved him off, it's true, but the Lord alone knows for how long. Bet your life he'll be on the worry again in a day or so. You're absolutely sure of your ground, I suppose?"

"Oh, absolutely, sir! No need for you to get worked up over that. My case now is the complete and finished article—*and* watertight. Leave the finish to me and I promise you that you shall have the person that murdered Griggs under lock and key within twenty-four hours."

As a result Sir Austin Kemble had replaced the receiver with a smile on his face.

Sutton now listened to Mr. Bathurst's final plans.

"If you think I can't pull it off single-handed—and I admit it's a good point that you've made—I'll get Oakley to help me," said Anthony, in conclusion. "As you say, if I go about the job in the way that I've indicated to you, I shall probably need his help. It should simplify matters considerably."

"Palliser's left the hotel," said Sutton. "He's in digs now, near Miss Fortescue. In Swynford Street. Till the end of next week, when the run finishes. She's at twenty-two. He's at eight. You say that you propose to go to the house? Is that wise, do you think?"

"Yes. More than wise. The safest plan in my opinion. Taking everything into consideration—that is. Tell me if you disagree. I'm prepared to hear your arguments against. If you have words, prepare to shed them now."

Sutton pursed his lips. "Never mind. Perhaps you're right. The boldest plan very often works out the best in the long run."

"'*L'audace. Toujours l'audace,*'" quoted Mr. Bathurst softly. "It shall be as we say, then. I'll 'phone Oakley at once—in case he's got anything else on. He's a much busier man, you know, these days, than he was. If I tell him that he's going to be in at the death, he'll jump at the chance. I know my Oakley. I can read him like a book. I'll get on to him now. Stay here for me, Sutton, will you? I shan't be a moment."

Anthony made his way to the telephone that was in the vestibule of the hotel. Sutton waited patiently for his return. Anthony obtained the number that he wanted and, luckily for him, because the last thing that he desired now was delay, found his man at home. He gave Oakley a brief resume of matters, and told him what he wanted him to do. As Anthony had anticipated, Oakley was a willing auxiliary. He took down the address that Anthony called out to him.

"I'll be along and join you right away, Bathurst. At the moment, I've nothing on here to prevent me leaving the place. Where will you pick me up? Where? At the corner of Swynford Street and Traquair Road? Righto. I'll be there to the tick. Look out for me where the cars stop. By the way, how do I stand with regard to the—er—you know what I mean?"

"The *Morning Message*?" chuckled Anthony. "My dear chap, your help has been invaluable. All that I can do for you in that direction shall be done."

Half an hour later Anthony's car drew up before an unpretentious-looking house in Swynford Street. Anthony, Oakley and Inspector Sutton came out of the car, and Palliser opened the door to them.

"Miss Fortescue is here," he said, "though why you've asked her to be here, I don't know." He was white-faced and obviously nervy.

"You will know," returned Mr. Bathurst; "all in good time."

Palliser took them to the room where Phillida Fortescue was waiting. Palliser saw to the conventions. Oakley took out the note-book that Anthony had told him to bring along and sat there, the perfect secretary, with pen poised in preparation.

Anthony looked at his watch and walked to the window. Then he glanced across to Oakley significantly. "Wells is late. That's a pity. I should have liked him to be here when the tapes go up. Still—there's no need for us to wait for him. Even if he should go to Staniforth in the first place, Staniforth will tell him where we are and send him on."

Mr. Bathurst turned to the others. Oakley, conscious of the part that he was expected to play, became a hundred per cent efficient. Bathurst had put his trust in him, and he was determined not to betray that confidence in any way at all.

Anthony began to speak. He had already assured himself that Inspector Sutton was occupying the position in the room that he had assigned to him when he had outlined his plans.

"I want to take you all back," said Mr. Bathurst, "to the night when Daphne Arbuthnot died on the pier at St. Aidans. You were there, Palliser. You were there, Miss Fortescue, and so was our mutual friend, Griggs. Griggs was there, if you will pardon my stressing the point, because you were there, Miss Fortescue? I take it that you will not contradict me on that point?"

Phillida Fortescue bowed her head. Her "Yes" was barely audible. But Oakley, listening for it as he had been instructed, heard it, and his pen began its rapid work in the note-book with which Anthony Bathurst had supplied him.

There should be no complaint regarding his obedience.

"Attached to your company," continued Anthony, "was a man named Fowles. In an industrial capacity. Working as a stage-hand. As an electrician. He was a comparative newcomer. Some weeks previously his two sons had been hanged. Murderers, you see, in this country have a knack of being hanged. The English people are inclined to be insistent on the point. The last decision as to their ultimate fate had lain in the Home Secretary's hands. He had refused to interfere with the course of justice, however, and the two brothers Fowles waited for a certain March morning and paid the inevitable penalty. Fowles, the father, determined, out of a mistaken sense of injury, to 'get' Griggs. The iron had entered into his soul. I am telling you these things, Palliser, because I feel that it is only fair to Miss Fortescue and you that you should know them.

"Becoming aware of Griggs's interest in you, Miss Fortescue, Fowles obtained employment in the Interference company, banking on Griggs showing up in contact with it somewhere before very long. Fowles was right in his conjecture, and the night at St. Aidans came . . . bringing Griggs into the arena. In describing how Miss Arbuthnot died, I will be brief. Unhappily, the crime will never be brought home to the guilty party. The proof is infinitesimal and a jury would never be convinced by it. When Griggs came into the men's dressing-room that night, during the *entr'acte*, Fowles poisoned the whisky that had been poured out for him. It was poured out, I think, in all probability, by Langley, your S.M."

Anthony swung round on to Palliser. "Here, Mr. Palliser, I shall want your help. You were there at the time: I was not. You saw and took part. I am merely reconstructing what I *think* took place."

The colour drained from Palliser's cheeks. Anthony made the slightest of signs to Oakley. The latter understood and prepared himself. He half-turned in his chair.

Palliser found words. "Any help I can give you, I will give willingly. I must do . . . now."

"Thank you, and listen carefully, please. Now, you, Miss Fortescue, did Griggs try to speak to you about that time? My case is built up on the idea that he did."

Phillida coloured. "Yes. He tried to speak to me . . . but I eluded him. I think that he heard me call out to Roger Langley, and when he heard my voice he attempted to get from one dressing-room to the other."

"Exactly." Anthony nodded eagerly. "That is just what I imagined occurred. Your voice, Miss Fortescue, was the voice of Fate. If you hadn't called out to Langley when you did, Griggs would not have moved from the table where his drink was . . . and Daphne Arbuthnot would most certainly have been alive to-day. Griggs, however, would have died a few weeks earlier." Anthony paused.

"What do you mean by that?" cried Basil Palliser hoarsely.

"I think," returned Mr. Bathurst quietly, "that you know, or at least, you suspect, what I mean."

There was a silence. Anthony made another almost imperceptible sign to Oakley. Again the latter shifted slightly in his seat.

Palliser groaned and put his face in his hands. All of them waited for him. But Palliser didn't speak.

Anthony Bathurst, therefore, continued. "Your actions tell me that you have guessed the truth, Palliser. Perhaps you had even suspected it for some time. As Griggs turned away and left his drink on the table . . . you came in, as you had done so many times before, for Miss Arbuthnot's 'pick-me-up'. There were, no doubt, several drinks there on the table in front of you. Fate dealt the cards, and you picked up the poisoned glass . . . there is no need for me to dwell on the remainder of the story. After Daphne Arbuthnot had drunk from it you replaced the glass on the table . . . without the slightest idea that Daphne Arbuthnot was dead. Fowles himself realised it first and recovered the glass to dispose of it in one of the fire-buckets that were hanging close at hand, where I eventually was fortunate enough to find it. And, as Meredith said to me on St. Aidans pier, 'nobody missed a glass' . . . which entirely commonplace sentence by a strange trick of chance . . . told me how Griggs died in his bed at the Lansdowne Hotel, and also who it was that had shot him."

Palliser's face now was haggard in the extreme, and beads of sweat glistened on his forehead. Oakley was writing hard, intent on every word that Anthony Bathurst spoke. Sutton, to the eye of the trained observer, was keyed up to the highest pitch of alertness. Action was not far distant.

Anthony began to speak again. "I will call this next recital 'part two' of my story. Griggs, all unconscious of having been brushed by the wings of the Angel of Death, comes to Lokingham. Objective? You, still, Miss Fortescue. He knows that you and other members of the *Interference* company are playing in Lokingham and once again, if I may put it in this way, the Griggs moth flutters to the Fortescue candle. Fowles, with his hangman's rope—thank you for that piece of information, Palliser, it proved to be extremely useful to me—is still awaiting Griggs's coming and his own chance. This time he promises himself there shall be no mistake. Griggs will die and the rope be used on him.

"But another factor has appeared in the equation. By name of Wells. Father of an attractive daughter. Your immediate predecessor, I fancy, Miss Fortescue. That is to say, from Griggs's point of view. Here's her photograph."

Phillida blushed.

Anthony produced the photograph from his pocket and passed it round the company. "That lady at whom you are looking had become another member of the Griggs Group. Wells senior had heard of it in time, however, and had put his paternal foot down. Had actually warned Griggs to 'lay off'. I believe that is the reigning expression at the moment, as applied amongst certain social classes to affairs of the heart. And, to complete his job of keeping an eye on friend Griggs, he also had turned up at the Lansdowne Hotel, Lokingham. That hotel was the mutual rendezvous. Now listen to this:

"Griggs, and you, Palliser, and Wells, and Fowles, were all playing billiards on the evening before Griggs was murdered. Griggs was no coward, whatever other faults he had, and he put a bold face on matters and ignored Wells completely. Treated him and all that he stood for with the utmost contempt. This angered Wells excessively, and he came to a decision which . . . well—we'll leave that for the moment. It can arise at the right time. For here, gentlemen, and Miss Fortescue . . . I come to the question of the secret society known as the 'Ku-Klux-Klan' and the melon seeds. These melon seeds, you must understand, were found between the pages of a book which Griggs had evidently been reading in bed just before the bullet was fired that killed him. They were extremely important clues . . . because we have learned since that they had figured elsewhere in Griggs's career."

Anthony turned sharply to the Inspector. "What was that, Sutton? The wheels of a car?"

Sutton sprang from his chair and went out of the room—to return almost immediately. He nodded to Anthony. "Yes. He's here and the girl with him. But everything's arranged, back and front, and I've told him what to do."

"Good! That's all right then. I'm sorry to appear unduly cautious . . . but I can't afford to take any risks. Now where was I? Oh . . . I remember . . . melon seeds. They came from a melon, not surprising that, which melon I suggest, though, had been purchased for the seeds thereof rather than for the fruit." Anthony went to the door and listened.

The others in the room could hear nothing. After a moment or so, he resumed his seat. Phillida Fortescue's eyes held a strange light.

"I now come to a stage of the story where I will again attempt to reconstruct," continued Mr. Bathurst. "Griggs finishes his billiards and puts up his cue. It is getting late and he goes upstairs to bed. But one of the people who has found a way there, and who has cause to hate him, is hiding in the darkness of the corridor where the bedrooms are and slips into the bedroom—Number Fifty-Four—soon after Griggs has undressed and got into bed.

"Consider the vital matter, gentlemen. A point which helped me considerably to the truth. A man, threatened by the murderous might of the Ku-Klux-Klan . . . does not trouble . . . when sleeping in a strange hotel . . . *to take the elementary precaution of locking his bedroom door*! This also must be remembered. That person who entered bedroom number Fifty-Four entered *unarmed*. An undoubtedly extenuating circumstance, Palliser. Which none of us, when we review the case afterwards—judicially and weighing everything—must allow himself to forget or overlook.

"A conversation then ensued in the bedroom between Griggs and his visitor. It was reported by Gladys Greene, a servant on the staff of the hotel, who happened to pass by the room at the time, to have contained these words and phrases, *'Murder', 'Fowles', 'They belonged to me and I'm entitled to please myself regarding them'*. Which brings me once again, gentlemen, to the sentence that I mentioned to you just now. It was spoken to me on St. Aidans pier by another member of the original touring *Interference* company. I refer to a man named Meredith. After the discovery of the death of Daphne Arbuthnot, and the inquiry into the question of the used and unused glasses, stage 'props' and otherwise, he said to me, amongst other things . . . 'and nobody missed a glass.'"

Anthony paused. "Which means, in effect, that the detective who has really solved the mystery of the death of Griggs—was not I—but another." Anthony waved across the room . . . vaguely.

Oakley half-turned and Sutton half-smiled. It was decent of Bathurst to apportion the glory to another and they, as allies of his, desired to demonstrate that they appreciated it. But both the Inspector and Oakley were doomed to disappointment, for Anthony, to their great surprise, nominated another.

"I refer," he declared, "to none other than the world-famous 'Father Brown', that marvellously clever creation of the mighty brain of Gilbert Keith Chesterton." Anthony Bathurst paused, and for some moments silence reigned again in that little room in Swynford Street.

Sutton was expectant. Phillida was amazed. Palliser was obviously a mass of tortured nerves. Oakley was frankly puzzled. Why was Wells being left to his own devices for so long? And again, why had Bathurst not played his trump card, Colonel Colquhoun of 222, East Fifty-Sixth Street? Surely, he should have been mentioned before now? The omission made him uneasy. But doubtless, he considered, Anthony Bathurst knew his own business best. He settled down in his chair again.

Chapter XXVIII
THE FIVE MURDERS

OAKLEY was right. As events were destined to turn out, all his anxiety was unfounded. For he heard Anthony's voice again, speaking quite clearly and distinctly.

"I will explain this unexpected intervention of 'Father Brown'. I owe all of you that much. You will find that in one of the 'Father

Brown' collections of stories, the voice of a man in a room behind closed doors is heard to say certain words . . . they are interpreted by the hearers as—'Mr. Glass'. Whereas, in reality, he is eventually proved to be a juggler, who, locked in his room, is practising a new trick with tumblers, and what he actually says is, upon making a mistake with one of his hand properties, *'missed a glass.'* You will observe the difference between the two expressions?"

Palliser's hand went to his lips. Where was he? Where were they all? What amazing revelation was coming next from this grey-eyed man who held them all with the magnetism of his projected personality?

"Now Gladys Greene, the maid," proceeded Anthony, "on her way to find a mislaid brush, had reported the words 'murder' and 'fowls' . . . or—as we might well be excused thinking—'F-o-w-l-e-s'. But, like our butter-fingered Chestertonian juggler, what Griggs actually said as she passed the door was not the word 'Fowles'. You will pardon me again if I endeavour to fill in some of the gaps.

"What Gladys Greene did hear was neither the word 'fowls', those tasty members of the poultry yard, nor the surname 'Fowles', known by now to all of us who have taken any part in this case."

Nobody spoke. But each one of them who listened hung on Anthony Bathurst's words. They were held spellbound.

Anthony went on: "What then *was* this word that Gladys Greene had heard? Using the idea that came to me from the juggler who 'missed a glass', I will tell you. The word was not fowls, or F-o-w-l-e-s . . . but *'vowels'*. And when I realized that, I began to build up quite an interesting little theory with regard to the murder, which, I imagine, will satisfy all the demands of truth and reason.

"Do you know, I'd pictured a conscientious teacher of—elo-cution—shall we say, whose business had suffered considerably, for various reasons, calling on our departed friend, the Home Secretary, even in the privacy of his bedroom, and remonstrating with him on such a matter, for instance, as the glaring imperfec-tions of his speech. That teacher would point out, his text-book in hand, of course, that precise consonantal attack depended almost entirely on correct manipulation of the lower jaw, that a vowel should be a mouthful of resonant tone, that many people ruthlessly murdered their vowels—all five of them—"

An interruption came—sharply and suddenly. Oakley sprang to his feet, his face and hands quivering with excitement. His note-book and his pen fell from his hands to the floor.

"Good God!" he cried in a hoarse voice. "You were hiding there in the bedroom! You heard me! You must have done—otherwise—" He paused—standing there swaying and trembling.

"Do you realize what Mr. Oakley says, Sutton?" observed Bathurst quietly. "It should be good enough for you to act on, I think."

The Inspector walked over to his man and uttered the usual charge and caution.

"Take your hands off me!" cried Oakley. "You can arrest me if you like, but you shall hear my story all the same. For heaven's sake give me a chance to justify myself. I claim to have killed the man in self-defence and I wish to God now that I'd never gone near him! For I never meant to kill him!"

Oakley broke off, sat down at the table, and buried his face in his hands. When he resumed, he had partly recovered himself, and he spoke evenly and steadily.

"Let me plead something in self-justification. Grant me that concession at least."

His eyes met Anthony's. The latter nodded. Oakley flushed and began to speak again.

"You know from what I've told you that I'm an elocution teacher. I get a modest living out of it, or rather, I used to. I'll explain what I mean. I advertise my little place as 'The Maxwell House Academy of Elocution and Dramatic Art'. Two of my slogans are 'Speech-Training our Speciality' and 'Commercial Elocution a National Necessity'. One of my most successful lines was what I call 'Elocution in Business'. If you think for a minute, you can see the idea behind it all. I teach my pupils to speak decently. Try to make them more efficient citizens. Teach them to express themselves plainly and clearly, to be audible, to hit their consonants properly, and illustrate the general value to them of such things as good enunciation, careful articulation, and pleasing modulation. I've tried to show them that from those things spring useful citizenship and efficiency, and that from efficiency comes a greater measure of commercial success, which spells promotion and improved prospects financially.

"Good Lord—the way the English people treat the glorious art of speaking is appalling! Like all other arts it requires preparation. No singer or musician would be suffered to attempt in public that for which he had never been trained. The Greeks and Romans of old knew better—believe me. They had their Schools of Rhetoric. Men were orators, not only by nature or accident, but by education and training. They reached eminence by reason of persistent practice and infinite labour. How else would Cicero have cured his vehemence and lung weakness, and Demosthenes his speech impediment?

"Then I've shown my pupils the reverse side of the picture and how careless, sloppily-spoken English is one of the most terrific handicaps under which it is possible to labour at the present day. How it keeps people under and in the ruck all their lives!

"I was doing splendidly, according to my standards, when what happened? The Right Honourable A.S. Griggs, M.P., spoke one night on the wireless! God!—he was appalling! He—no less a person than the Home Secretary, mind you—committed every speech fault against which I was warning fifty-three specially selected pupils daily and nightly, who, you can bet your life, were listening-in! Didn't I hear of it next morning when I started to take my class? Had to answer several very nasty and pertinent questions. How had a man like that, and who spoke like that, become Home Secretary, etc., etc.? Hadn't I told them the opposite? Time and time again! How could I substantiate my statements about commercial success in face of this supremely successful man, Griggs? The upshot was that I lost seventeen pupils in a week.

"Next time the ignorant swine broadcast, I think, if possible, his performance was even *worse* than the time before. Result—the next week saw fourteen more pupils turn down my classes. That made thirty-one out of fifty-three all told. Twenty-two of them left. It worried me no end, as you may guess, and I dreaded his third wireless effort beyond anything. And after that there were still two more advertised to come!

"I felt absolutely disgusted with the man, with his horrible voice and revolting accent, undoing in two short talks my hard work of months and months. In fact, I doubted whether I should have a single pupil left to me. When I heard that he was in the Lansdowne Hotel at Lokingham it seemed like the intervention of heaven and I determined, if possible, to see him and point out certain things to him. So I went there that evening. My grand chance came when he finished playing billiards. I hung about in the Corridor and spotted Griggs pass upstairs. After a time I followed him into his bedroom. I had noticed that he didn't lock the door.

"You should have seen his face when I walked up to the bed. I was pretty well wound up, you know, and when I got there I told him a few home-truths and showed him some elementary rules in one of the text-books that I use and which I had purposely brought along with me. I suppose the contempt and aggression of my voice stuck out a mile, for he showed his teeth and came for me with a revolver.

"Of course, I wasn't having any of that and in the struggle I got the best of him and . . . the revolver, I think, went off. I was horrified. After some thought, I laid a few false clues for the Police, hoping that by so doing I should throw them off the scent. Griggs had some billiard-chalk in his room and I had some melon seeds. I used them both. I put the seeds in the books and chalked his shoes with the skull and cross-bones. I left my book behind on the bed, and placed one of my visiting-cards in his wallet. I thought that the story I would put up about that would clear me completely should I ever come to be suspected. The revolver, I considered, might show finger-prints, so I took it out of the hotel with me when I cleared off and dropped it over the Dennet Bridge. But his death was as much his fault as mine . . . I swear it! More . . . because he flew at me first." Oakley broke down again and sobbed into his hands.

Anthony rose and accused him. "If you went there with no intention of killing Griggs—as you say that you did—explain this. Why were you carrying the melon seeds in your pocket?"

Oakley looked up at him wearily and shook his head. "I was down to lecture, on the following morning to the remnant of an advanced class on 'The Methods of the Ku-Klux-Klan'. They were to speak on it afterwards. I had sent my wife to buy the melon so that I could exhibit the seeds to them. We never have one in the house—I loathe the things. As I looked at the dead body of Griggs on the bed, the idea of the Ku-Klux-Klan came to me . . . I thought it would help to put the Police off the scent . . . so I used the seeds. I'd been reading a lot about the Society just recently in preparation of my intended lecture."

He rose and faced the Inspector. Sutton tapped him on the shoulder and took him away.

"What will he get?" asked Palliser impulsively.

"Two years at the most," returned Anthony; "he can plead self-defence, you know. I had to kid him all the time to-day—with regard to my preparations—and he fell for everything beautifully."

Anthony turned to the two others. The girl was still trembling. Palliser was subdued.

"Thank you for your assistance, Miss Fortescue. And you too, Palliser. You must forgive me if I took a liberty with your personal characters. I'm afraid that the story I told Oakley implicated you both rather strongly. By getting him here as an auxiliary, under false pretences, I admit, I was enabled to 'play' him and eventually cast him on the bank high and dry."

Palliser nodded anxiously. "You virtually forced a confession from him."

"Yes. I'll admit to you that that was my intention. He thought I was after both you and Wells. The story that I unfolded to him *made* him think that. I don't believe that he had the slightest suspicion that I hadn't accepted him on his own terms and at his own valuation. Ah, well, it's been a complicated case, right from the beginning, and I fear that few bouquets are mine in connection with it. Good-bye, Miss Fortescue, and once again, many thanks. Good-bye, Palliser."

Anthony shook hands with each of them. "I've an appointment at seven o'clock this evening with the Commissioner of Police, Sir Austin Kemble of New Scotland Yard . . . shall I—er—may I—drink your health?"

Miss Fortescue blushed deliciously as Mr. Bathurst turned away. His diagnosis, evidently, had been correct.

CHAPTER XXIX
MR. BATHURST SWEEPS UP

SIR Austin Kemble murmured impatiently and looked at his watch. The hands showed him that the time was almost seven o'clock. His two guests would have to hurry to be in time for their appointment. He detested unpunctuality. As the Commissioner thus mused, a hand touched him on the shoulder from behind. He turned clumsily, to see the tall figure of Anthony Lotherington Bathurst standing behind him.

"This is Inspector Sutton," said Anthony, indicating the man at his side, "your other guest for this evening. Inspector—Sir Austin Kemble."

"Good evening, Inspector."

"Good evening, sir."

"Sit down, Bathurst, will you? And you, Inspector. Good heavens—I'm damned hungry! Can't make it out. I shouldn't be. I had a fair lunch. Ah—here's Murillo himself. I've taken the liberty of ordering you a 'Clover Club', Bathurst, and you, Inspector, a Martini. When you aren't sure of a man's particular taste, a Martini is usually a fairly safe proposition."

He turned to the *maître d'hôtel*. "Now, Murillo, we're all ready. Tell your fellows to serve at once."

The *maître d'hôtel* bowed. "At once, milord. I will see to it." He vanished with Latin alacrity.

For two courses Sir Austin paid assiduous attention to the matters immediately on hand. Towards the close of his whole-hearted attack on a *sole au gratin* he growled ominously.

"Below par, this sole, Bathurst. Not enough white wine in the cooking—I shall have to speak to Murillo about it. It's not good enough. This is the second occasion on which I've noticed it. Damned place is falling to the level of a 'good pull-up for car-men'."

"Quite right, sir," said Anthony encouragingly. "Speak to him about it. Murillo mustn't be allowed to slack. 'Twould be an unspeakable calamity."

"H'm," mumbled the Commissioner, "that's all very well—but when you come to weigh things up, he wants beating. When I think of some of the damned English places with which I'm sometimes inflicted—faugh! D'you know what I always say, Bathurst, when it comes to a criticism of cooking?"

"No, sir. What do you say? I'd be charmed to hear." Anthony drooped an eyelid in the direction of Inspector Sutton.

The latter, however, was by far too perturbed to respond.

"Why, this," declared Sir Austin: "In France—I say in *France*, particularly—a chef of my acquaintance will take a piece of ordinary brown paper, he'll sprinkle a little salt on it, some pepper, perhaps a *soupçon* of sauce, the veriest suspicion of mustard, cook it to a turn and put it in front of you—and you'd consider it, my dear Bathurst, directly you tasted it, to be like a most glorious piece of beefsteak."

"Really, sir," said Mr. Bathurst, his eyes twinkling, "is that so ... now ... and what's your point behind all that?"

"My point?" The Commissioner's eyes glared fiercely. "Why this! That in this wretched country of *ours* a cook takes a glorious piece of steak, fries it in an appallingly dirty pan—and when you get your teeth in it—if you're particularly gifted in that direction, that is—you think it's a piece of ruddy brown paper! Fact. I've tasted it ... so I know."

Sir Austin raised his glass and drained it. Anthony smiled. The Inspector laughed heartily.

"Now, Bathurst," declared a mollified Commissioner, "let's hear all you have to tell us about this Lokingham Hotel case. Congratulations, of course, in advance—on the successful issue."

Anthony laughingly disclaimed the praise. "I don't deserve any, sir. So don't talk about them. I take it that you want my résumé of the case?"

"As soon as you like! There are still several points about it that aren't at all clear to me."

Sutton, at this, became a changed man. His eagerness to obtain information regarding Anthony's settlement loosed the strings of his tongue.

"When did you first get on to him, Mr. Bathurst? That's the point that has been troubling me for some time now."

"He told me a lie, Sutton. A deliberate lie. But a lie that seemed, from his point of view, to put him completely outside the circle of my suspicions. He took a risk over it—but it wasn't exactly a big risk—and he took the chance."

"What was this?" demanded Sir Austin.

"He went to St. Aidans," said Anthony, "and he came back with what he described as 'evidence'. Carefully planted evidence. Evidence which he knew would suit admirably my main line of theory with regard to the Ku-Klux-Klan."

Sutton intervened. "You mean—he brought back *false* evidence?"

"Oh, absolutely, Sutton! He went even one step beyond that. He brought back *concocted* evidence! Concocted by himself. The melon seeds on Griggs's luggage at St. Aidans, as described by the luggage porter, existed only in his imagination. That was where he took the chance that I mentioned just now, and he came within an ace of pulling it off."

"How?" queried Sir Austin.

"In this way, sir. He ascribed the evidence of the melon seeds to a luggage porter at St. Aidans. By the name of Kennedy. This man's particular job was to collect luggage from hotels. *Oakley knew that this man had left his job and gone to America.* He discovered that fact while he was making his inquiries at St. Aidans. This is how his brain worked: he calculated that it was a thousand to one that I would accept his evidence . . . because it *fitted* . . . and was all part of the general pattern—in other words, it suited my book. I couldn't *test* it by going to St. Aidans myself . . . because Kennedy wouldn't be at St. Aidans to deny it. He—Oakley—was, therefore, seventy-five per cent safe from me, as far as that matter was concerned. And . . . I shiver to think how near he was to bringing it off."

"What turned the scale against him, Bathurst?"

"The fact that I *did* follow up his St. Aidans inquiry . . . and while I was there, ran into the damning fact that this man Kennedy had left for America *days* before Oakley had arrived at St. Aidans. It was by the merest chance, though, that I *struck* the fact. I was lucky enough to interview a garrulous inhabitant of the town who gave it away to me . . . and I realized with a shock some little time afterwards that there was something radically amiss with Mr. Oakley's *story* and therefore, in all probability, with *Mr. Oakley himself.* That realization came to me in the watches of the night . . . if it interests you to know such things as that. Thank you, Sir Austin." Anthony took the cigar that the Commissioner offered him.

Sutton came in again. For some time his face had shown that he was puzzled. "Colonel Colquhoun, 222, East Fifty-Sixth Street? Where did he fit in? How do you account for the strange coincidence that both Kennedy, the former luggage porter at St. Aidans, and Jayne, Griggs's butler at Great Astill, went to the same American address?"

Anthony smiled at his bewilderment. "It wasn't a coincidence, Inspector. I haven't troubled to verify it . . . I haven't really had time for it . . . but I have little doubt that the truth of that is this: the Colonel of East Fifty-Sixth Street was a close friend of the late Home Secretary. It was Griggs's habit to give introductions to the Colonel of East Fifty-Sixth Street of anybody who went out there. Kennedy told Griggs probably during the time that Griggs was in the St. Aidans hotel that he had American 'intentions'. Wanted to emigrate there if ever the opportunity arose. Griggs put him on to Colquhoun. Jayne, of course, had known of the East Fifty-Sixth Street connection for years. So that what seemed a coincidence to us, when we met it, heavy with meaning and significance, was quite simply explainable."

The Commissioner nodded at Anthony's statement. "Yes. I see. So that, after all, the case proved less difficult than we had anticipated, eh?"

Before Mr. Bathurst could reply, Sutton made a further contribution. "All the same, we were unlucky. Looking at everything fairly. Anybody might have been excused thinking that the word which Gladys Greene heard and which eventually proved to be 'vowels', was 'Fowles'." He shook his head rather despondently.

"I don't know," said Anthony judicially. "I blame myself severely for not having seen through that before. I was painfully slow. The book on elocution should have served us better than we allowed it to. Don't forget that, Sutton. The clues were there for us, if we'd only had the brains to see them. They stuck out a mile. Consonantal attack! Resonance of vowel tone! No," he shook his head as Sutton had done a few moments previously, "there is no excuse for us; we have only ourselves to blame."

"One more point, Mr. Bathurst. Did Griggs really call on Oakley and arrange for those lessons?" The question came from the Inspector.

"Never in his life. All eye-wash. Boloney—to Colonel Colquhoun. That was Oakley's story. It wasn't a bad one, either, when you come to consider it. He had suffered so—because Griggs had died. The man's death was a minor disaster for him. No *cui bono* as far as he was concerned. For a long time he took me in completely. The picture that he drew of dashed hopes was most convincing."

"Why did he leave his text-book behind in Griggs's bed?"

"Publicity! A position of centre-stage. A condition for which he had craved for years. It would bring him and his book into the limelight that was playing on the murder. Any more questions, Sir Austin?"

"Yes—one. And it's been on the tip of my tongue for some time. What was his real idea with the chalk and the chalk-marks on the soles of the shoes?"

Anthony shrugged his shoulders. "I would explain them in this way, sir. Griggs took the cube of chalk into the bedroom after he had finished playing billiards. One constantly finds a cube of billiard-chalk in one's pocket after a game or two. He placed it, I suggest, when he undressed, on the dressing-table or on the mantel-piece. Oakley saw it there and resolved to work it in with his melon seeds as the 'secret-society' pointer that he described to us. As he confessed, it would complicate the case even more. So he chalked the dead man's shoes, and when he had finished with it dropped the cube into the breast-pocket of the dead man's pyjamas."

"I see," commented the Commissioner. "Once you had detected that lie that he told you about the St. Aidans luggage porter, you felt no doubt, I suppose?"

"Hardly any, sir. Because I very soon proved the case to the hilt. I was able to trace the purchaser of the melon. I was lucky, perhaps. But in the front part of his now notorious book on elocution there was a photograph of himself and his wife. I cut it out, hoping that the chance would come for me to use it. It did, and when I showed this to Westwood, the fruiterer, he was able to identify the lady at once. The murder of Griggs, as he explained to me when I visited him, gave him the clear association with the date. But I think this—if Oakley hadn't shot Griggs, Fowles would have got him the very next night, perhaps."

The Commissioner nodded and ordered liqueurs. "Ah, well," he declared pontifically, with a glance in the direction of Inspector Sutton, "it shows these local chaps what the Yard *can* bring off when it likes. Doesn't do any harm, either, once in a while. Wakes 'em up a bit."

"Exactly," murmured Bathurst. "Although . . . do you know . . . I hadn't altogether looked at it in that light."

The Commissioner glanced at him somewhat suspiciously. There was something about the tone . . . But Mr. Bathurst's face was impassive—he was lost, apparently, in keen appreciation of an old brandy. And inasmuch as a man is all the better for companionship, Sir Austin Kemble decided to accompany him.

THE END

www.ingramcontent.com/pod-product-compliance
Lightning Source LLC
Chambersburg PA
CBHW031015190726
48286CB00003BA/866